P

for the Ri

"Millennials will love following Riley Ellison, junior reporter, on her laugh-out-loud adventures in the quaint town of Tuttle Corner, Virginia.... Riley is a heroine for the twenty-first century, struggling, like others of her generation, with such contemporary concerns as online dating and obnoxious coworkers. Her romantic misadventures provide most of the comedy here, but there's plenty of suspense, too; an additional source of appeal is Tuttle Corner itself, a thoroughly quirky but realistically drawn small town full of eccentric and amusing characters.... Orr's series is perfect for fans of Janet Evanovich's Stephanie Plum and Kyra Davis' Sophie Katz, witty protagonists who always mix fun with murder. *The Ugly Truth* is a great vacation read for comic mystery fans."

— *Booklist* (starred review!)

"Delightfully comic...highly amusing... Quirky characters enliven the carefully constructed plot."

— *Publishers Weekly*

"Jill Orr hits an almost impossible combo with *The Ugly Truth*; page-turning suspense, laugh-out-loud humor, and a delightfully complex mystery you just can't put down. If you like smart criminals, smarter women sleuths, and endearing side characters you care about, Orr delivers with the third book in her charming Riley Ellison series."

— **Libby Kirsch**, Emmy Award–winning journalist and author of the Stella Reynolds Mystery Series and the Janet Black Mystery Series

"The small town nature of this mystery, with the requisite fish-bowl local politics, relationships, and grudges, makes it perfect for cozy lovers who want something more modern. Readers will enjoy Riley's humor and determination even when things turn sad."

— ***Booklist***

"Here comes Riley Ellison, the journalist-slash-hero we need right now. She solves murders! She writes obits! She lets a really cute guy get away but she'll survive! I loved this fresh page-turner—it's fun, funny, and moves like lightning. Jill Orr has created a complex plot and complex contemporary characters that make murder quite delightful. Can't wait for the next in the series."

— **Lian Dolan**, Satellite Sister and author of the best-selling novels *Helen of Pasadena* and *Elizabeth the First Wife*

"A ray of sunshine cloaked in a mystery. Jill Orr is the best humorous mystery writer around, with a voice all her own."

— **Laura McHugh**, best-selling author of *The Weight of Blood* and *Arrowood*

"Fresh and funny, romantic and sunny, Orr's book checked three genre boxes for me: a smart cozy series, a Southern small-town setting, and, my favorite, a newspaper mystery.... I loved the hilarious emails the author interjects into the narrative from Riley's 'Personal Romance Concierge' at Click.com."

— **Carole Barrowman**, *Milwaukee Journal Sentinel*

"The laughs keep coming."

— ***Kirkus Reviews***

The Full Scoop

By Jill Orr

Also by Jill Orr

The Good Byline

The Bad Break

The Ugly Truth

The Full Scoop

By Jill Orr

Prospect Park Books

Published by Prospect Park Books
2359 Lincoln Avenue
Altadena, California 91001
www.prospectparkbooks.com

Distributed by Consortium Book Sales & Distribution
www.cbsd.com

Library of Congress Cataloging-in-Publication Data
Names: Orr, Jill, author.
Title: The full scoop : a Riley Ellison mystery / Jill Orr.
Description: Altadena, California : Prospect Park Books, [2020] | Series: Riley Ellison mysteries
Identifiers: LCCN 2019047137 (print) | LCCN 2019047138 (ebook) | ISBN 9781945551802 (softcover) | ISBN 9781945551819 (hardcover) | ISBN 9781945551826 (ebook)
Subjects: GSAFD: Mystery fiction.
Classification: LCC PS3615.R58846 F85 2020 (print) | LCC PS3615.R58846 (ebook) | DDC 813/.6--dc23
LC record available at https://lccn.loc.gov/2019047137
LC ebook record available at https://lccn.loc.gov/2019047138

Cover design by Susan Olinsky
Cover illustration by Nancy Nimoy
Book layout and design by Amy Inouye
Printed in the United States of America

To Jimmy, again and always

Prologue

It's amazing how quickly—and slowly—a month can go by when you've been blindsided by shock and grief. It had been exactly thirty-one days since Hal Flick died, alone, in a hospital bed. The medical examiner listed the official cause of death as acute internal hemorrhage, but those words didn't mean anything to me. That was just rhetoric, a slippery way of defining something with itself to avoid a harsher truth. It was like saying the cause of global warming was the rise in the Earth's temperatures, or the cause of the opioid epidemic was too many people addicted to pain meds. The harsh truth here was that Hal Flick died because someone forced his car to crash, at full speed, into the rocky side of a mountain on a dark highway in rural Virginia. The harsh truth, in this case, was murder.

Images from the past month flashed through my mind like a slideshow. I closed my eyes and saw Holman driving me to the hospital that night. *"I'm so sorry, Miss Ellison."* The ER doctor's long gray ponytail. *"Did you know Mr. Flick had given you power of attorney?"* Talking to the Brunswick County sheriff. *"Can you think of anyone who might have wanted to harm him?"* The sun glinting off the mahogany casket as it was lowered into the ground.

There were moments when it felt like I was a spectator watching the whole thing as if it were happening to someone else on film, and then there were moments when I felt Flick's loss so sharply, I thought I might suffocate under the weight of it. Most of the time, though, I was somewhere in between, just trying to get from one moment to the next without feeling anything at all.

Another harsh truth was that when someone dies, the world does not stop turning. There are certain responsibilities that must be dealt with even when all you want to do is sleep or cry or shake your fist and vow revenge. So, day after day you find yourself in one office or another—hospital administrators, lawyers, insurance agents—having conversations you don't fully understand because your bandwidth for such things is limited by your heartache, and because none of this was supposed to happen in the first place. But despite your grief-induced apathy, you make the phone calls, you sign the documents, you file the paperwork.

It isn't until much later—thirty-one days later, actually—that the numbness begins to subside. And when it does, it's replaced with a deep sense of injustice that washes over you like acid rain. It's not just the loss, which exists in its own emotional ecosystem; it's the audacity of the crime that keeps you up at night. *They took your friend. They took your grandfather.* You may not know who "they" are yet, but it doesn't matter, because you know you will find out. It's that certainty that pushes past the shock, past the sadness, past the grief, and grabs you by the throat. *Do something,* it urges.

But the problem with bossy inner voices is that they are, almost without exception, infuriatingly vague. The fact of the matter is that you don't know what to do. You don't know how to begin to seek justice. You don't even know that if you could somehow figure out who was behind these terrible crimes, it would help heal the mile-wide hole in your heart. *Do something*, the voice calls again, this time more insistent. So you do. You claw your way out of your sorrow, you go back to work, and you start to live your life again. Everyone says that's what Flick and Granddad would have wanted, but you know that they'd also want justice. And so, to the outside world, you look like a woman moving on. But on the inside, you're making plans: You will not only find out who did this and why, you will make them pay.

Voicemail transcript: Jeannie Ellison to Riley Ellison. Sunday, December 26, 4:43pm

Hi honey. It's Mom. I'm calling because I've been a little worried about you lately. The other day when you were going on about "making people pay" and "hunting people down" and whatnot...well, to be honest, it was a little disturbing. I mean, I know you've been sad—we've all been sad ever since...you know [clears throat], but you're young and you have your whole life ahead of you! You should be focusing on your future!

So, in the spirit of focusing on the future...SURPRISE! I signed you up for one of those astrology websites! I got the idea from Sheila Nixon—do you remember Mrs. Nixon? Her daughter Lilith was a year ahead of you in school? Anyway, Sheila told me that Lilith told her that all the kids are super into astrology these days. [Lowers voice] Lilith lives in West Hollywood and has a tattoo of a lotus flower, so I feel like she would know.

Anyway, it seemed like the perfect little pick-me-up—to learn about all the wonderful things that the universe has in store for you! Hope you don't mind that I shared your email address and birth date, place, and time with them. I'm sure it's super safe.

Okay, sweetie, that's it for now! Sorry this message is so long. [Laughs] I'm surprised it hasn't cut me off yet. Seems like these machines are forever hanging up on—[Click]

Sign Overview: Scorpio

Oct. 23–Nov. 21

Symbol:	Scorpion
Element:	Water
Ruling planet:	Pluto
Best qualities:	Magnetic, passionate, loyal, protective, brave
Worst qualities:	Oversensitive, vengeful, insecure
Favorite things:	Your home, books, a good meal, comfortable shoes
What you hate:	Simple-minded people, insincere flattery, social-climbing users

Fiery, independent, and unafraid to blaze their own trail, Scorpios aren't afraid of controversy. They love debates and won't back down from a fight, especially if it involves defending those who can't defend themselves. Protective of themselves and others, when they attach themselves to a cause, they will go down swinging every time.

In their personal life, Scorpios yearn for the very thing they fear: true intimacy. Allowing themselves to become vulnerable is difficult but worthwhile. As Scorpios open up and learn to trust others, they can heal in ways that are truly profound. But those who dare to cross you will feel the powerful sting of your revenge!

Scorpio's ruling planet is Pluto, which is associated with depth, passion, intensity, and death. In this case, death is figurative, representing endings of all forms—relationships, projects, phases, ideas, and more. Scorpios use this concept of regeneration to grow, often killing off the ventures, activities, or relationships in their lives that no longer serve them to make room for something new. That is, if they can allow themselves to let go.

Chapter 1

I sat at my desk in the newsroom pretending to look busy. Again. Kay Jackson, my editor at the *Tuttle Times*, had been enormously understanding about my level of distraction in the month since Flick's death, but I knew her understanding had its limits. I wasn't the only one grieving. Flick had been a member of the *Times* family and we all felt his loss, Kay included. Besides, practically speaking, we were a small staff, and with Flick gone, we were down one.

I'd taken an entire week off when Flick died and had been coming in to the newsroom since then to do just the bare minimum—editing, fact-checking, updating stories—things that didn't require much from me. The rest of the team had taken over the beats I normally covered to give me the time and space to work on Flick's obituary. It was their way of honoring him and his contributions to our newsroom. But now that the funeral had passed, the obit had run, and Christmas had come and gone, it felt like some unseen line of demarcation had been crossed and I was expected to become a fully functioning member of society again—or at the very least, a fully functioning member of the press.

"Knock, knock," I said as I hovered at the threshold to Kay's office.

"Come in," she said without looking up. Kay was always doing the jobs of at least three people, and this necessitated her dropping all extraneous pleasantries like greetings and eye contact.

I sat in the chair opposite her desk. “I think I’m ready to take on—take back—my usual workload.”

Kay put down her blue editing pencil and looked up at me. She lowered her chin. “You sure?”

I nodded.

“Good.” She paused and then added, “Where are you with the other stuff?”

By “other stuff,” I knew she meant my unofficial investigation into Flick’s so-called accident.

“I’m still in touch with Sheriff Clark, but he says there’s not much more he can do at the moment. The case is still open, and he acknowledges that this doesn’t feel like an accident to him, but without any witnesses or cameras in the area, he says they’ve hit a brick wall. I’ve got a call into a guy at the Department of Transportation who used to be on a forensic crash investigative team in Maryland. I’m hoping to pick his brain about what places with bigger budgets do in these situations.” Flick had the misfortune to be murdered in one of the poorest counties in Virginia, which made finding his killer that much harder.

“Good thinking,” Kay said.

The connection to the guy in the DoT was tenuous at best, a friend of my ex-boyfriend Jay, who also worked for the government. I’d left Hank Jorgensmeyer a rambling message reintroducing myself and asked if he might give me some insight into how he would have handled a case like this back in the day. I was waiting for him to call back.

Kay tapped the blunt end of her pencil on her desk. “And the file?”

Before his death, Flick had entrusted Kay with a tattered, brittle manila folder held together by rubber bands and tenacity. He instructed her to give it to me "in the event something happened to him." She gave it to me the night of the crash.

"Safe and sound."

"Do you want to tell me where?"

I shook my head. The file contained notes about what Flick was working on, presumably what got him killed. I figured the fewer people who knew the whereabouts of that file, the better.

"You sure?"

I knew Kay well enough to know this wasn't a challenge. It was a genuine offer of help. I smiled. "Yes."

"Okay then," she said, looking back down at the proof sheet she'd been working on when I walked in. "Talk to Henderson and find out where he is with the bridge-repair story. You can pick it up from here. And Skipper Hazelrigg is supposedly announcing his candidacy for sheriff soon—you might want to track that down. Oh, and Holman has been covering the new botanical poisons installation at the Apothecary Museum for you. You can let him know you're back, though he might want to keep it."

"Holman does love that place," I said with a small laugh. I started to leave, then turned around before walking out. "Thanks for being so understanding, Kay."

She made some sort of noncommittal sound and kept her eyes down on her work. Someone else might have misinterpreted this as dismissive, but I also knew Kay well enough to know she was terribly embarrassed by any show of emotion, even gratitude. It was one of the qualities she shared with Flick—probably why they worked so well together. The second that similarity struck me I left, lest my misty eyes reveal that I might not be *quite* as ready to move on as I'd claimed.

Chapter 2

I spent the morning getting up to speed on my assignments and thanking the people who covered for me over the past few weeks. Everyone had really pulled together. Even Gerlach Spencer, who is the closest thing I'll ever have to a nemesis, had been uncharacteristically helpful.

"Let me know if you want me to finish up that piece on the grand opening of The Grind coffeehouse," he'd said. I felt a rush of unexpected warmth toward him a split second before he added, "The lady that runs that place is suuuuper hot. I wouldn't mind giving her something to grind on!" He stretched his hand over his cubicle wall to high-five Bruce Henderson, who (unfortunately) responded by saying "booyah."

When I refrained from pointing out to them that if they weren't such misogynistic pigs, they might not die alone, I considered us square. That level of restraint constituted repayment of my debt as far as I was concerned.

Around noon, Holman stopped by my cubicle and asked if I wanted to go to lunch at Mysa, formerly Rosalee's Tavern. Ridley and Ryan bought the restaurant from the bank after its former owner, Rosalee Belanger, went to prison. "Rosalee is synonymous with *murder*, and murder is unappetizing," Ridley reasoned. So she chose a word from the Swedish language, her mother tongue, as a start of the rebranding process. "*Mysa* doesn't have an exact translation in English—kind of like me," she explained with a giggle to a small group of regulars who gathered out front the day they hung up the new sign. "*Snuggle* is closest but not quite the same. *Mysa* is the act of being cozy. You can *mysa* by yourself, with friends, family, lovers. Technically, it's a verb, but it's more like a feeling."

"Ohhhhh, okay," Betsy Norbitt had said with a furrowed brow. "So...Mai-zah?"

"Actually, it's Mee-sah," Ridley corrected.

"Meeza."

"No, it has a hard 's.' Mee-SAH."

"Mee-SAHHH!"

"Well, you don't actually accentuate the 'sah.' "

"Okay, mm-hmm." Betsy looked more confused than ever, but being the good Southern girl that she was, she added brightly, "That's a real pretty shade of blue on your sign there, sweetie."

As the group turned to leave, Charlotte Van Stone—another good Southern girl—whispered loudly, "Honey, just call it Rosalee's. No one's ever gonna remember that new name anyhow."

I told Holman I couldn't go to lunch with him because I had an appointment, which strictly speaking wasn't exactly true. The real reason was that I already had lunch plans with Ash, the new director of Campbell & Sons Funeral Home. I would have told Holman the truth, but lately I'd gotten the feeling he wasn't a member of the Ash Campbell fan club. He'd never said anything directly, but a few times over the past month when I'd mentioned Ash's name, either in the context of funeral arrangements for Flick or just times we'd hung out, I'd felt a distinct chill from Holman. Better he should think I was at the dentist.

Ash and I planned to meet at my house for lunch so I could walk Coltrane before going back to work. My sweet dog had gotten spoiled over the past month by having me home, so I wanted to ease him back slowly into being alone for hours during the day. Plus, if there was ever a cure for the midday blues, it was a ninety-four-pound German shepherd looking at you like you were a combination of steak, bacon, and a slow-moving squirrel.

When I pulled into my driveway, Ash was sitting on my front porch swing holding a bag from Landry's.

"Hey," I said as I walked up.

"Hey." He gave me a big smile and moved like maybe he was going to follow it with a hug, but I buzzed past him to unlock the door before he had the chance.

When Ash moved here from Texas about six weeks earlier, our relationship flip-flopped between flirty one minute and contentious the next—or more accurately, Ash had. He came to Tuttle Corner to run his family's funeral home after his grandfather had a debilitating stroke. He was just out of law school and had given up his dream job at a law firm in Austin to take over the family business, so he was understandably conflicted about the new direction his life had taken. We'd met when I was doing a story about a murder victim whose body had gone unclaimed, and he'd quite literally slammed a door in my face on Monday; by Friday he suggested we go out for a drink. It nearly gave me whiplash.

Ash Campbell was smart, witty, and good-looking—and he knew it. I'd found his arrogance both appealing and repellent, and when you combined that with his mercurial nature, I wasn't sure how close I wanted to get to a guy like that. But for all of his volatility, when I showed up bleary-eyed and overwhelmed at Campbell & Sons to make the arrangements for Flick's funeral, Ash had been amazing. He'd walked me through everything, helped simplify my choices, and literally held my hand through the tough decisions. He'd shown me more compassion than I would have expected from him.

We started talking every day because of funeral stuff, but somewhere along the way we'd settled into a pattern. Calls, texts, pop-in visits to each other's work, offers to walk Coltrane or bring over pizza. And yes, over the past few weeks there'd been a few moments when if circumstances had been different—if I hadn't been mired in grief—something might have happened between us. But as of now Ash and I were just friends. Pretty much.

"They were out of Cubans so I got you a turkey club," Ash said, pulling a foil-wrapped sandwich from the bag. "Hope that's okay."

"Perfect. How much do I owe you?"

"Don't worry about it." He shrugged.

"No, seriously. You don't have to pay for my lunch..."

"I know I don't have to." He smiled. "I want to."

"Fine," I said, looking down to conceal the involuntary blush I could feel spreading across my cheeks. "My treat next time."

"How was this morning? Did you tell Kay you were ready to go back to full speed?" Ash had been gently encouraging me to get back into my normal routine. He said that was one of the best ways he found to move forward after his mom died.

"Uh-huh," I said, my mouth full of sandwich. I held up one finger as I chewed. Ash waited with an amused look on his face as I swallowed the way-too-big bite I'd taken. "She was great about it. Classic Kay. Gave me a handful of assignments and plugged me right back in."

"That's good. There's nothing like being busy to keep your mind off..." he let his sentence trail off. "By the way, did you find anything in Flick's office about your grandfather's book?"

I'd recently found out that at the time of his murder, my granddad was putting together a collection of obituaries about people who had died and had no one to bury or mourn them. The working title was *The Lonely Dead,* and his goal, according to Flick, was to find out what happened in these people's lives to isolate them so thoroughly—and then to give their story a voice. It was so like Granddad to want to shine a light on the less fortunate among us. As a journalist, he'd spent many years tuned into the imbalanced distribution of privilege in our country. It was one of the many things I'd admired about him. Flick's theory was that Granddad had been killed because of something he found out while researching that book.

"No," I said. "Not that I can make sense of anyway."

Flick had never been able to find a shred of evidence that Granddad had been working on this book. The only reason he knew anything about it was because Granddad mentioned it in passing during one of their morning coffee sessions. It was like the entire project—his notes, files, source lists—just evaporated the moment he died. Even his laptop had been destroyed. Sheriff Tackett told me at the time that Granddad must have knocked over a glass of water and fried the system, but the computer expert I'd taken it to said, based on the amount of damage, it looked to him like the machine had been submerged in water "for a significant length of time." Flick was the only person with whom Granddad had discussed the book, so no one else knew anything was missing. His notes in the file were messy, disjointed, and cryptic. I'd been working my way through Flick's file every chance I got, trying to make sense of what was in there.

"I'll keep on looking, though," I said. "Hopefully, I'll find something eventually." I changed the subject and asked Ash about how things were at the funeral home, and if there'd been any change in his grandfather's condition.

"Not really. He eats just enough, opens his eyes just enough, squeezes my grandma's hand just enough...but he's not getting any better."

Franklin's sudden illness had been hard on the whole Campbell family, perhaps Ash most of all. With his mother gone, his father in and out of prisons and rehab centers, and his sister living out in California as a single mom to three kids, Ash was the only member of the family in a position to take over the 143-year-old business. But it didn't come without a cost.

"Have you decided when you'll go back to Texas to get your stuff?"

He sighed like he always did when we talked about Texas. "I'd like to go before the end of next month, so I can stop paying for the storage locker. I've just been putting it off, I guess. I've been busy, but really I think I'm just delaying the inevitable." He let out a small laugh that was one part humor and three parts regret. Making the decision to leave behind his career in Austin had been a very difficult one, fueled more by obligation than choice.

"But you like your new place, right?"

"Yeah, I really do," he said. "I love being on the water. It's so peaceful out there. I can just sit out on my back porch, have a beer, and watch the sun set. I still can't believe that place was available."

Debbie Forrester, a retired P.E. teacher from Tuttle Middle School, had decided to take up a second career as a cruise ship dance instructor. She was a widow and said she'd always loved to dance, so she couldn't think of a better way to spend her post-retirement years than dancing while out at sea. "It'll be just like living on the *Love Boat*!" she told Ash when they'd met to sign the rental agreement for her cabin on the James River. Debbie signed a nine-month employment contract with the cruise line, "with an option to extend indefinitely," so Ash did the same.

"You need to come out and see it," Ash said. "We could watch the sunset...open a bottle of wine..."

This wasn't the first time Ash had invited me over to see his new place. He'd suggested I come over a few times over the past couple of weeks, but I'd always made some vague excuse to get out of it. It just seemed like going over to his house to watch a movie or have a drink was more of an official date than meeting for lunch or seeing each other at Campbell & Sons. I liked Ash and was learning to trust him but wasn't sure I wanted to take that next step. And given how his amber eyes sparkled under my kitchen lights, I didn't trust myself to resist them during a Virginia sunset.

"Sure," I said, taking our glasses over to the sink. "Hey—did you know that Skipper Hazelrigg is planning to run for sheriff against Carl in the next election?" I turned on the water and started washing the dishes.

I didn't need to turn around to know Ash had followed and was right behind me. I could feel the heat from his skin a split second before I felt his fingers sweep the hair off the back of my neck. My whole body went still.

He leaned in close. "Riley Ellison, are you trying to change the subject?"

I shut off the water but didn't turn around. "No, I—it's just—" I stammered, confused by the electric sensation of his fingertips. "It's just—"

Ash put a hand on each of my shoulders. It was like time slowed down. I stood frozen, afraid to move. I knew I could stop this by wriggling out from under him, and I knew I could escalate it by turning around to face him. The only thing I didn't know was what I wanted.

I closed my eyes. "Ash—"

He pulled back slowly, running his hands down my arms and squeezing my hands before letting go. "It's okay," he said softly, taking a step back. "I just thought that maybe since you were ready to get back to work, you might be ready to move on in other areas, too."

I turned around now that we would no longer be nose-to-nose, but when I looked at his face, the slight pink in his cheeks, those sexy hooded eyes, I completely lost what I was going to say. My mind went blank, and I just stood there looking at him.

After a few moments, Ash let out an embarrassed sort of laugh. "Okay, I guess not. I'm sorry—"

"Don't be sorry," I said quickly. "I'm just a mess right now."

"No—I misread the situation, clearly."

"You didn't, it's just—"

"It's okay, Riley. Really."

I took a deep breath. "I just don't know about a lot of things right now. I've probably sent mixed signals—I'm sorry—it's not on purpose, I promise. I just don't know whether I'm coming or going these days. But I like you...and I like our, um, friendship, or whatever we have. And I know there's, like, this chemistry between us, but I'm just not sure what the best thing to do is, you know? I'm not sure if I'm ready for whatever this is, if it's anything at all."

"Wow, you really like to complicate things, don't you?" He was joking, but the comment still stung. I looked down.

He sighed, sounding frustrated that his joke didn't land. "I like you too, Riley. Obviously." We stood there silently for a few seconds marinating in the awkwardness. "Let's just forget about it for now, okay? We can revisit our raging sexual tension another day."

That made me laugh, and as I did, all the weirdness went out of the room. We were friends again. Or something like that.

"Hey, my cousin Toad is having a New Year's Eve party. Wanna come?"

I'd nearly forgotten about the holidays this year, given everything that had happened. I'd spent a somber Christmas with my parents. None of us felt much like going to church, though we did anyway, and my mom prepared her infamous tofurkey and we all sat around their house trying not to talk about the man we'd just buried. It hadn't even registered that soon we'd be ringing in a new year.

"Um, sure," I said, mostly because I didn't know what else to say. I didn't want Ash to think I was saying no because of what happened earlier, and besides, it was probably not a bad idea to get out of the house and spend New Year's with people my own age.

"Cool. He's going with a Gatsby theme this year."

"Like, costumes?"

"Yeah, he gets really into his themed parties. He's kind of known for it, but you don't have to if you don't want—"

I'd never met Toad, he was several years ahead of me in high school, but I'd heard about his legendary parties for years. It was kind of exciting to think I could be going to one. "That actually sounds really fun. I'll do some research."

"Great," Ash said. He'd finished cleaning off his place from the table and had put his coat on. "All right, well I've got a one-thirty so I should go."

"Thanks for lunch," I said. Just before he turned to walk out, I added, "Hey—"

He turned around.

"I...um, I..." Now that I'd started the sentence, I didn't know exactly where I was going with it. *I think you look amazing in that color blue. I like how a strand of hair falls down and covers just one eye, and you have to flick it away every so often. I hope you'll try to kiss me again someday.* In the end, all I could come up with was, "I think you'd make a really good Nick Carraway."

Ash titled his head to the side. "I can't remember, was he a good guy or a bad guy?"

"Both—neither," I said, then laughed. "More complicated than anything else, I guess."

Ash flashed me a mischievous grin. "But he was handsome, right?"

"Definitely."

"Does he get the girl in the end?"

"Afraid not," I said, feeling the smile slide off my face. "He actually decides he was in love with an illusion and heads west."

Ash winked and said, "Oh well, guess you can't win them all."

CHAPTER 3

By the end of the day I was feeling pretty good about my reentry into the world of the *Tuttle Times*. I'd already filed two stories and had picked out the subject for the weekly editorial obituary. Since most of the obits that ran in our paper were technically death notices—small tributes sent in by families or funeral homes—Flick had had the idea to bring back the obituary in its traditional form, a news article detailing the life of someone who had an impact on our community. The column had been a huge success, increasing our circulation with many readers citing the "Life in a Day" column as the reason they decided to take the paper after all this time.

I'd decided (and verified with Kay) that this week's subject would be Myrna James Rothchild, known to all in Tuttle Corner as the "Christmas lady." Myrna kept her house decorated for Christmas, inside and out, year-round. You'd often see her dressed up as Mrs. Claus on a sunny day in April or raking leaves in October, though her husband, Doug, refused to dress up as Santa during any month other than December. Throughout the years her obsession with the holiday grew, and she began offering tours of her 2,400-square-foot home that boasted more than thirty-seven Christmas trees, twelve bunches of live mistletoe, and 350-plus nutcrackers. And for two weeks every December, Myrna would rent a buck from Swanson's Venison Farm in West Bay and tie up the poor beast in her front yard for photo ops. Whenever someone would point out that Rudolph looked more like a white-tailed deer than a reindeer, Mrs. Rothchild would wag her finger and say, "Santa doesn't visit doubting Thomases."

Myrna had been struggling with a heart condition for the past few years. She died in her sleep on Christmas morning, and although she would be missed, it was almost hard to feel sad, because Myrna herself could not have designed a more fitting exit.

Doug Rothchild cried when I'd called to let him know I'd be featuring Myrna for the New Year's Day edition of the paper. "Bless you, Riley," he'd said. "She'dve been so honored."

On my way out of work for the day, I stopped by Holman's office to let him know I was heading home. He certainly didn't need to know where I was every second, but checking in with Holman about my comings and goings from the office was a habit I'd gotten into. He'd often do the same to me as he passed by my cubicle on his way into or out of the newsroom. He was on the phone and held up a finger when he saw me in his doorway.

"I'm leaving," I whispered. "Just wanted to say goodbye."

"Stay," Holman whispered back. His face looked serious as he returned to his phone conversation. "Yes, yes, okay. I understand."

Something about his tone told me he didn't like what he was hearing. I set down my bag and sat in the chair across from his desk.

"Okay, thank you, Lindsey," he said. "Yes. I'll tell her." He pressed end and lowered the phone from his ear.

"What is it?"

Holman blinked, looked at me, then blinked again. "That was Lindsey Davis." Lindsey Davis was the Tuttle County prosecutor. "Joe Tackett says he has information about a cold case and would be willing to trade it for a reduction in his sentence or a prison transfer."

I knew even before Holman finished his sentence what case he was talking about. My heartbeat suddenly felt bigger inside my chest. I held my breath as Holman said the words.

"He says he knows who killed your grandfather."

Tears pricked at the back of my eyes. I'd always suspected Joe Tackett had been involved in my granddaddy's death—or at the very least, in covering it up. Tackett had been the sheriff of Tuttle County at the time, and I always thought he'd been too quick to close the case out as a suicide. Plus, he was a mean sonofabitch. I didn't like to use the word *hate*, but my feelings for Joe Tackett came close. Then a few months ago my suspicions about him were confirmed when it came to light that Tackett had gotten in deep with a Mexican drug cartel and was looking the other way as they distributed their product in the region. My childhood best friend and Holman's co-worker at the *Times*, Jordan James, figured out what was going on, and Tackett and the cartel had her killed. Holman and I worked the story together, and partly due to some good reporting (but mostly due to some ridiculously good luck), we managed to bring Tackett to justice without getting ourselves killed.

Just hearing his name filled me with a restless kind of rage. Tackett was as crooked as a barrel of fishhooks. He was all about selling his power to the highest bidder, and my gut told me—had been telling me for years—that his handling of Granddaddy's death had been bought and paid for. This was the validation I'd been searching for.

"Let's go see him. Tomorrow—no, tonight! We could leave right now." I stood up, adrenaline coursing through my veins. "I wonder why he decided to talk now after all this time? Do you think it has something to do with Flick's death? Wait—but no—he might not even have heard about that. I mean, he's in prison, after all. Do they have access to newspapers? TV? Do you think he'll talk to us? I'd think if he's planning to give the authorities the information anyway, surely he'll at least give us something..." My mind felt like it was filled with firecrackers.

Holman sat motionless and said nothing.

"C'mon," I said. "Let's go! If we leave now, we could get to Greensville Correctional before...well, okay, maybe you're right—maybe it's too late tonight. We'd better wait until the morning. Do you mind driving? I know I already owe you like a million dollars in gas, but I'll pay you back, I promise. Why aren't you saying anything?"

Holman gave me a look that could only be described as pity. "Riley..."

"What? What's wrong with you? Why aren't you freaking out—this is a *huge* deal, Holman."

"Riley," he repeated, his voice soft and gentle. "They're not going to give him the deal."

For a split second, the entire world stopped turning. "What?"

"Sit down, please."

I sat.

"The DEA has been after Tackett to flip on members of the cartel, but he won't cooperate. He says he might as well sign his death certificate if he does that."

"So, what does that have to do with anything?"

"The feds aren't interested in your grandfather's case. They want the cartel. They've been in touch with Lindsey and have 'encouraged' her not to make a deal with him. They want to keep pressure on him."

"Are you kidding me?"

Holman shook his head. "Lindsey thought you had a right to know."

To say I was gobsmacked would have been an understatement. The federal government didn't care about the murder of one of its citizens, a man who fought in the Korean War, a man who served his country as both a soldier and a journalist covering war zones? Albert Ellison was in many ways a hero—and not just to me. The fact that some asshat in the DEA would so flippantly reject information about his death was unacceptable.

"I want to talk to her."

"It won't do any good. It's out of her hands," Holman said.

"Still."

"She said she was leaving for the day—"

"Then I'll catch her," I said. I grabbed my coat and was out of Holman's office in three seconds flat.

CHAPTER 4

One of the benefits of living in a town the size of Tuttle Corner was that the majority of our businesses were distributed in a single square block around Memorial Park. On the south end of the park was the largest of the municipal buildings, the Tuttle County courthouse. From the *Times* newsroom on the east side of the square to the courthouse, it was about a four-minute walk. Three, if you were fueled by righteous indignation. I caught Lindsey Davis just as she was walking up to her car.

"Riley." She did not seem surprised to see me.

"Can we talk?"

"There's not much to talk about. I already told Holman everything I know. I'm sorry," she said.

I believed her. Lindsey Davis had moved to Tuttle to take over the District Attorney spot after Kevin Monroe had been arrested for taking bribes in the Tackett corruption scandal. She agreed to move here from Washington, DC, as part of an American Bar Association program that helps pay down school debt if lawyers agree to practice in an underserved area for at least five years. She was young, probably under thirty, but was hardworking and had already earned the respect of the community.

"Please," I said. "I need to understand."

She sighed and was about to say no, I could feel it.

"I'm not asking as a reporter," I said, lowering my voice. "I'm asking as a granddaughter."

She opened her car door, chucked her briefcase inside, and closed it again. "Fine, but let's do this over a drink."

We sat upstairs at James Madison's Fish Shack, Lindsey on the distressed-leather loveseat and me across from her on the chintz club chair. The fireplace in the corner crackled and hissed and sent out a warm glow into the converted attic space. They still had their holiday decorations up, which added to the cozy feel. There was a handful of other people there, but Lindsey and I were tucked away into a corner so no one would hear us.

"This is off the record," Lindsey said, holding her mug of mulled wine with two hands. "And just to be clear, I mean *way* off the record. You cannot print any of this—not even without a source."

Lindsey Davis had thick, dark hair, which she wore in a pin-straight, blunt-cut bob, the left side always tucked behind her ear. Her dark brown eyes were wide set with long lashes, giving her face a doe-like quality, which I think was what the no-nonsense hair was supposed to counteract. I could only imagine how tough it was to be a woman in her field in this part of the country, especially a young African-American woman.

I nodded. "Understood."

"Okay, well, I really don't know a whole lot more than what I told Will on the phone," she said. "The federal agent in charge of the case against Tackett has been trying to persuade him to give up information about the Romero family's drug operations. But Tackett has been locked up tighter than Fort Knox. He says if he utters one word against the cartel, he'll be dead before breakfast. Then about a week ago, he tells this agent that he has some information about a crime that took place in Tuttle County when he was sheriff. He said he'd be willing to tell the state what he knows about that crime in exchange for 'helping him out.' " She paused. "The agent naturally asked what crime he was referring to, and Tackett said, quote, 'Albert Ellison's supposed suicide.' "

"I knew it," I said automatically. "I knew he didn't kill himself." Before I could stop it, a bubble of emotion crept up on me. I tried to bite it back but only succeeded in looking like someone who had just swallowed a frog. "I'm sorry..."

Lindsey looked down, giving me some privacy as I fought to collect myself. After a minute she said, "I can only imagine how painful this must be."

I took a deep breath in and blew it out slowly. "I've been searching for answers since I was eighteen years old." I paused, shaking my head. "I knew it couldn't have been suicide, but no one believed me. Tackett made sure of that... but now—"

"Don't get your hopes up, Riley," she said, firmly cutting me off. "The feds were clear with me: They want to hold out for information about the cartel."

"Who cares about the feds?" I leaned forward. "My grandfather was killed in Tuttle Corner, that's your jurisdiction, right? Can't you make a deal with Tackett? Recommend a transfer to Judge Giancarlo in exchange for the information?"

She started shaking her head before I had even finished talking. "It's not that simple. They've warned me not to step on their toes. I could face a lot of static for doing it anyway."

I sat, openmouthed, silenced by the injustice of the situation.

"I know," Lindsey said, her large brown eyes filled with compassion. "I'm frustrated too."

"I don't understand." I slumped back in my chair. "How can the government not care about who killed my grandfather? Do we all of a sudden not care about apprehending murderers?"

"As of now, the official cause of death in your grandfather's case is a self-inflicted gunshot wound. In the eyes of the law there's been no crime. There's no case. And the government is looking at it through the lens of the DEA. If they can get to the leadership of the Romero cartel, they can potentially save thousands of lives."

"But..."

"It's also possible that Tackett's lying. He's certainly not above that," Lindsey added.

I hadn't considered for a second that Tackett was lying, probably because I knew in my heart all these years that he knew what happened to my grandfather. Flick knew it too. *Flick*. The thought hit me like lightning.

"Lindsey," I said, scooting to the edge of the chair. "I've been working on the theory that my grandfather's and Hal Flick's deaths might be connected. What if the information Tackett has would do more than just shed light on an old case? What if it could help solve a murder that just happened?"

"Connected? How?"

I explained everything to her about the file and Flick's unofficial investigation, the trip to Chincoteague, his cryptic phone calls, Granddad's missing research.

"Have you told the Brunswick County sheriff about your suspicions?"

"I tried, but Sheriff Clark said there is literally almost nothing to go on in the investigation. No witnesses, no cameras—"

"Yeah, but this could provide a motive," she said.

"Sometimes that's as effective as a witness in tracking down who committed a crime."

"I guess, but I don't have any hard evidence of the connection."

She arched one eyebrow. "Then I suggest you get some."

"Do you think that'd make a difference? If I could prove that the two deaths were related, could Tackett be forced to give testimony in that case?"

"No one can compel him, but if he has information about a person who has killed twice and is still at large? That might give me more leverage in defying the feds. I'm not saying it's a slam dunk, but it's better than what we have now."

"Thank you, Lindsey," I said, feeling as close to hopeful as I had in a long time.

She held up her mug. "To catching the bad guys."

"And taking them down." I held up mine and clinked it against hers.

We hung out for a little while longer and talked mostly about how she liked living in Tuttle. "It's different from DC for sure," she said, "but the people here are really nice, and the cost of living is great. I just wish I could meet more people our age. That's been the hardest part."

I could see Tuttle being a hard place to meet friends if you hadn't grown up around here. Most Tuttleans in the sub-thirty-five age group were either lifelong residents who all knew one other or had married young and already had kids.

"We don't exactly have a killer social scene around here, do we?"

Lindsey laughed. "Honestly, it's fine. I work so much, I barely have time for a life, but there are moments when I miss going out to bars or concerts or whatever. That's actually how I met Will."

This surprised me. "You met Holman at a bar?"

She nodded. "Karaoke Night at Lipton's Books & Brew."

"I'm sorry—hold up." I almost spit out my drink. "Holman sang karaoke?"

"Yeah, he was really good, too! He did a haunting rendition of 'Blank Space.' "

That time, I really did spit a little of my Revolutionary Rum Runner out of my mouth. "Holman sang Taylor Swift?"

"He did this really slow, sexy version of it. Everyone went nuts. I mean, granted there were only like nine of us there, but it was amazing. He's really talented."

It was like she was describing a completely different person than the Will Holman I knew. I'd never so much as heard him sing along to the radio in the car, let alone belt out a pop anthem in front of a crowd. And to describe him as sexy? I was dying! *Dying.*

"What?" she asked. "Is that out of character or something?"

"No, it's just you never know what you're gonna get with Holman. He's full of surprises."

"So, um, are you two like...?"

"Oh God no!" Lindsey flinched and I felt badly, like maybe I'd reacted too strongly to the question. "Don't get me wrong, Holman's great, but we're more like brother and sister." An awkward silence hung in the air for a moment. "Why do you ask?" I was pretty sure I knew why she was asking.

Two scarlet patches came into focus on her cheeks, confirming my suspicions. "I was just wondering, that's all."

"You like him!" I said, a smile spreading across my face. This was big news. Holman had been devastated when

Rosalee, on whom he'd had a major crush, used him, literally, to try to get away with murder. I was giddy thinking about how flattered he'd be to know a woman like Lindsey Davis thought he was, um, sexy. (I had trouble using that word even in my own mind in relation to Holman.)

"Let's just say that I'd be interested in getting to know him a little better."

"We can definitely arrange that," I said, waggling my eyebrows.

"Oh no." She held up a finger at me. "No setups."

"Not a setup *exactly*—we can just engineer a situation in which you are both in the same place at the same time."

"That is the definition of a setup." Lindsey gave me crocodile eyes that I imagined worked very well on uncooperative witnesses.

"Actually," I said, a new thought rolling around in my mind. "I just found out about a New Year's Eve party that a friend of a friend is having. Do you have plans?"

"Not unless you count a *Gilmore Girls* marathon as plans."

"Perfect!" I said. "I'll see if I can wrangle you an invite and one for Holman too. Trust me—it'll be fun!" I didn't dare mention that it was a themed party. I didn't know Lindsey well enough to know her stance on costume parties. I was pretty sure Holman could be persuaded to play along, especially if it meant getting to spend the evening in the company of a smart, accomplished woman who just happened to think he was, um, sexy.

CHAPTER 5

I was wired after my meeting with Lindsey, as much about her interest in Holman as with the possibility of finding a connection between Flick's and Granddaddy's deaths, so Coltrane got an extra-long walk when I got home. Being a large, long-haired German shepherd, Coltrane did not mind the near-freezing temperatures half as much as I did. He trotted happily along the sidewalks in my neighborhood, ears up, tail aswish. Sometimes I imagined that Coltrane was the king of the four-block radius around my house, and our daily constitutionals were like visiting his royal subjects. *Nice to see you again, Elm Tree. How's it going today, Magnolia Bush? I shall pee on you now, Crabgrass.*

"What're you smiling about?" The voice came out of the darkness and made me jump about three feet in the air.

"Ryan, you scared me half to death!" I said once I'd caught my breath.

"Sorry." He set down the bag of trash he'd been carrying to the curb and bent down to greet his canine soul mate. He then proceeded through several rounds of *Who's a good doggie*?

"How's the house?" I asked, finally interrupting the lovefest. "You guys getting settled?"

In a somewhat uncomfortable move, Ryan had recently

purchased the house that backed up to mine. It was only uncomfortable because as recently as six months ago, Ryan declared his undying love for me, before mentioning Oh-yeah-I-got-another-girl-pregnant-and-she's-moving-to-Tuttle-to-raise-the-baby-but-we're-not-together-and-I-love-you-let's-make-out. I declined his invitation for obvious reasons.

The pregnant girl in question was Ridley, and the three of us had mostly worked through whatever weirdness there had been between us. The fact is that I liked Ridley a lot. I liked Ryan a lot too, for that matter (when he wasn't being a clueless idiot), and their baby Lizzie was just about the most adorable thing I'd ever seen, not to mention my goddaughter. After telling Ryan in no uncertain terms that we would never, ever, get back together, Ryan decided that he wanted to give things another try with Ridley. I wasn't sure what exactly was going on with them lately. Mostly because I hadn't asked.

"Yeah, it's just been crazy." Ryan stood up. He was wearing basketball shorts, an Adidas T-shirt, and flip-flops, and I could see his breath when he spoke. He had to be freezing. "Between the baby, buying the restaurant, and moving... we've hardly had a chance to catch our breath. But we love the house. It's got a good soul, you know?"

Ryan beamed at me from under his thick lashes, and I was struck by how genuinely happy he seemed. It was hard to believe that this was the same Ryan Sanford whom I'd dated for seven years, and instead of proposing to me after college graduation as planned, took off to Colorado like a thief in the night without so much as a "See ya later." So much had happened since Ryan had come back to Tuttle six months ago. He was now a father, a homeowner, a local business owner, and living with his beautiful, smart, practically-perfect-in-every-way Swedish baby mama. Whoever said life is what happens when you're busy making other plans sure got it right. I don't think anyone—including Ryan himself—could have predicted the direction his life had taken.

"I've been meaning to come over with a plate of something," I said, suddenly realizing that I had yet to properly welcome Ryan and Ridley to the neighborhood. My mother would be horrified.

"Nah, don't worry about it. You've had a lot going on. How're you holding up?" He and Ridley had both come to Flick's funeral, both given me extra tight hugs when it was over.

"I'm okay," I said. "Busy with work, which is always a good distraction. And..." There was a part of me that wanted to tell Ryan about Tackett offering information on Granddaddy's death. Ryan had been the only person in town who believed me that Granddad hadn't committed suicide, who didn't write me off as a grief-stricken young girl. There was a part of me that would always love him for that, but I knew that, if anything, Ryan and I needed to disengage rather than revisit the things that had held us together in the past. We were doing a pretty good job of learning to be friends, and I wanted to keep those boundaries firm. "Yeah...all good!"

He smiled at me. "Well, you look great."

"Thanks." I smiled back. "You too."

Just before the moment got awkward, Coltrane whipped his head around, his ears shooting up into perfect triangles, his eyes opaque with purpose. He stared down the dark road and let out a low growl. As a former police dog, Coltrane never growled without reason. Both Ryan and I followed his gaze.

"What is it?" Ryan whispered, as if Coltrane might answer. "What do you see?"

I scanned the darkness but didn't see anything unusual. To the left, the Dorseys' three cars with West Virginia plates were parked in and around their driveway (probably family in town for the holiday). To the right, Gill Littrell was walking back up to his house after putting the trash out. And at the top of the street, a Prius was turning left at the stop sign. Nothing seemed out of place.

"It's probably nothing," I said, though not quite as sure as I sounded. I clipped Coltrane's leash back on. "C'mon, buddy. Let's go home." But Coltrane wouldn't budge. He crouched down on one leg, the way dogs do when they're stalking something. He took a step forward and growled again, this time lower and longer.

"I'll walk you home," Ryan said. The spot Coltrane was focused on was just back and to the left of Ryan's driveway, which put it in the woods directly next to my house.

I shrugged him off. "No, you'll freeze to death. I'm fine."

"I'm gonna grab a coat, stay here," Ryan ordered, already turning to run back up the brick path to his front door. "Don't leave."

I debated taking off before he got back, but I had to admit I was a little spooked. Coltrane wasn't jumpy or prone to overreacting to strangers or stray cats or whatever. If he growled at something, it meant he was warning me. Or warning whoever was out there. I looked around again. Mr. Littrell had gone inside, and the Prius had driven on. Coltrane and I were very much alone on that street, at least as far as I could tell.

A few seconds later, Ryan came back with a puffy down coat, a wool hat, and a flashlight. But he was still wearing shorts and flip-flops. (Clueless idiot.) "Let's go."

We walked quickly along the sidewalk of Beach Street. Coltrane seemed more relaxed now that we'd left Ryan's street, though he was not the same jaunty monarch he'd been earlier. Maybe it was my imagination, but he seemed a bit more on guard.

I asked Ryan about Lizzie and what fun new things she was doing these days (grabbing her feet, blowing spit bubbles, giggling) and how his parents felt about him taking time away from working at their Farm & Home store to get Mysa up and running. Ryan said his parents were over the moon about it all. They'd all agreed that once the café got established, Ridley could run it and he'd go back to work for the family business. They'd volunteered to help with any and all babysitting needs. Sounded like they were just as smitten with Lizzie as the rest of us.

"And how are things with Ridley?" I wasn't sure if it was weirder to ask or not to ask at this point. A few weeks ago, Ryan had come to me seeking advice on how to best declare his newfound love to Ridley. When I'd tried to tell him that maybe he ought to ask someone else for advice, he'd wrongly assumed it was because I was jealous that he had someone since I was still single. I'd tried telling him he was wrong, that I'd long since let go of any romantic feelings for him, and I was perfectly happy being on my own. To that, he'd basically ruffled my hair and said something along the lines of, "Sure you are, kid." It made me want to dunk him in a vat of boiling oil. After a while though, I'd forgiven him as usual. He didn't mean to be so self-centered; he just couldn't help it.

"Things are good." Ryan smiled into the darkness. "We're taking things slow, but we're in a really good place right now."

"I'm glad," I said, ninety-seven percent because I meant

it, and three percent to prove I wasn't carrying a torch.

When we got to my driveway, I unleashed Coltrane and gave him the "Go see" command, which meant that he took off to sniff the perimeter of the house. It was a neat trick he'd learned in the doggy police academy before he was retired for being gun-shy. Ryan trailed behind him with his flashlight. I waited on the front porch, scanning the street and trying not to look freaked out.

After about three minutes Ryan came back, Coltrane trailing behind him. "All clear. Must have just been a raccoon or something."

"Yeah, I'm sure you're right," I said, not at all sure. "Well, thanks for walking me home. Say hi to Ridley and kiss Lizzie for me."

"You got it—though I might switch those around."

I rolled my eyes. "Bye, Ryan."

"'Night, Riles," he said. "Night, buddy," he called to Coltrane.

I went inside, slid the deadbolt into place, and threw a little prayer into the universe that whatever "raccoon" had been skulking around my house earlier didn't own a set of lock picks.

CHAPTER 6

I spent the rest of the evening going over Flick's file. Again. I'd been through it ten times already over the past month, but now I attacked it with renewed purpose. I needed to find evidence that Flick's and Granddad's deaths were connected in order to persuade Lindsey to deal with Tackett. I knew in my gut that the two crimes were related—possibly even committed by the same person—I just had to find a way to prove it.

The problem was that Flick had told me very little about what he was working on. It was his way of keeping a promise he'd made to Albert to "keep me safe." I still didn't know if Granddad had asked Flick to do that as a general measure, or if he said it because he was worried about a particular threat to my safety. Either way, Flick's interpretation of keeping me safe had led us down a rocky path. Right after Granddad's death was ruled a suicide, I'd begged Flick to help me investigate it, to help me prove it had been a crime, but he refused to even talk to me about it. He shut me down and shut me out completely. At the time, I assumed it was because he was selfish or lazy or a coward. I had no idea he was just trying to keep the last promise he'd made to his best friend. And until very recently, I'd had no idea that Flick shared my suspicions about how Granddad died.

I started, as I often did when I was feeling stuck, by

making a list. I carefully selected a brand-new journal from my growing collection (and possible indication of hoarding tendencies). This one was gray, eight and a half by eleven, leather-bound, and had my initials stamped into the bottom right corner. It had been a birthday present from Flick. I opened it to the first page and wrote the words **WHAT I KNOW** across the top.

1. Flick went to Chincoteague Island to follow a lead about Granddad's murder.

Just days before he was killed, Flick told me he was going to Chincoteague to look into something. I didn't even know he'd left the island until I received the phone call from Kay saying his car had been found on Highway 58. That was more than 200 miles from Chincoteague. Among the many things I needed to figure out were: What exactly was Flick doing on the island? Why did he leave? And where was he going when he was run off the road?

2. Shannon Miller / plane crash.

The last conversation I had with Flick was on the day before he died. I remembered the call so clearly. I could still hear his gruff voice across the line, the cutouts from bad reception, the background noise that made it sound like he was in a war zone, rather than a vacation destination off the coast of Virginia. I'd asked him to tell me what he'd found out, what lead he was chasing. He was characteristically vague and said only that he was following up on something Albert had been working on right before he was murdered.

"...an entire family was tragically killed in a plane crash outside their home state of–" the line cut out and I didn't hear that part. *"The youngest daughter was only four years old at the time. Her name was Shannon Miller...I came over*

here to Chincoteague because this is where their plane went down–"

When I told Flick that I was worried about him and maybe he should just come back, he'd laughed and said, *"Don't worry about me, kid. I've confronted worse than a pack of professional liars...I'll call you back later tonight, okay?"*

But he didn't call me back. Instead, he'd left the island and had driven west. I would never hear his voice again. A wave of sadness swept through me thinking about that night. If only he would have told me what he was working on, whom he was meeting, where he was going. I don't know that I could have saved his life, but it sure would have made it easier for me to find who killed him and hold them responsible.

Other than Granddad's missing book research, this was the biggest clue I had to work from. And it wasn't much. I had the name of Shannon Miller, a four-year-old who died along with her entire family in a plane crash off the coast of Chincoteague Island in 1959. I'd been able to find a couple of old newspaper articles online about the crash that had been digitized by the Chincoteague Historical Society. The reports said that the pilot, a man by the name of Daniel Miller, was flying his family to Wilmington Beach, North Carolina, when the plane crashed. All five family members were killed. Investigators were not sure of the exact cause of the crash, but the theory was that Daniel lost consciousness while flying the single-engine Piper PA-32, and the plane dove into the Atlantic Ocean. Listed among the dead were Daniel Miller, thirty-eight, his wife, Robin Miller, thirty-six, and their three children, Eric Miller, ten, Joseph Miller, eight, and Shannon Miller, four.

While it was certainly a tragic story, I didn't know what

this plane crash from sixty-plus years ago had to do with my grandfather. Why would Granddad have been looking into an aviation accident that happened when he was just a teenager? My only thought was that perhaps Granddad had been planning to include this family in his *Lonely Dead* book. But that didn't seem to fit either. How could five people die and have no one to bury them? Also, why did Flick specifically tell me to remember the name Shannon Miller? I needed to find more information on this family and its connection, if any, to my grandfather.

3. Doodle

I'd found a piece of yellow legal pad paper in the file upon which there was a hand-drawn doodle of two hands cupped together. It looked familiar to me—almost like the logo for that insurance company, but the hands were wider, the fingers spread farther apart, almost as if they were reaching out to grasp something. Flick had circled the drawing and taken the time to put it in the file, so even though I had no idea what possible significance this might have, I put it on the list anyway.

Close to midnight, I set my notebook aside, no more enlightened than I'd been when I'd sat down. I'd asked a few questions but uncovered no answers. And even worse, I had no ideas about how to get any answers. Had Flick and Granddad started out with these same questions? Was that the reason they were both dead? Was I now heading down the same path that had led two of the most important men in my life to their deaths? If I was being honest, I knew that I probably was. Surprisingly, while there was definitely a part of me that was scared, most of me just felt angry. I would not—could not—allow whoever committed these crimes to get away with it. They'd taken too much from me.

So, as scared and lonely and overwhelmed as I felt, I knew I had to keep chasing the answers to my questions. No matter where that chase might lead.

Daily Astrological Forecast

Scorpio

Saturn is at odds with Neptune today, stoking the fires of controversy and combat. This energy may bring an old enemy or issue back into your orbit. Proceed with caution. Emotions can run high, especially when you feel threatened. And while you are generally easy-going, as a Scorpio you are capable of a distinctive venomous sting. Like your celestial spirit animal, you prefer to lie in wait and strike when least expected.

Remember to slow down, dear Scorpion. Life is a game of chess and you are continually plotting to score the eventual checkmate you so desire. As Mars enters analytical Virgo, today is a good day to survey the chessboard. Work on your patience. The time to make your move is coming soon.

Tonight: Take your taste buds on a culinary odyssey! Consider trying the cuisine of Southeast Asia!

CHAPTER 7

Acting Sheriff Carl Haight was in a foul mood when I arrived at his office the next morning to get his reaction to Skipper Hazelrigg's declaration of intent to run against him for Tuttle County Sheriff in the upcoming election.

"How do you think I feel about it, Riley?"

I'd known Carl Haight since preschool and had rarely heard him snap like that. "Um, you know I'm interviewing you for the paper, right? Do you really want me to use that quote?"

"No," he said, the word coming out with a sigh. Carl took off his hat, ran a hand through his red hair, and then placed it back on his head. "My official answer is that I hope the people of Tuttle County will look at my record of service, my dedication to this town and this county, and give me the privilege to continue to serve and protect as I've done for the past six months as acting sheriff and as a deputy for the three years before that."

"Better." I quickly scribbled the quote down in my notepad, word for word.

"Coffee?" He motioned to the single-serve machine that sat on the credenza behind his desk. I nodded and he dropped a pod into the machine and pressed start.

"You doing okay, Carl?"

He shot me a look from under the brim of his hat.

"Just asking as your friend now."

I knew he was hoping to run uncontested for the position of sheriff, especially since he'd stepped in after Tackett's arrest and handled some very high-profile cases in his short time as acting sheriff. When Skipper Hazelrigg, Tuttle County native and former Virginia Big Buck bowhunting contest winner, decided to challenge him, it didn't surprise me that Carl would be upset. Or worried. Skipper owned a company that manufactured firearms components and accessories that worked mostly with law enforcement agencies and the military. A few years ago, he made a run for Virginia State representative for district sixty-two. He ran against incumbent Hope Lauder and lost by a narrow margin.

A lifelong Tuttle County resident, Skipper had always been an active member of our community, often monopolizing town council meetings to complain about the things he felt were not being done correctly. Everyone knew he'd been itching to get into politics, and after his loss at the state level, I guess he saw this sheriff's race as a good place to start.

"Hazelrigg is a good man," Carl said. "And he's an accomplished businessman. I just don't think he's the right person for this job—and I'm not just saying that because he's my opponent."

I actually believed him. Carl may have been overly officious at times, but he did not suffer from a big ego. If anything, it was the opposite. That was one of the areas in which Carl and I connected. We were both relatively new in our respective positions, and as the next generation of Tuttle County, we often felt slightly in over our depth. It was that intermittent sense of inadequacy that fueled both of us to try harder, work longer, and be more thorough than other people.

"Have you spoken to him since he officially entered the race?"

Carl nodded. "He came by my office on his way to file his paperwork. He said he wanted to tell me in person."

"That was nice."

Carl shrugged. "He also said he thinks Tuttle County is headed in the wrong direction and needs a 'stronger hand' in order to deal with the recent rise in criminal activity."

"Was he suggesting that was your fault?"

"He didn't say that exactly, but I got the feeling that's what he meant. He implied that because I'm young, I'm not equipped to handle the kind of challenges we're facing as a community."

"That's ridiculous! Being young doesn't mean you're not capable." I know as the press I'm supposed to be impartial where local politics are concerned, but I couldn't help but take that comment a little personally.

"Coffee's done."

"Thanks." I took the mug and two packets of sugar off the credenza.

"I just have a feeling this race could get ugly." Carl's mouth flattened into a thin line, the way it always did when he was worried.

I wasn't sure what to say. I didn't disagree with him. I'd once covered a city council meeting in which Skipper Hazelrigg ranted for forty-five minutes about how allowing a Dollar General to open up would plunge Tuttle Corner into an economic tailspin that would leave our streets empty and our citizens penniless. He made a twenty-slide PowerPoint, set to music from *Les Misérables*. By the end of his public comment, he had almost every person in that room convinced that Dollar General was an outpost of the devil himself.

"What does Lisa think?" I asked. Lisa Haight was a teacher at Tuttle Elementary and perhaps the sweetest person who ever walked the Earth. She was one of two kindergarten teachers at the school, and people were known to hold their kids back a year if they didn't get into her class.

"She says I shouldn't worry, says Skipper may have more business experience, more contacts, and more money than me, but I have more heart." He rolled his eyes. "Like that's what people want in a sheriff."

"I don't know," I said. "You might be surprised."

"Enough about that. How're things going with you? Any news from Brunswick County?"

Carl had reached out to Sheriff Clark when he heard about Flick's death and offered his assistance. He'd also vouched for me, which I think had been one of the reasons Sheriff Clark had been open to talking with me about the case.

"Not yet," I told Carl. "I talked to him a few days ago, but he said they were at a dead end. I'm worried they're just going to let the case go unsolved."

"Did they ever determine why Flick was on that particular stretch of road at that time of night?"

"Not that I know of."

Carl made a face. "They don't know where he was going? Or why?"

I shook my head.

"Hmm...I'd think..." He hesitated.

"What? Carl—tell me."

"Nothing, I mean, I don't want to tell anyone how to do their job, but if it were me investigating a hit and run, one of the first things I'da done was get phone records of the deceased to determine who they'd been talking to right before they were killed. I'd have checked with all the local hotels and motels in the area to see if Flick had been staying anywhere nearby—or was planning to. I'd check credit card statements, bank transactions, email accounts. All of it. Seems to me if you're looking to find out who committed a crime, you have to start by finding witnesses, if not to the crime itself then at least to what the victim was doing right before, who he'd been talking to, things like that."

I wondered if Sheriff Clark had been asking these questions, investigating these angles. It's entirely possible he was and that he just wasn't sharing his process with me. After all, he didn't know me like Carl did. For all he knew, I was some buttinsky journalist with an ax to grind.

"You're the executor of his estate, right?" Carl asked.

"Uh-huh."

"Then you should have access to a lot of that stuff, you know."

I hadn't thought about that before, but he was right. Not only had Flick given me power of attorney, he'd also named me as the executor of his will.

"Thanks, Carl," I said. "See—this is why Tuttle Corner needs you as our sheriff!" I drained the rest of my coffee in one gulp and stood to leave.

"Where're you going?"

"To make some calls."

"Riley, be careful," he said, his voice taking on that ominous warning tone that I'd become familiar with over the past few months.

"What?" I was halfway into my coat, anxious to get back to the office and request some of these records. "You just said—"

Carl walked over and held the corner of my coat so I could slip my arm inside. "I know what I said. And now I'm saying be careful. Whoever killed Flick is out there. They could be watching the investigation and watching you."

"I know," I said. The image of Coltrane growling last night popped into my mind. "Trust me, I will be."

"Will you?"

"Geez, Carl." I rolled my eyes. "Yes, I said I would."

"Because *careful* is not really your thing."

I laughed. He didn't.

"I hate to say it," Carl said. "But I agree with Skipper Hazelrigg. Tuttle County has become a much more dangerous place than when we were kids."

"It's gonna be all right, Carl. Don't worry." I didn't say whether I was referring to tracking down Flick's killer or Carl's race for sheriff, mostly because I didn't know which, if either, would actually be okay.

CHAPTER 8

On my walk back to the office from the sheriff's station, my phone rang. It was Hank Jorgensmeyer, Jay's friend from the Department of Transportation.

"Thanks for calling me back," I said, digging out my notebook. I parked myself on the nearest bench, even though it was thirty-five degrees outside. The freezing temperatures at least guaranteed me privacy out here.

I explained the situation to Hank, including a little bit of background context, that Flick had been ruffling the feathers of some people who had possibly killed in the past. That may have been a teensy bit of guesswork on my part, but whatever. Hank told me he was sorry, and then told me what he would have done if he'd been the lead investigator.

"In a case like this where you have very little physical evidence to work off of, you want to focus on motive. You want to examine who had incentive to kill the victim, check their alibi, check whether or not they'd had any recent communications with the deceased. You have to work from the outside in, especially if you have some idea of who might be behind it."

"And if you don't?"

"Well, then you scour the victim's life for clues. In my experience, people aren't murdered for no reason. Something your friend was up to got the attention of the wrong person. If you can figure out what it was, you can trace out the tentacles from there."

I wrote all of this down.

He added, "But this takes time and resources, two things most small-town sheriff departments are short on."

"Do you think they'd take leads from, um, outside sources?"

"Are you planning to run your own investigation into the accident?" He laughed, a big round bubble of a sound.

"Maybe. And it wasn't an accident."

"I'm sorry." He cleared his throat. "It depends. Some offices will appreciate the help, some won't. All I can tell you is whatever you do, do not mistake yourself for a law enforcement professional. If you want to do some background legwork on paper trails and things like that, fine, but the minute you overstep, you could find yourself in a world of trouble that could jeopardize the entire case, not to mention your own safety."

"I'm not a moron, Hank," I said.

"Oh, I can tell," he said without any sarcasm in his voice. "I'm just telling you to be careful."

"I see someone has been well coached." When Jay and I were dating, I'd received many a similar lecture from Jay about the dangers of crossing the line between reporter and cop.

Hank let out another jolly laugh. If he had a big belly and a white beard, he could moonlight as a mall Santa. "Just watch yourself is all I'm saying."

This was the third time in twenty-four hours that I was told to 'be careful' by some man. I'd be lying if I said I didn't resent it just a bit.

"I appreciate you taking the time to talk to me," I said, sidestepping his warning.

"Riley?"

"Yes?"

"Jay just thinks the world of you. I know he'd want to make sure you're being safe."

His words knocked me off balance. Jay and I had a brief but intense romance a few months ago. Our breakup had been due to logistics more than anything else, and I was aware I had some unresolved feelings for him. He'd actually come to my rescue not too long ago when my car broke down in DC, where he was now living. He'd invited me over to his place and just when I was beginning to rethink the whole breakup thing, he introduced me to his new girlfriend, Chloe. They were so cute together, it quite literally almost made me puke.

"That's nice." And then unable to resist, I added, "I'm sure he and Chloe talk about my safety all the time."

"Chloe?"

"Jay's new girlfriend?"

"Oh," he said, sounding embarrassed. "I didn't know that he had a new girlfriend. Whoops, I'm sorry. Well, in any case, Jay's a good friend to have."

A million responses came to my mind: *Is he? We're not exactly friends. Jay is good at a lot of things...*but in the end, I simply thanked Hank for his time and hung up.

Chapter 9

No one had been more surprised than me to find out that Hal Flick named me executor of his will. Flick and I had been close when I was younger, but after Granddad died everything changed. When he refused to listen to my theory that Albert hadn't killed himself, I'd locked Flick out of my life completely. And he didn't really fight it. He'd pulled away from me too, and over the years a deep chasm of bitterness and resentment grew between us. I was hurt by what I perceived as his abandonment of his best friend, but mostly I was young, angry, and immature. I was mad that Granddaddy had left me—whether it had been his choice or not—and needed to blame someone. Flick became that someone for me.

It wasn't until I'd started working at the *Times* that Flick and I reconnected. It had been a slow process, but over the past several months we'd talked about everything from our shared memories of Albert Ellison to the fundamentals of obituary writing. We spent hours working together at the paper, and recently he'd even started coming by my parents' house again like he used to back in the day. In fact, my father had invited him to spend Christmas Eve with us. Flick was planning to bring the cranberry sauce.

After he died, I went through his paper address book and called everyone with the last name Flick I could find. It was a small list. He had an ex-wife to whom he'd been briefly married, but they'd had no children and weren't in touch anymore. Upon hearing the news, she'd said she was "saddened." It felt like a response of theoretical sadness and reminded me of what someone would say about the death of an ancient celebrity or a former politician. Flick also had two nephews and a niece, his brother's children, whom he hadn't seen since his brother's funeral seven years earlier. None of these people came to the funeral; only two sent cards.

In light of his small family, it made more sense that he would have chosen me as executor. But why not choose my father? Or my mother, for that matter? I couldn't help but think that Flick wanted me to be the executor of his estate because of something to do with his investigation. That had just been between us. As far as I knew, I was the only person who knew what he was working on. I suppose it made sense to leave me in a position to carry it on. That's why he'd left the file for me, wasn't it? *In case something happens to me*...he'd told Kay.

I called Flick's lawyer, Stanley Calhoun, and asked him what records I could access.

"As executor, you can request phone records, financial records, medical records—anything really. Why do you ask?"

I hesitated for a moment. "Is this between us?"

"It can be."

I lowered my voice. "I've been disappointed with the progress the Brunswick County sheriff's department has made in the accident investigation. I was thinking maybe I'd see if I could help out."

"So, you're going to do some amateur sleuthing?"

"I'm a reporter. Technically, I am simply doing research on an important news item."

"Uh-huh," he said. "Riley, listen, if you—"

"Let me stop you right there," I said, gall rising in my throat. "I appreciate your concern, but please do not tell me to be careful. I am a grown woman who is perfectly capable of assessing the risk associated with my decisions."

"Um, I was going to say you can drop by my office and pick up the documents you need to request those sorts of records. It can take a while to get them, so the earlier you start on it, the better."

"Oh," I said, glad he couldn't see my reddening face through the phone. "Sorry."

"Had enough of people trying to tell you how to behave, have you?"

"To last a lifetime."

"Well, you won't get any warnings from me. I'm actually glad to hear you're looking into it. Flick was a good man. He didn't deserve what happened to him, and if the cops aren't able to figure out what happened, someone needs to."

"My thoughts exactly."

"I'll get the documents prepared and you can run by and sign them later today," Stanley said.

I spent the next few hours making phone calls on the "Life in a Day" column. Myrna Rothchild's sister, who lived in West Virginia, kept me on the phone for nearly thirty minutes telling me story after story about how Myrna's love for Christmas had grown from the time she was young. I also spoke to Myrna's daughter, Beth, and also to Ed Sutherland, the electrician who helped create her Tuttle-famous "magic tree." As I started to write the piece, I felt Flick's loss like a phantom limb. We had always worked on these together, talking through which details would best illuminate the individual life we were focusing on. Flick had a special eye for that sort of thing. This column was his legacy, and I hoped I could do him proud.

About ten minutes later, Holman walked into the newsroom with his earbuds in (I wondered if he was listening to Taylor Swift). I grabbed his elbow as he walked past. "Hey, what're you doing on New Year's Eve?"

He took the right earbud out. "What did you say?"

"New Year's Eve...do you have plans?"

He looked at me like I had just handed him a carton of milk and said, *Smell this*. "Why?"

I crossed my arms in front of my chest. "Why are you asking why?"

"Why are you asking why I am asking why?"

"*Holman!* It's a simple question: I just want to know if you'd like to come to a party with me on New Year's Eve."

Holman took out the other earbud with a sigh. I heard him mutter, "Here we go again..." under his breath. "Can you come into my office a minute? I think we should talk in private."

"No, Holman this isn't—"

"Please." He held up his hand. "Let's not make this harder than it has to be."

Having been down this road a number of times, I knew where this was going. Holman was going to attempt to let me down easy. Again. Despite my never, *ever*—not even once—having expressed the slightest bit of romantic interest in him, Holman seemed to forever be explaining to me why it was best if we just remained friends.

I followed him into his office and waited for the familiar lecture to begin.

"Riley," he said, his voice dripping with gentle condescension. "The holidays can be a difficult time of year, and I know this year has been particularly hard for you. But you have to accept that you and I—" he broke off and steepled his fingers together, "we're just better off—"

"Yeah, yeah, we're just friends. I get it."

"You do?"

"Yes."

"What a relief," he said. "Are you okay?"

"I'll try to pick up the pieces and move on."

Holman, who was completely impervious to sarcasm, smiled. "Brave girl."

I bit back a thousand snarky responses and moved on. "Listen, Ash's cousin is having a Great Gatsby–themed New Year's Eve party. You should come!"

"A Great Gatsby party? What does that mean?"

"Nothing really. It's just like a theme for decorations and stuff. And some people will probably dress up like people from the twenties, but you don't have to."

"The roaring twenties," he said. I could practically see the intricate cogs and gears of Holman's mind twisting and turning as he attempted to process this information. "It was a time of tailored fashions for men, I believe. Suits and ties were de rigueur for day, tuxedos and top hats were often worn for an evening out. In fact, I believe that was when the zoot suit rose to—"

"No zoot suits." I cut him off. "It's pretty much just a regular party. Do you want to go?"

"With you?"

"Don't look so horrified. Yes, with me—and Ash."

"Oh, right, Ash..."

"Why do you say it like that?"

"Like what?"

"Like his name tastes bad in your mouth."

"Names don't taste like anything, Riley. They're just words."

I had a feeling Holman was being purposely obtuse.

That was too literal, even for him. "*Anyway,*" I said, "Ash invited me, and I'm inviting you. I think there will be a fun group of people around our age there. And it beats sitting at home. Do you want to come with or not?"

Holman stared at me while he considered the invitation. After a moment he said, "Sure, it'll be the cat's pajamas!"

"No, Holman—you don't have to—"

"We'll get our glad rags on and have a swell old time!"

I was already starting to regret this. "So, you're in?"

"Like Flynn."

"Great." I stood up to leave. I was excited to tell Lindsey the good news.

"Actually," Holman held up a long, bony finger. "The expression 'in like Flynn' didn't appear in common parlance till closer to 1940, referring to the professional prowess of actor Errol Flynn, of course, so technically that would be incorrect in the context of the party. Perhaps a more apt colloquialism for the Jazz Age would be—"

I walked out of his office before he could finish the rest of that sentence. I had a feeling I'd hear quite enough about "colloquialisms of the Jazz Age" before the clock struck twelve on New Year's Eve.

CHAPTER 10

I texted Lindsey and told her Holman was in for the party, and that I hadn't mentioned to him that I'd invited her also. Since she seemed so opposed to the idea of a setup, I thought I'd space out those conversations. Then I texted Ash and told him. His cousin had said it was cool to invite whoever. The party was still four days away, but I was starting to get excited. It'd been a long time since I'd gone to a party like this, longer than I cared to admit. And the past few weeks had been so bleak, so depressing, it felt good to have something to look forward to. I'd call my mom later that night to help me decide what to wear. Jeannie would love this sort of a project.

I was all caught up on my assignments for the paper, so I dedicated some time to trying to get more information about Shannon Miller and the plane crash that killed her and her family. There wasn't a whole lot of information beyond the details of the accident in the few articles I'd found online, but since the ones I had found were from the Chincoteague Historical Society, I wondered if maybe they could point me to more resources.

"I'm sorry, Miss Ellison. I don't have much on that particular accident. It was before the NTSB was formed, and I'm afraid they just didn't keep good records back then," a docent named Roberta told me when I called. I was about to thank her for her time when she added, “Did you try the local historical society in Hudson Falls, Texas?”

“Hudson Falls?”

“Yes. That’s where the family who perished was from.”

“They were from *Texas*?”

“Yes,” Roberta said. “It says right here in our ledger. Daniel Miller’s pilot license has a home address in Hudson Falls, Texas.”

“Can you email me a copy of that?”

“Sure,” she said. “I’ll see what else I can dig up and will send along whatever I find.”

“Thanks, Roberta,” I said. “You’ve been super helpful.”

“I’m happy to have a project. You’d be surprised—it can be fairly slow around here.”

I was not at all surprised; I would not have imagined the Chincoteague Historical Society being anything other than slow. But I didn’t say anything. We hung up and I immediately looked up Hudson Falls, Texas. It was a tiny town, population 2,347 at the last census. Tuttle Corner was bigger than that, but I knew from experience that small towns often had less red tape when it came to information sharing. I called their county records office and spoke to a nice woman named Elaine. I explained that I was doing a story on a family who had lived in Hudson Falls in the 1950s but had died while on vacation in Virginia. Elaine surprised me by asking, “The Miller family?”

I almost swallowed my tongue. “How did you know that?”

“You’re the second person to call today about the Millers,” she said. “Is it some sort of anniversary of their death or something?”

“Something like that,” I mumbled. I wondered if the first person to call had been someone from Brunswick County. I decided to see if I could find out. “Um, oh gosh, I hope I’m not duplicating efforts. Was it Sheriff Clark who called?”

"No," Elaine said. I heard the sound of shuffling papers. "Says here it was a woman named Jane Smith. We faxed her some information on the Millers first thing this morning."

Jane Smith. I'd never heard such a fake name in all my life. Sounded like someone else was also doing some digging into the Miller family.

"Oh yes, *Jane*," I said, hatching a plan on the fly. "We used to work together when I was at a different paper." I laughed again, then lowered my voice to a conspiratorial whisper, "Hey listen, Elaine, is there any way you could help me out and send me what you sent Jane?"

"Um, well..." She had the sweetest lilting accent. "I suppose so...they're just some records from our archives, free and open to the public. All we need is your name, phone number, and email address. There's a real handy form I can send you to fill out."

"You're the best. Thank you!" I paused. "Um, one more thing...do you think you could give me Jane's phone number? I'd love to reach out and see if we can share sources and that sort of thing."

"But I thought you said you two know each other?"

I could tell I was making poor Elaine feel uncomfortable. I felt my conscience squirming from somewhere deep within my internal ethics department. Journalism 101 teaches you it is not okay to lie to get information from a source. But I wasn't *exactly* researching a story here, was I? I was a private citizen looking for information to help solve the murders of two innocent men.

"We do!"

"Then, uh, shouldn't you already have her number?"

Good point, Lainey. I quickly rerouted. "Of course I do—I mean, I did. This is kind of embarrassing, but I actually just dropped my phone in the toilet and lost all my contacts."

Elaine gasped.

"Tell me about it," I said. "And I haven't been able to afford a new phone—you don't exactly get rich working at a small-town newspaper, am I right?"

"Or working at the records department in one," she said with a laugh, and I knew I almost had her. I just needed to press on the gas a little bit harder.

"Jane is such a good reporter. She was like a mentor to me at one point, and I'd bet she'd help me out if I could just reach her." I paused for dramatic effect. "If I'm being honest, Elaine, I think my boss is like two seconds away from firing me. If he's not happy with my work on this story, Nibbles and I could be out on the streets."

"Nibbles?"

"My cat." Then in a last-minute spark of inspiration I added, "She's diabetic."

"Oh, my word," Elaine said. "Well, I suppose it wouldn't be a big deal. I mean, you two being friends and all. And you used to have her number and all before you, uh, had the mishap with the, uh..."

I lowered my voice. "They say toilet water is just like the rest of the water in your house, but I don't believe it."

"No, no, definitely not," she whispered. I heard the sound of shuffling papers again. "Okay, it says here Jane's phone number is 252-555-4378."

"You're amazing," I said. Guilt aside, I felt like I was writing down the winning Powerball numbers. Elaine emailed me the form I needed to fill out to request the documents. I didn't exactly know what I was asking for, so in the Materials Requested box, I just wrote: copy of materials sent to Jane Smith. Elaine said she was the only one in the records office, so she'd know what that meant. I thanked her profusely again.

"Best of luck with the story," she said before hanging up. "And with Nibbles!"

CHAPTER 11

The records that "Jane Smith" requested (and I so deftly cribbed) were a little underwhelming. They painted a picture of the Millers as a normal American family. Between 1948 and 1959 the Miller family had lived a pretty typical life in Hudson Falls, at least according to their paper trail. Daniel and Robin had gotten married, bought a house, and paid their taxes. Since I was neither family nor law enforcement, I couldn't access any of their birth certificates, but I could tell from Department of Health immunization schedules that the Millers' three children, Eric, Joseph, and Shannon, definitely existed, because the records show they'd been vaccinated on a regular age-based schedule.

There was not a single record filed after May 1959, when the plane crash occurred, not even death certificates. I learned that death certificates are filed in the place you die—not where you were born or even where you lived. So, because they died in Virginia and not Texas, their story had never been given an ending, at least not in Hudson Falls. Birth and death records weren't cross-referenced across state lines back then, so technically as far as the state of Texas knew, the Millers could still be alive. It was sad and actually sort of poetic. They'd have to be living off the grid and would be in serious violation of about 700 tax laws, but still. It was strange to think that an entire family could vanish from the face of the Earth, and because of a failure in data management procedures, it could look like the whole thing never happened.

As I integrated this new information, I did a quick mental assessment of what I knew: Granddad was writing a book about people who had died alone. Flick said something Granddad was working on got him killed. Flick told me to remember the name Shannon Miller. Within forty-eight hours of telling me that, Flick was killed too.

As a general rule, I tried not to jump to conclusions, but when you have no place else to start, sometimes you have to start from a hypothesis and work backward. I knew from reading Arthur Conan Doyle's Sherlock Holmes stories (and binge-watching Benedict Cumberbatch's version of the same on Netflix) that he relied on the method of deductive reasoning. Granted, he was a fictional character with a serious drug habit, but with no better plan in place, I decided if it was good enough for Sherlock Holmes, then surely it was good enough for Riley Ellison! I would start from the hypothesis that Granddad was planning to include the Miller family in his book. If that premise was true, then under the rules of deductive reasoning, the next most logical question would be, *Why* had the Millers died alone? The whole family was wiped out by one cruel swipe of fate's paw, so where were the grieving grandparents, aunts, uncles, cousins, neighbors, and friends?

Another central question was, Why did Flick tell me to remember the name Shannon Miller? There had been five Millers who perished. What was special about Shannon? She was only four years old when she died. Had she been extraordinary in some way? My Google search quickly revealed that looking up Shannon Miller was about as productive as looking up someone named Jane Smith. Of the approximately one zillion Shannon Millers who came up in my search, one was a famous Australian performance artist, one was the CEO of a large multinational corporation based in California, one was a nail technician in Boca Raton, and on and on. There was nothing written about a four-year-old who had died five decades ago. And in fact, there was nothing I could even think of that a four-year-old could do that would bring them notoriety, other than being a famous child actor (negative) or becoming the poster child for a tragic disease (unlikely). But I made a note to contact the hospital in Hudson Falls to see if anyone there remembered a Shannon Miller being associated with any sort of fundraising drives or the like.

After I hit a dead end with the Shannon Millers of the world, I decided to grab a late afternoon pick-me-up (in the form of something caffeinated and possibly something chocolate) at Mysa. I bundled up in my yellow wool peacoat and braved the five-minute trek. Tuttle winters weren't typically too bad, usually bottoming out in the forties during the day, but this year we were having an unseasonably cold winter. Chase Brommer on Channel Eight news this morning said we were on our sixth consecutive day of subfreezing temperatures. It was a bad time of year to be without a car.

About a month ago, my sweet little Nissan Cube (Oscar, may he rest in peace) went to the great scrap heap in the sky. Oscar needed some repairs that were going to cost almost as much as I had paid for the car. My mechanic Ivan convinced me it was probably best to just sell it and get something else. "This cube car is not reliable transportation. You are young woman, you need better. Ivan will find good car for you. You wait and see."

Ivan had actually been able to sell Oscar to a guy he knows who resells parts and got me way more than I could have gotten on my own. He'd also been in touch to let me know about a couple of cars he'd found at auctions, but I'd been so consumed with everything going on with Flick and the funeral that I just hadn't gotten back to him yet. The truth was that most places I needed to go to in Tuttle Corner were walkable, and on the rare occasion I needed a car during the past month, I asked my parents or Holman. But as the cold wind blew hard against my cheeks, I realized it was probably time to let Ivan know I was ready to buy something.

I pulled open the door to Mysa, thankful for the blast of warm air that came at me. Taking off my hat and gloves, I looked around—or rather gaped—at all the changes Ridley and Ryan had made over the past month during their rebranding campaign. The café looked like a completely different space! They'd painted over Rosalee's signature yellow walls with a soft white, making the space appear much larger and more modern than before. Gone were the red café curtains with the small fleur-de-lis pattern that had hung in the windows for as far back as I could remember. The front window now stood uncovered, and they'd painted the casement black for a chic, updated look. They'd replaced the old wooden chairs with molded plastic white ones with stainless steel legs. And although they were still using the marble-top tables, they replaced the bud vase and single faux red rose with a low rectangular white ceramic candle in the center of each table.

Along the back of the café, the pastry case was still there, as it had always been, but the wire racks had been switched out for glass ones and an entire wall of floating shelves on the wall behind the case had been added. The shelves were arranged with an artful display of white ceramic dishes, dried goods in glass jars, and some new products they were now selling for at-home consumption, like imported Swedish biscuits, green tea, specialty hot cocoa, and of course everyone's favorite, Swedish fish.

I stood at the front door admiring the new look, my eyes swiveling from one new thing to the next. It wasn't every day that familiar institutions got a facelift in Tuttle Corner.

"What do you think?" Ridley floated out from behind the pastry case, leaning down to give me a kiss on each cheek.

"It's amazing. I can't believe how much you've done," I said as I mentally added interior decorating to the long list of things Ridley Nilsson was good at.

"We've basically been living here." She smiled, giving me a shot of her perfect white teeth. "But it's good, right? It looks cozy?"

"It's incredible," I said, and I meant it. I would have complimented it whether or not I liked it (I was a good Southern girl), but in this case I didn't have to fake it. "I'm so impressed."

"Come in the back," she said, leading me through the swinging door that connected the front and back of the house. "Let me show you what else we've done."

Just as they'd done in the dining room, they'd completely streamlined and cleaned up the kitchen. What used to be a small cramped space overflowing with equipment was now an efficient, organized workspace. And Rosalee's old office, which was basically a glorified broom closet, had been reconfigured, repainted, and repurposed as a tiny little nursery for Lizzie. Ridley pulled back the heavy hanging curtain to reveal a beautiful modern bassinet on large wooden rockers. Lizzie slept peacefully inside, swaddled within an inch of her life. She looked like a beautiful pink cotton candy burrito.

"Amazing," I whispered, staring at the baby.

Lizzie's plump cheek twitched, and her eyelashes fluttered. Ridley pulled the curtain closed. "She loves it in there."

She led me back out front and to a table near the window. I ordered a mocha latte and a croissant, and when she brought it out, she sat down.

"So how are you doing? You're back to work?"

"Uh-huh," I said. "Feels good to be busy."

"Have you found out anything more about who—" she stopped herself from actually saying the words.

"Killed Flick?" I filled in the blank. "No, not yet. I'm working on a few things."

Ridley tucked a strand of her long blond hair behind one ear and leaned forward. "Ryan said there might have been someone following you last night?"

I shook my head. "Coltrane probably just saw a squirrel or something. Everything's fine."

"Are you sure?"

"Yes."

"Good."

I could have kissed her for not telling me to be careful.

"By the way, are you going to Toad's New Year's Eve party?" she asked.

"How do you know Toad?" Ridley had lived in Tuttle Corner for only a few months, and I swear she already had more friends than I did.

"He sold us the insurance on this place."

"He did?" I didn't even know he was an insurance salesman.

She nodded.

"How'd you know I'd be going?"

"Aren't you dating his cousin Ash?"

"Um, I...I mean...it's—we're—"

Ridley waited patiently as I stammered through my nonanswer. When I finally stopped making sounds, she said, "You like him but aren't sure you want to get into a relationship."

I stared at her openmouthed. I had never confided any such thing to her. "How did you know that?"

"You know I have a heightened sense of intuition," she said with accountant-level seriousness, then flashed me a wicked smile. "So, what's the hesitation? He's very cute..."

"Yeah, he's cute for sure." I felt a blush begin. "What kind of coffee is this? It's delicious."

"No changing the subject."

"There's nothing to say," I said, looking down. "It's like you said: I like him, he's cute, we're just going slow, that's all."

"But you are going to the party as his date?"

"Yeah, I guess." I hadn't exactly thought about it in those terms, but I supposed she was right. It was a date. "Speaking of dates, whatever happened between you and David Davenport? You guys still seeing each other?"

It was Ridley's turn to blush, something I'd actually never seen her do in the whole time I'd known her. Ridley was perhaps the most confident person I'd ever met; she was not prone to self-conscious blushing. "David is a great guy, but with the baby and all...it just didn't work out. We're in two completely different places in our lives." She paused, then looked up at me, her crystal blue eyes boring into mine. "Ryan and I have been spending a lot of time together, obviously, and we've sort of reconnected—romantically."

Before I had a chance to say anything, she reached across the table and clasped my wrist. "Does that bother you?"

It was the first time she'd ever asked me point-blank what I thought of her relationship with Ryan. We'd talked around the subject of my being in Ryan's past and of course about them raising Lizzie together, but Ridley had never asked how I felt about it. It was sweet of her to care, even though we both knew my feelings on the subject were (and should be) irrelevant.

"Not one bit," I said.

At that, her face broke into the kind of smile that countries went to war over. She'd been looking for my approval, and although she didn't need it, I was glad to give it to her.

"I want you both—you all," I corrected myself, "to be happy. You deserve it."

She gave my arm an extra squeeze before letting go. "You deserve it too. Be careful not to talk yourself out of it."

CHAPTER 12

I hadn't gotten three steps into the newsroom before Kay leaned her head out of her office. "Ellison, can you come in here a sec?" She'd obviously been waiting for me.

I walked in and saw Holman sitting in one of the two chairs opposite Kay's desk. I caught his eye. He gave a slight shrug.

"What's up?"

"Close the door."

I did and then sat down next to Holman, my heartbeat ticking up a few notches. "What's going on?"

"It's Joe Tackett." Kay said.

"What about him?"

"He sent a letter addressed to Riley Ellison and Will Holman, care of the paper."

Holman's face betrayed nothing. I tried to follow suit. Lindsey Davis had told us about Tackett with the understanding we would not report it. I didn't want to do or say anything that would betray that agreement. I'd given her my word. Plus, getting crosswise with the county prosecutor was never a good idea.

"Neither of you look surprised." Kay looked from Will to me.

"Did you open it?" Holman asked.

"Of course I didn't open it," Kay snapped.

"Can I see it?" I held out my hand, seized by a strong and sudden impatience to see what that sonofabitch wanted from me.

Kay gave me a long look, then took an envelope out of her top drawer and handed it to me. "If I didn't know he was in prison, I would have had that checked for ricin."

I slid my finger under the seal and worked it across the top of the envelope. Inside, there was a single piece of unlined paper. I unfolded it. There was no greeting, no pleasantries, just three handwritten sentences followed by his signature: "I know what really happened to your grandfather. It was not suicide. I am ready to talk if my conditions can be met. Joe Tackett."

A fuzzy sort of numbness started to crawl up my neck toward my face. I passed the letter to Holman. He read it, then handed it back across the desk to Kay. The three of us sat in silence for at least ten seconds until Holman finally said, "Do you think he's talking about your grandfather, Riley?"

I shot him a look that could have cut glass.

"What?" he asked.

"Of *course* he's talking about my granddad, Holman."

"Well, technically the letter was addressed to us both, so an argument could be made that he might have been talking about *my* grandfather."

Both Kay and I stared at him, our mouths hung open in twin expressions of bewilderment.

"I have two grandfathers, actually," he continued, undeterred by our reaction. "Both are still living, though, so the part about suicide wouldn't fit. Then again—"

Kay cut him off. "I think we can safely assume Tackett is referring to Riley's grandfather, Will."

Holman opened his mouth to say something, but thankfully his good sense prevailed, and he closed it.

"I want to go see him," I said to Kay. "There's a story here." This is what I'd wanted to do since the moment I heard about Tackett's sudden desire to talk—and now was my chance to do it legitimately for the paper.

"I don't know if that's a good idea." Kay pursed her lips.

"Holman will come with me, right?"

"Yes. Of course."

"Kay, this is newsworthy. Albert Ellison wasn't just my granddad. He was a part of our community. If his death wasn't a suicide, then it was murder. That is a story we need to tell."

Kay had to know I was right, but she was probably worried about sending Holman and me to face Joe Tackett, the man who in the not-so-distant past had ordered both of our deaths. She tapped her pencil rapidly against the desk. "Fine." The word shot out like a dart. "But you know he's going to push you to help him trade his information for something he wants, right?"

"I know."

"And you know that the odds are overwhelmingly against Tackett ever actually telling you what he knows—now or at any point in the future?"

"I know."

"And you realize that reporting on this story is going to open up a lot of old wounds for you personally?"

"I know."

Kay held my gaze for a few seconds and then said quietly, "You can't trust him. He's a bad guy, Riley."

"Believe me, I know."

Kay sighed. "Call Greensville. If you're lucky, they'll get you in before the end of the year."

"I've interviewed the director before," Holman said, standing up. "I did a piece a couple of years back on the lower recidivism rates coming out of Greensville. It was favorable. Maybe he'll remember me and get us in sooner?"

"Oh, he'll remember you," Kay said, but it was impossible to tell from her tone whether or not she was happy about that.

Chapter 13

I don't understand," my mother said to me later that evening. "Why do you have to go talk to him again?"

"I told you," I said, trying (and failing) to keep the frustration from my voice. "We're trying to see if the information he supposedly has about Granddad can be connected to Flick's death. If it can, there's a chance the judge will grant him a reduced sentence or a prison transfer or whatever."

"Yes, but why you?" She pulled the car over and looked into the backseat. "Here you are, Mrs. Foley. Bingo should be just about ready to start!"

Old Mrs. Foley nodded, clutching her brown cracked-leather purse handles with two hands. "And you're sure I don't pay you in cash?"

"All the payments are done right through your phone, remember?" my mom prodded, pointing to the phone in her hand.

Mrs. Foley's daughter, Susie Ryerson, was one of my mother's oldest friends. She worked odd hours at the hospital and wasn't always available to drive her mother places, so when she heard Tuttle Corner got its very first Uber driver in the form of Jeannie Ellison, she was all over it. My mom had driven Mrs. Foley a few times a week over the past month, but she still seemed to distrust the process.

"I'll never understand how tapping on this thing translates to money, but I suppose it's a new world." She sighed. "And Riley honey?"

"Yes, ma'am?" I turned around.

"You be careful going to see that horrible old sheriff, okay?"

"I will, Mrs. Foley."

"I sure hope you find out what happened to Albert." She shook her head sadly. "He was such a dear, dear man. Did I ever tell you he took my little sister out for ice cream one time when they were seniors in high school?"

She had, many times, but I knew the memory made her happy, so I let her tell me again. He'd picked her up in his powder-blue Mercury and taken her out for mint-chip cones at Landry's General Store. "There wasn't a spark between them, but it was just as well. He wanted to travel the world and Janie wanted a more traditional life. He was so handsome, though, just like your daddy." She smiled at my mother.

"You'd better get in there before all the best cards are gone," Mom said.

Mrs. Foley got out of the car, and my mom pulled out her phone, clicked a few things, and said, "All right. I'm officially off the clock. Dinner?"

"Dinner." I nodded.

My father had an Elk's Club meeting, so it was just the two of us. We decided to pick up salads from Landry's and eat back at their place. She said she had a dress that would be perfect for me to wear to the New Year's party, an old beaded number she'd picked up at an estate sale years ago. "I always knew if I hung onto it, eventually I'd find a use for it!"

We settled into our familiar places around the kitchen

table and I explained more about the situation with Tackett as we ate.

"And tell me again why it has to be you?"

"My guess is he thinks I'll push the hardest to bring this story to light. If there's public interest, it could help sway the lawyers in the case to consider making him a deal." I speared an apple chunk out of my salad. "It's smart, actually. It wouldn't be the first time journalists were used to bring attention to a cold case."

"Do you think he's telling the truth? What if he's just making something up in order to reduce his sentence?"

"I've always believed Joe Tackett knows more than he's said." That was putting it as diplomatically as I could manage.

While I'd been unwilling to believe that Granddad committed suicide from the start, my parents had accepted that explanation, despite the complete absence of warning signs. Granddad wasn't depressed, he had no history of mental illness, and he didn't even own a gun. When you threw in the fact that Tackett closed out the case with only the most cursory of investigations, the whole thing felt wrong to me. But my parents hadn't seen it that way. They'd met Granddad's suicide with deep grief and then quick acceptance, which was the easiest path forward for them. I tried not to resent them for their attitude. It was consistent with who they were, who they'd always been. And it was probably a form of self-preservation, particularly for my dad. The agony of losing a parent to suicide could easily swallow a person whole.

My mother looked down at her plate, pushing the same four farro grains around and around. I could tell she was working up the courage to tell me something. "The day after Granddad was found, Dad went over to his house—your house now," she looked up and gave me a sad smile. "I offered to go with him, but he said he wanted to do it alone."

I set my fork down. I had not heard this story before.

"He was still in shock about the whole thing, of course, but the anger was starting to set in. He kept repeating, 'I can't believe he'd do this to us. I can't believe he'd do this to Riley.' "

A lump started to build in my throat.

"That night he went over there, he was particularly angry, which as you know, is not an emotion Skip is used to. It was understandable given the situation...but anyway he went over there on a mission." She paused. "He told me later he went over there and tore through Albert's house looking for some clue as to what would have caused him to take his own life. He looked through his bank statements, files, combed through his desk drawers looking for anything that might help explain. Was he sick? Was he in trouble somehow?"

A picture of my dad, wild with grief and anger, tearing through Granddad's things appeared in my mind. It nearly knocked the wind out of me.

"He looked under the mattresses, behind the bookshelves, even took Albert's desk apart, piece by piece," she said. "He didn't find anything that explained what happened, but he did come across something kind of odd that night."

I looked at her, moisture rimming the edges of my eyes, the question evident on my face.

"It was a small scrap of paper that had been taped flush to the underside of his desk drawer. It was only visible if you pulled the drawer all the way out and turned it over. He'd clearly hidden it for some reason."

I swallowed audibly. "What'd it say?"

My mom got up, walked into the study, and came back a few seconds later. She handed me a plastic zip bag containing the piece of notebook paper. In my grandfather's thin, slanted handwriting it read: "You shall chase your enemies and they will fall by the sword before you. Leviticus 26:7."

I stared at the note, trying to bypass my emotional reaction to seeing his handwriting after all these years. I'd never seen this particular verse before, and while my grandfather was technically a Christian man, quoting scripture was definitely out of character. He was your typical twice-a-year churchgoer, Christmas and Easter. As far as I knew, he had no real feeling about religion at all. "What does it mean?"

"We don't know," she said. "But in light of everything that's happened with Flick and the file and...well, we think it must have had something to do with something he was working on. We thought maybe you should have it. Maybe it could be helpful to you as you look into what really happened."

After Flick died, I had told my parents all about his investigation into why Granddad was killed. I'd also told them I was going to pick it up where he left off, to the extent that I could. Though they never explicitly said it, they seemed more open than ever before to the idea that Albert might not have committed suicide. And this here tonight—my mom giving me what she hoped might be a piece of evidence and hearing her admit we still don't know what "really happened"—was her way of saying they believed me. I felt a surge of love and gratitude wash over me. "Thank you, Mom."

She sniffed her emotion away—Jeannie didn't do weepy—and after a deep breath in, she said, "Now let's go see about that dress!"

Daily Astrological Forecast

Scorpio

Teamwork is the name of the game today, as a spontaneous Uranus trine inspires you to form a surprising alliance. Conversation, connection, and your keen powers of observation will unearth a treasure trove of much-needed intelligence. However, the effects of the recent double eclipse are still reverberating throughout the universe. This cosmic concealment has a habit of flipping up with down, front with back, and good with bad. You'd be wise to focus a questioning eye on all information gathered today. Remember that while problems can masquerade as solutions—the opposite can also be true. Watch your back today, Scorpio.

Tonight: Light some incense and indulge in a mani-pedi of the DIY variety!

CHAPTER 14

We were issued an approval for a sixty-minute interview with Joe Tackett and were on the road by eight the next morning. Just as Kay suspected, the director of Greensville did remember Holman, and when he reached out to ask if our application to visit Tackett could be fast-tracked, the director agreed by saying, "Anything for a friend of the facility." It took me fifteen minutes to talk Holman out of sending the email he'd written in response denying that he was a friend of any of his story subjects, accompanied by a three-paragraph written lecture on how one of the most important tenets of good journalism was impartiality. In the end, I think it was my promising to buy bear claws for the drive that convinced him.

It wasn't a super long drive, but so far most of it had been spent in relative quiet. I was nervous about seeing Tackett again, about what he might or might not tell us, so I guess I'd been less talkative than usual. Holman must have picked up on my apprehension because he kept asking me if I was okay.

"I'm fine," I said. I looked out the window at the bean fields stretched out wide on either side of the highway. The crops were dormant now, and dried-out husks, cracked mud, and brittle sticks lay where lush green abundance had been just a few months ago—and would be again come spring. This decay was a necessary part of the life cycle, but it was ugly and bleak all the same.

I could feel Holman looking at me. "Coffee is a diuretic, you know."

"What?"

"Your travel mug looks like it holds about sixteen ounces. That's nearing the upper limit of what the average female bladder can comfortably hold. Studies have shown that while the bladder is elastic like a balloon, it will eventually reach capacity when your body produces enough ur—"

"Holman!"

"What?"

"I'm *fine,*" I repeated, then shifted in my seat, suddenly feeling sewn in by the safety belt.

He dropped the topic and was quiet again. For about ten seconds. "All I'm saying is that we've been in the car for a while now and you've consumed several fluid ounces of a diuretic. It stands to reason that your bladder is nearing its limit. Holding it for too long can lead to an overgrowth of bacteria and increased frequency of bladder infections."

"*Ohmygod,* fine," I sighed. "I'll go if you'll stop saying the word *bladder.*"

Holman took the next exit and pulled into a Sunoco station. He switched off the engine but made no move to get out of the car.

"Aren't you coming in?"

"No."

"But you've been drinking coffee too! Didn't you just lecture me on the importance of not stressing the limits of the human bladder?"

"No, I said the *female* bladder. While there is little functional difference in bladder size between males and females, female anatomy is such that the nerve receptors leading to the exit tube, or the ureth—"

"Seriously, please just stop. I'm begging you."

He looked up at me and blinked. "What?"

I opened the door and put one foot out. "I'm going inside now. When I come back, can we please talk about something else?"

"If you tell me a subject you're interested in, I can think about it while you're—"

I shut the door on the rest of that sentence. Sometimes you just had to do that with Will Holman, bless his literal heart.

I walked inside the small convenience store, and the woman behind the counter barely looked up at me. Her long brown hair was pulled back into a low ponytail, and she wore oversized glasses and a T-shirt with a picture of a fox on the front. She was reading what looked like a tabloid magazine and was listening to a fire-and-brimstone-type sermon on the radio. Evocations of devils among us and the unquenchable thirst of Satan curled out into the quiet of the store. When she looked up and saw me, she turned down the radio and muttered a tepid greeting.

I used the bathroom, tried not to touch anything, and came back out to the front. Even though the lady working probably couldn't have cared less, I decided it was only right to buy something in exchange for using their facilities. Years of hearing my dad's best friend, Vern Wexler, who was the owner of Tut-Tut-Tuttle Gas 'n Go, complain that people use his business like a porta potty had had an effect on me.

I walked up and down the aisles looking for something to buy. I wasn't hungry—and I sure as hell wasn't going to get a drink, lest Holman refresh his discourse on the intricacies of bladder function, so I grabbed a copy of the

Times-News from the wire rack near the checkout counter.

"That'll be a dollar fifty-seven."

I handed her the money.

"You just passing through?"

"Um, I'm on my way to visit someone."

"Greensville?" She gave me a knowing look.

"Uh-huh."

"You been before?"

"This'll be my first time."

The lady nodded. She had small, thin lips that almost disappeared when she closed them together. In the background, I could hear the radio preacher reach a fever pitch as he called out, "*...eternal damnation for the unrepentant!*"

"You take care now." She handed me my change and receipt.

I smiled as repentantly as I could. As I walked out, the lady turned her radio back up and the preacher's voice boomed out into the empty store. "*Remember, the devil doesn't come to you wearing a red suit and horns, he comes dressed as everything you ever wanted!*"

Once we were back on the highway, the preacher's words echoed in my mind. There did seem something a little too convenient about Tackett offering up the one thing in the world he knew I wanted more than anything. It wasn't like I'd ever make the mistake of trusting Joe Tackett, but was it stupid of us to go see him? To engage with him? What if Tackett was just using the promise of telling me everything I ever wanted to hear and really had no information about my granddad?

"You're biting the corner of your lip." Holman's voice interrupted my thoughts. "In my experience, that means you're worried about something."

I turned to him. "Do you think Joe Tackett is playing

us?"

"Depends on what you mean by 'playing us.' He's been up front about wanting to use his knowledge about Albert's death to get better conditions, so if you consider that playing us, then yes."

"But do you think there's another reason, some hidden motivation for wanting to get us to come out and talk to him?"

Holman thought about this for a moment. "It's possible."

"What do you think it could be?" I twisted a strand of hair around my first and second fingers.

"Any guesses I could make would be pure speculation," he said. "Luckily for us, we won't have to wait long to find out."

CHAPTER 15

Greensville Correctional Center was situated at the end of a long two-lane road. I'd never been to a prison before and was surprised to see that it wasn't just a single building; it was more like a complex, laid out in a hexagonal pattern. There were four large, long rectangular buildings, which I assumed were where the prisoners were housed, because they were guarded by six tall, armed guard towers. The entire area was surrounded by a high metal fence, topped by big loops of razor wire.

We followed the signs to the visitors' parking area and walked inside. After checking in at the front window, presenting our identification, and signing several documents, we were led into a room where we were asked to take off our shoes. There they searched us for weapons, checked our shoes for heaven-knows-what, and made us empty our pockets. Then we were taken into a secured area through two locked doors and finally into a small room with a table and four chairs.

After what seemed like forever, Joe Tackett was ushered into the room by an armed corrections officer. I was glad to see that they had shackles around his legs and a waist chain hooked to his right arm. Not that I seriously thought Tackett would try to hurt me or Holman during our conversation, but the chains provided a little extra insurance in case things went sideways. After the officer got him settled in a chair, I thought for a minute that he was going to leave the room, but he didn't. He took up a position in the corner, which was only about six feet away from Tackett, and stayed there throughout the entire visit. It was another measure of safety. Another reminder that Tackett was no longer a free man.

For the first few moments, Tackett and I just stared at each other. The past six months had not been kind to him. His long, angular face looked pale and waxy—the color of cold oatmeal—and his wiry frame was swallowed up by his shapeless orange jumpsuit, making him appear smaller and thinner than I remembered.

"I knew you'd come." His voice was as cocky and biting as ever, despite his diminished physical appearance. Hearing it again caused a ripple of fear inside my chest. The man had tried to kill me, after all.

"We received your letter," Holman said, allowing me a moment to collect myself.

"Yeah, I knew that'd get you. I know Riley here is desperate to find out what happened to her old granddaddy."

Hearing him mention my grandfather made me want to jump across the table and start clawing at him like a wild dog. I started to react, then quickly caught myself.

Tackett saw my temper flare, and it made the bastard smile. "The way I figure it," he said, leaning back, emboldened by my momentary slip, "I'm the only one who really knows what happened to him, 'cept for the person who did it."

My stomach felt like it was filling with acid. I needed to get control of myself. I was giving Tackett all the power, which was definitely not what this conversation was supposed to be about. I took a deep breath in and out through my nose. "Was it you?"

He laughed and rolled his eyes. "Why would I think confessing to a murder would get me outta this place? How dumb do you think I am?"

"We know you are not dumb, Joe," Holman said. "Cruel and sociopathic, yes, but not dumb."

Joe smiled a hyena's grin. "Right. So this is what I'm offering: I will give a sworn statement revealing the identity of who killed Albert, how they did it, and why, in exchange for a reduction in my sentence, or at the very least a prison transfer. I hate this fucking place."

"Don't you have a lawyer? Shouldn't you be telling them this?" I asked.

"Fired her ass. She was incompetent."

His narcissism was unbelievable. "So why not bring this directly to the prosecutor?" I asked, already knowing the answer, of course. But I couldn't pass up the opportunity to make him admit how powerless he was. He spent years abusing his authority...it was so satisfying to see him squirm under the weight of his own impotence.

He slid his eyes away from mine and glowered at the wall. "Tried that. She didn't seem interested."

"What can you tell us about Flick?" I asked. I didn't want to lose sight of the fact that one of my primary goals of this interview was to prove a connection between Granddad's and Flick's killings.

Tackett shrugged. "How am I supposed to know what happened to him? I was in here when he bought it."

"Pretty big coincidence both Albert Ellison and Hal Flick, two obituary writers from Tuttle Corner who were best friends, both being killed, don't you think?"

He glared at me. "Maybe being an obituary writer in Tuttle is becoming a dangerous occupation."

Holman, sensing the mounting tension, stepped in. "Joe, we think the prosecutor would be much more likely to work with you if your information could be used to solve two crimes, particularly one that just happened."

His eyes flicked over to the guard in the corner. "I *might* know something that I *might* be willing to share with the proper authorities in exchange for getting what I want," he said, his voice lower and more conciliatory than before.

"Okay, but you understand that we're reporters," Holman said. "You know we don't have any agency over your sentence."

"But you have two things I don't—one is your goddamn freedom," he hissed. "The other is access to the newspaper. That lady prosecutor acts like she doesn't want to deal with me, and I believe what she needs is a little public pressure to change her mind."

Holman kept his voice even, neutral. "My sources tell me that you tried to offer this information to a federal agent and that he or she wasn't interested in helping you make a deal."

"He's only interested in the Romero cartel. Problem is, if I said one word about that, I wouldn't need a deal 'cuz I'd be dead. Feds say they can protect me, but they can't—not forever, anyway." He turned his watery pig eyes to me. "And I know how much you want to find out what happened to your granddaddy, so surely you'll figure out a way to persuade that lady prosecutor to deal on this."

"You can just say prosecutor," I said.

"Huh?"

"You don't have to keep calling her a 'lady prosecutor.' Her gender isn't relevant."

"You want to give me a lesson in political correctness now? I don't give a shi—"

"I don't know, Joe," Holman jumped in again. "Albert was killed nearly seven years ago. His killer could be dead by now, and then your information wouldn't be worth much."

"I can assure you that is not the case. The person responsible is very much alive. Very much in the public eye, in fact."

My eyes snapped to him.

"Oh?" Tackett's eyes widened. "Didn't know that, did you? I thought maybe you might have had some ideas who it was by now."

The man was taunting me. I opened my mouth to snap something back, but Holman put a hand on my arm. He was right. There was no point in letting Tackett get the best of me, if for no other reason than that was exactly what he was trying to do.

"If what you say is true—that the person who killed Albert is alive and some kind of public figure—that may rise to a level of interest that will get you something," Holman said. "But you're going to have to give us something before we're going to help you."

Tackett scoffed. "You think I'm going to give up my trump card?"

"We won't print your vague 'promise of information.' That isn't newsworthy," I said. "And no prosecutor in her right mind would cut you any sort of deal without something more concrete. You're a convicted criminal. Your word doesn't count for much."

I was trying to flip the tables, to bait him, and I could tell by the bulging vein on the left side of his forehead that I'd done it. He leaned forward and put his free elbow on the table between us. The officer in the corner made a move, and Tackett immediately shrank back.

"I think all parties would be *highly* interested in what I have to say. And it's not just their word against mine. I have proof."

"What sort of proof?" Holman asked.

"The audiotape kind, Lurch."

Holman blinked. "My name is Will."

Tackett looked confused. "Huh?"

"You called me Lurch, but my name is Will. Will Holman. I believe you knew that, at least at one point, because you addressed the envelope you mailed to the *Times* to both Riley and me. Also, a few months ago, you ordered your henchman, Fausto Gonzalez, to kill me. And I'd assume when ordering someone's death you pay attention to details like their proper name."

A deep crease appeared between Tackett's eyes.

Holman continued undeterred. "However, the stress of incarceration has been shown to negatively affect cognition, so I suppose it's possible—"

I leaned over and whispered in Holman's ear, "Lurch is slang for a tall, skinny person."

"Oh," Holman said.

"Listen." Tackett's stinging, nasal voice came out loud in the small room, and the guard took a step forward. Tackett, knowing he'd crossed a line, leaned back and held both his palms up. He then continued in a lower voice, "I don't know what you two idiots are talking about and I don't care. Are you gonna help me or not?"

Holman motioned for me to turn our backs on Tackett, then whispered. "What do you want to do?"

"I want to kill him."

He cocked his head to the side. "Hyperbole?"

I nodded, letting my eyes flit back over my shoulder to Tackett. He was such a cockroach, the thought of helping him made me feel sick to my stomach. But in order to get the information I wanted, I guess we had to—or at least it had to appear like we were. "Let's see if we can talk to Lindsey again," I said, taking my voice down as low as possible. "If we tell her about the fact that he supposedly has proof, maybe she'll change her mind."

Holman nodded, then turned back around. "No guarantees, but we'll take it to our managing editor and see what she says."

"Good." Tackett sounded relieved, and it wasn't until that moment that I realized how much he wanted this.

"We'll come back when and if we have more information to share," Holman said and then stood up. The guard in the corner, who had obviously been listening to every word we said, stepped forward and grabbed up Tackett by the elbow. His chains clinked and jangled as he was led out of the room back to wherever it was he'd come from. There was no goodbye—we were not old friends. This was a transaction and our business was concluded, at least for the moment.

Chapter 16

Holman and I left Greensville and made the forty-five-minute drive to the Brunswick County sheriff's office. I'd called ahead and asked Sheriff Clark if we could come by for an update on Flick's case. He'd agreed.

The Brunswick County sheriff's department looked almost exactly like the Tuttle County sheriff's department except instead of a cream and brown color scheme, they had a white and powder-blue one. The entire department basically was housed in one large room filled with a number of desks. In the far-right corner, it looked like there was a break room or kitchen and a small hallway leading back to the bathrooms. From where we stood in the entry, it seemed like there were four desks for deputies, only two of which were occupied at the moment. The place had a "government office" feel to it—that is to say, it felt like a place where people worked hard but not necessarily quickly.

Sheriff Clark came out to greet us. He was a tall man, probably over six-four, which I hadn't remembered. I'd only met him once, and that was right after Flick died. I didn't remember his height or his large, bushy mustache. As he led Holman and me back to his office, it was clear from his stiff posture and clipped tones that he wasn't super excited to see us again.

"I'm sorry that you came all this way, but like I said on

the phone, I don't have a whole lot more to share with you about your friend's case."

"We were actually in the area visiting an inmate at Greensville prison, so it wasn't out of our way," Holman said. "A man named Joe Tackett."

Sheriff Clark's eyes widened, but he didn't say anything.

I was hoping for a bigger reaction. "You might remember him?" I said. "He was the sheriff of Tuttle County until a few months ago, when he pleaded guilty to a boatload of corruption charges?"

"I know Joe." His tone could have sliced through leather.

"Holman and I worked on that case together."

"Story," Sheriff Clark corrected me. "Reporters work on *stories*. Law enforcement works on cases."

Warmth started rising up my neck and into my cheeks. "Right. Anyway, it's come to our attention that Tackett has some information about a cold case, a murder, that we believe might be connected to what happened to Flick."

Sheriff Clark arched an eyebrow. "Would the cold case in question happen to be that of your grandfather? The one that is currently closed and listed as a suicide?"

I felt like a child who'd been caught with her hand in the cookie jar, but I wasn't about to let him make me feel small over this. I lifted my chin and said with as much dignity as I could muster, "Yes it is, as a matter of fact. Tackett may be a horrible excuse for a human being, but I didn't believe my grandfather committed suicide then, and I don't believe it now."

Holman spoke up and gave Clark a short summary of how Tackett rushed to close out Granddad's case and went through all the reasons why it didn't add up to suicide. He also told him about Tackett's letter and what he was asking for. At the end, Holman added, "Riley and I have been working on a theory that Flick's 'car accident' and Albert's 'suicide' were engineered by the same person and for the same reason."

Sheriff Clark, who had taken a few notes while Holman was talking, set down his pen and looked at us. "Interesting..."

"What's interesting?" I asked.

Sheriff Clark opened a file on his desk and took out a sheet of paper. He handed it to me. "That's an incoming call log from Greensville Prison."

I scanned the document. There was one entry highlighted in yellow. "That's Flick's number," I said.

Sheriff Clark nodded. "I spoke to the operator who answered the phone that day and she said she remembers the call. Said Flick asked how he might go about getting an appointment with an inmate."

"Tackett," I said. *I knew that sonofabitch was hiding something.*

"Did he make the appointment?" Holman asked.

"The operator told him he was not on Tackett's list of approved visitors, so he needed to go on the Department of Corrections website and fill out a form."

"Did he?"

"Not that I can find a record of," Sheriff Clark said.

I had been troubled from the start by the fact that Flick's accident occurred on Highway 58, miles away from Chincoteague and Tuttle Corner. Now I wondered if maybe he'd been heading to see Tackett in prison. "I guess he could have taken 58 from Chincoteague into Greensville...maybe that's what he was doing that night—heading to see Tackett?"

Sheriff Clark gave a curt shake of his head. "Lawrenceville. We believe Flick was heading to Lawrenceville." He said it with the kind of authority that gave me the impression that this was more than just something he thought.

"What's in Lawrenceville?" I asked.

"Not what," he said, "who."

"Okay," I said, growing weary of his slow-drip style of communication. "*Who* is in Lawrenceville?"

"I'd rather not say until we have more information."

"But—" I began, my frustration beginning to boil over. "Why not?"

"We're simply not ready to talk to the press about our investigation."

"We're here not as reporters. We're here as Flick's family."

"Even still," Sheriff Clark said. "When there's information to share, we will share it. For now, you have to trust that we're running down leads as best we can with our limited resources. It's just gonna take some time."

Right after Flick had been killed, I'd quite frankly been scared to share any of my theories with Sheriff Clark. One of the last things Flick had told me was that I should be very careful with the information we were uncovering about Granddad's murder. I didn't know Sheriff Clark and therefore didn't know if he could be trusted. I hadn't told him much about what Flick had been investigating, and now I was beginning to rethink that decision. If I shared with him, maybe he'd be inclined to do the same? It was becoming abundantly clear that I was not going to be able to figure this out alone.

"Sheriff Clark, my grandfather was working on a book when he was killed. Flick believed—as I do—that something he uncovered while researching that book was the reason he was targeted."

He ran a hand over his mustache, looking interested now. "What sort of book?"

I explained what I knew about *The Lonely Dead.* "Flick

told me the day before he died that he'd been to Chincoteague Island to look into something about a family of five who'd died in a plane crash years earlier. The Miller family out of Hudson Falls, Texas."

Something flashed in Clark's eyes.

I seized on it. "What? Does that mean something to you?"

With a reluctance that was almost palpable, he again opened the file on his desk, took out a business card, and pushed it across the desk to me. "Charles Miller is the *who* we're looking at in Lawrenceville."

Since Sheriff Clark seemed mildly impressed, I fought the impulse to let my mouth hang open in surprise.

Holman took the card from him and read aloud, "Silver Meadows. Raising the standard of senior care." Holman blinked at Sheriff Clark. "What does this mean?"

"We know that Hal Flick called Silver Meadows two days before he was killed. He spoke with Ms. Eggers, the director, about visiting one of their patients."

"Charles Miller?" I asked.

Clark nodded. "Pretty big coincidence that guy being a Miller and all, wouldn't you say?"

"I don't believe in coincidences," Holman said flatly, his standard response.

My brain was already six steps down the road. "Sheriff, have you gone to talk to this guy yet?"

"No. Haven't had time."

I scooted toward the edge of my chair and looked him dead in the eye. "Can we?" And then before he had a chance to say no, I added, "We'll record the whole thing, provided he doesn't mind, of course, and come straight here afterward and let you listen to the tape."

Sheriff Clark held my gaze but said nothing.

"Please."

After what seemed like far too long, he gave a brisk nod and mumbled something about this being a free country. We were out the door before he had a chance to say anything else.

CHAPTER 17

Silver Meadows sat at the end of a long tree-lined road. It was a large one-story building made of red brick with freshly painted white trim. The front windows were decorated with teak boxes full of colorful flowers—real, as far as I could tell—and there were magnolia and glorybower trees, boxwoods, and Japanese maples to round out the impeccable landscaping. Silver Meadows must be where seniors go who have more money than family members willing to take them in.

A woman named Rhonda met us at registration and had both Holman and I fill out a visitor's form before we were allowed to proceed. We told her we were doing a story for the paper on some of Charles Miller's relatives. It was obvious Rhonda liked the old guy. "He's pretty amazing for a guy of ninety-one. He's a quiet one, though. Mostly, he just sits and reads. Matter of fact, that's where he is now."

She led us back to a large room with a high ceiling and windows lining the back wall. An elderly man in a wheelchair sat facing out looking over a large open field with walking paths and a lake with a mermaid-shaped fountain in its center.

"Charlie?" Rhonda said as we approached. "You've got a couple of visitors."

As he turned around, I could see that Charlie Miller

was straight up *old*. He had two tufts of white hair above each ear, skin the texture of ancient parchment, and cloudy blue eyes that I could tell were showstoppers back in the day. On his lap was a worn leather-bound book.

"Thank you, Rhonda," he said in a thin voice. "Can I trouble you for a Coke?"

"It's no trouble at all, sugar," Rhonda said. "You want your usual—7UP, no ice?" He nodded and she went off to fetch his drink.

"Hi, Mr. Miller." I stepped forward to hand him my business card. "I'm Riley Ellison and this is Will Holman."

He lifted his arm to take the card, but it stayed bent at the elbow. "Pleased to meet you both."

I spoke slightly louder than I would have in normal conversation. "Mr. Miller, we're reporters with the *Tuttle Times* and we were wondering if we might be able to ask you a couple of questions."

At first, I couldn't tell if Charlie had heard me, because he didn't react for several seconds. I was about to open my mouth to repeat myself when he said, "Don't know what use I can be, but I'm happy to help if I can."

I took that as consent for the interview and sat down on the opulent beige sofa across from him. Holman remained standing. I took out my notebook and my phone. "Do you mind if I record our conversation?"

He shook his head. I pressed record. "Mr. Miller, in 1959 there was a plane crash just off the coast of Chincoteague Island." I scanned his face for any sign of recognition. I didn't see any. "A family of five perished in the crash. The Miller family."

"Miller?" He asked, looking from me to Holman.

"Yes."

Charlie furrowed his brow, like this information was

upsetting to him.

"Was that your family? Are you related to the Millers who died in that plane crash?"

His gaze fell down toward the bottom of the sofa, and for a moment he looked like his mind was somewhere far away. "I have a daughter, you know?"

This was apropos of nothing, and Holman and I shot each other an uncertain glance. I said, "You do?"

Charlie smiled and it changed his whole face. He instantly looked ten years younger—which meant that he still looked old, but happy-old instead of tired-old. "She and her husband live in North Carolina. They visit when they can."

A quick calculation told me that this man's daughter would be no spring chicken herself. If he was ninety-one, his child was most likely in her sixties or seventies. I smiled. I wanted to get back to talking about the plane crash but didn't want to seem rude, so I waited for him to finish his thought.

"She's an angel. A God-fearing woman." He absently touched the Bible in his lap. "And my granddaughter... Ella. She lives over in...in..." he looked up as he struggled to catch the thought. "Texas. Yes, that's right. And my grandson, Nicholas. He's a CPA."

"You must be very proud," I said. "Um, Mr. Miller, do you know anything about that plane crash I mentioned? Do you know if you're related to the family who died?"

The smile lines around his eyes faded like footprints at the edge of the ocean. "No."

"No, you're not related to them, or no, you don't know if you are?" Holman asked.

"No, I'm not related to them."

Charlie's response struck me as odd. For starters, it was the first thing in the entire conversation he'd been definitive about. Secondly, he hadn't asked any questions—what were the names of the people who died, how old were they, why did the plane go down? These were all things you'd think someone would want to know, particularly if you shared a family name with the victims.

"Are you sure?" I asked.

"My family's not from around here. We're from the West Coast—no relation to any of the Millers in these parts."

Without reasonable grounds to argue, I let it drop. "Do you—I mean, did you—know a man named Hal Flick?"

He shook his head, his face blank. "No, I don't believe so."

"How about someone named Albert Ellison, did you know him?" Holman asked.

"Ellison," Charlie repeated. "That sounds familiar..." Then he looked down at the card I'd given him, still in his lap. "Riley Ellison. That's you."

"Yes."

"Do I know you?" he asked, tilting his head to the side.

I wasn't sure if he was asking because I looked familiar or if he was confused by Holman's question. Either way, he suddenly seemed frailer, more vulnerable. A feeling of guilt started to creep up on me.

"We've never met before today. Albert Ellison was my grandfather. He was a journalist too, an obituary writer, actually."

"Obituaries," he said with a small, breathy chuckle. "I used to read them, but I've outlived all my friends. Don't know anyone in there anymore."

Rhonda came back with his 7UP and we took the opportunity to say goodbye. "Thanks for talking with us today, Mr. Miller," I said.

He said goodbye but looked agitated or maybe

confused. Either way, I had the feeling our visit had upset him.

As soon as we got in the car, Holman said, "Charlie Miller is not from the West Coast."

"What? How do you know?"

"He called his 7UP a Coke."

"So what?"

"So a 7UP is not a Coke."

"Sure it is," I said.

"No," Holman said in the overly patient voice he reserved for teaching me things. "Technically, a Coke is a Coca-Cola. A 7UP is a colorless lemon-lime soft drink."

"Same difference." I rolled my eyes. "Besides, how do you know that means Charlie Miller isn't from the West Coast?"

"Everyone knows that there are regional differences in the word for soda and in—"

"—they do?"

"Yes."

"*I* didn't know that."

"That's probably because you've never lived anywhere but Virginia."

Well, I supposed he had a point there. I aborted my halfhearted argument. "Go on."

"On the West Coast, people say *soda,* unless you live in the upper Northwest, in which case you might say *pop.* Calling a soda *a coke,* in addition to being a trademark infringement against the Coca-Cola Company, is a decidedly Southern affectation."

"Interesting," I said. I'd never heard that, but as Holman pointed out, I wasn't exactly Mrs. Worldwide. "Why would he lie about where he's from?"

"That's the question, isn't it?"

"Should be easy enough to do a little digging on his background. I'll start tonight."

We stopped back by the Brunswick sheriff's office and told Sheriff Clark what we'd learned and what we suspected. He said very little in return, took a few notes, and we agreed to talk again when there was some news. We got back on the road to drive home. My brain needed a break from talking about Joe Tackett, so I decided to surreptitiously bring up Lindsey's name and see if I could gauge Holman's interest in her.

"Do you want to call Lindsey and tell her about our meeting with Tackett?" I said, fishing.

"I can if you like."

"She seems like she'd be willing to help if she could. I mean, she's certainly no friend of Tackett."

"Mm-hmm."

Holman was not taking the conversation bait. I tried again, "She's cool, don't you think?" As soon as I said it, I worried I'd gone too far, been too obvious, so I scrambled to do something nonchalant to make it look like I was super relaxed with no ulterior motive whatsoever. "Do you want a piece of gum?"

"Yes, thank you."

"Oh," I said as I dug through my purse. "I guess I don't have any."

Holman frowned. "Why would you offer me—"

"So anyway, back to Lindsey," I said, cutting him off. "I think if it weren't for the pressure from the feds, she'd be willing to make the deal. She seems like a super reasonable person, you know?" I peered at him from the corner of my eye.

He made some vague sound of agreement.

"And smart, too."

"She is actually a rather gifted songstress as well."

Songstress? I fought the urge to mock his old-timey word. Now that he was finally talking, I didn't want to make fun of him and risk him clamming up. "Really?"

"She came to karaoke night at Lipton's last week. She sang 'Natural Woman' by Aretha Franklin. Difficult song. I was impressed."

Holman did not impress easily. I took this as a good sign and waded in a little deeper. "Hey, I was thinking of inviting her to come with us to that New Year's party so we'd have an even foursome. Plus, she's pretty new to town and it might be fun for her to meet some new people. What do you think?"

"Sure." Holman kept his eyes straight ahead, betraying nothing. Then, after a beat, he added, "But I wouldn't be surprised if a woman like her already had plans for New Year's Eve."

"Oh, you never know," I said and turned my face away, toward the window, to hide my smile. *This was going to be fun.*

Daily Astrological Forecast

Scorpio

Today's movement of sensual Venus into your fourth house could result in fireworks of the carnal kind, so be sure all your personal grooming is up to code! You've been so focused on your career recently that you may have been neglecting the interpersonal relationships that are your raison d'être. But all that is about to change. Your powers of attraction are on point, making you irresistible to almost everyone you interact with. Go with it—all work and no play makes Scorpio a dull girl!

Unfortunately, erratic Uranus is stagnant over your rising moon, creating instability and uncertainty. Changes may be on the horizon that force you to leave the days of wine and roses behind. A difficult choice may present itself sooner than you thought, Scorpio, so do your homework. A small misstep could have severe consequences for the people you care most about.

Tonight: Rock your highest stiletto and show off those calves!

CHAPTER 18

I had another restless night of sleep (or not-sleep, as it were) and finally gave up at about 5:30 a.m. and got out of bed. I bundled up and took Coltrane for a predawn walk, which he seemed to appreciate far more than I did. My winter coat—really only meant to protect against mildly cold temperatures—was no match for the unseasonably arctic weather we'd been having lately. When we got home, I started the coffee maker and stood underneath a near-scalding shower for at least fifteen minutes. Once sufficiently thawed, I bundled myself in my warmest PJs and robe, slipped my feet into my pom-pom slippers, and poured myself a large mug of steaming hot coffee. I still had over an hour and a half until I had to be at the office.

I was halfway through the online obituary section in the *Guardian* when a faint knock on my door sent Coltrane into guard-dog mode, shattering my morning peace. It was 7:07 a.m.—way too early for a visitor. I checked my phone to see if I'd missed any calls or texts from someone telling me they were coming over. Nope.

"Who is it?" I called out as I made my way to the door, half expecting it to be Holman with doughnuts or maybe one of my parents on their way to coffee with friends.

"It's Jay."

Jay? Jay, my ex-boyfriend who lived in Washington,

DC? He was here, at my house, at seven o'clock in the morning? I swear my heart stopped beating for a fraction of a second. I did a quick inventory of what I was wearing and quickly debated whether I had time to go put on clothes. Or brush my teeth. Or get a complete makeover.

"I'm sorry to come by so early without calling..." he said through the still-closed door.

Damn, no time. I quickly smoothed down my hair and opened the door. Jay stood on my front porch looking like he'd just walked out of a J. Crew catalog. He wore a crisp white shirt under a navy suit, a hot-pink pocket square, and rich brown leather wingtips. In sharp contrast, I wore a puffy peach-colored robe over lobster-print flannel pajamas.

"Hi," I said, peering out from behind the door. "Is everything okay?"

"Yeah, yeah," he said, stepping inside. "I'm so sorry to just stop by like this."

I tucked a strand of hair behind my ears. "No, it's fine. I was just—"

"Drinking coffee and reading the obits?"

He knew me well. I turned toward the kitchen to hide my smile. "Can I get you a cup?"

"Sure." He followed me into the kitchen but hung back by the breakfast bar as I got down a mug—the cheesy "Virginia Is for Lovers" one he always used to use at my house in the mornings—and poured. The last time I'd seen Jay it had been at his apartment in DC, about two months ago. That was also the night I met his new girlfriend, Chloe. Given the circumstances, it was almost strange how not-strange this early morning visit felt.

"So," I said, arching a brow, "to what do I owe the pleasure?"

He smiled and looked down at his feet. "I'm actually

passing through on my way to a meeting."

Jay worked as a special agent for the DEA. We met when he was undercover posing as a criminology professor at a nearby college in order to get close to a drug cartel's operation in Tuttle County. We had started dating, but shortly after, he was promoted and moved to Washington, DC. We'd decided not to do the long-distance thing...a choice I'd questioned more than a few times in the months since he moved away.

"And you just stopped by to say hello?"

"You always did have a pretty good bullshit detector," he said with a laugh. "No, I wanted to talk to you about Joe Tackett."

The second I heard Jay say the name, it was like all the pieces clicked into place: Jay was the arresting officer on the Tackett case. Jay must be the fed who Tackett tried to give his information to. Jay was the person standing in the way of me finding out who killed my grandfather. I can't believe I didn't see it before. All of a sudden, I felt like I'd swallowed a pair of socks.

He read my expression as clear as if it were a headline on the front page of the *Times*. "You already know."

I nodded, not trusting my voice at that moment.

"Listen, Riley," he said. "You have to understand the position I'm in."

"I don't," I said, not even trying to conceal my anger, my disappointment.

"Tackett has a lot of information that could be really helpful to us. He was sent to Greensville prison for a specific reason. We *want* him to be uncomfortable, so uncomfortable that he'll consider giving us the names of some of his cartel connections."

"He's never going to do that."

"If we can apply enough pressure, he might."

"He told me yesterday if he breathes one word about the cartel, he's as good as dead."

"We could protect him, move him to another facility, change his name." Then, as if he suddenly realized what I'd said, he crinkled his brow. "You spoke to Tackett?"

"Yesterday. At Greensville." I folded my arms across my chest, which would have looked more foreboding if it weren't for the fluffy bathrobe. "You're not the only one he's been talking to," I snapped.

Jay let out a sigh, and I knew what he was going to say before he uttered a word. I'd heard that sigh before. "Riley, what are you doing going to visit Tackett? He tried to kill you, for God's sake."

"Holman was with me."

"He tried to kill Holman too," he said, his voice rising. Then he closed his eyes and shook his head before saying in a softer, calmer voice, "Tackett can identify some very dangerous people who are currently—"

"He can also identify one very dangerous person who murdered my granddaddy and his best friend!"

"Wait—what?" he said, clearly confused.

"Flick."

"Flick is dead?" Jay was visibly shaken. He lowered his voice. "Oh my God...what happened?"

I should have realized that Jay wouldn't know. News of Flick's death wouldn't have traveled up to DC, and I hadn't thought to tell him. A decision I suddenly felt badly about. "Flick had been looking into something Granddad was working on years ago. He was tracking down a lead in Brunswick County when he was run off the road, his car smashed into the side of a bluff. By the time the ambulance got to him—" I broke off, unable to finish the sentence.

"Was this what you called Hank about? I had no idea it was Flick..."

I nodded. "We buried him three weeks ago."

"Oh, Riley." Jay stood up and before I could stop him, he had his arms around me. "I am so sorry."

That small gesture of kindness was all it took for me to crack like an egg. I melted into Jay's arms and let him comfort me. Part of me wanted to push him away, to tell him he was now part of the problem, an obstacle standing in the way of the thing I'd wanted more than anything for the past seven years. But another part of me knew Jay was just doing his job, carrying out the mission of the DEA like the dedicated professional he was. Besides, it felt really good to have him hug me. We stood like that for a long time. When he finally released me, neither of us looked the other in the eye. I couldn't have told you what Jay was thinking, but I was embarrassed at how much I'd needed that moment.

I wiped away the moisture from my cheeks. "Holman and I believe whoever killed Flick is the same person who killed Granddad—and Tackett knows who that person is."

Jay took a step back and put both hands in his pockets. He looked lost in thought. I waited for him to say something, anything that would make this situation better. When the moment stretched on, I said, "We are so close to finding out, Jay."

"I'm sorry," he said quietly. "I know this has to be killing you—that's why I came here this morning—but it's out of my hands. My direction is to keep the pressure on Tackett."

"Who's directing you?"

He didn't say anything, his standard response when something was classified.

"You're not just passing through, are you?"

Jay looked down. "I'm meeting with Lindsey Davis at eight."

I cinched my robe tighter and stood up as straight as I could. "You should know Holman and I are going to fight this. In the press if we have to."

"Riley, that's not a good idea. The Romero cartel does not like loose ends. Press coverage about Tackett striking a deal with prosecutors—even if it doesn't have to do with their operation—could make them act."

"Act?"

Jay gave me a dark look. "These are very dangerous people, Riley." His tone was almost pleading.

I turned away and started wiping down the counter, so I didn't have to look him in the eye. "Well, you've got your job to do, and I've got mine."

Jay brought his coffee cup to the sink and rinsed it, which sparked an irrational flare of anger at him for reminding me of what a good guy he was.

"There's more at stake here than you know," he said.

Jay's words stoked the low-burning fear that had been with me ever since my first run-in with the cartel six months ago. They had tried to kill me. And Holman. And Ryan. They had a well-established habit of taking out whatever and whoever they saw as obstacles.

I stuffed the fear down to the faraway place I needed to keep it in order to function. "Maybe so," I said. "But I think you're underestimating just how important this is to me. It may not be as lofty a goal as the war against drug traffickers or whatever, but the stakes—as you say—are every bit as high to me."

Jay hung his head and for a moment it seemed like he wanted to argue, but instead he said, "I'm really sorry to hear about Hal. I wish you would have let me know. I would've come to the funeral."

I shrugged. "I didn't think Chloe would appreciate me calling you." The minute I said it, I felt like a fool. We were over and had been for months. I had no right to be mad that he had moved on.

"Right. Chloe..."

"Sorry," I said, quickly. "That was unfair."

"Listen, I know this is ancient history, especially in light of everything that's going on now, but I feel like I should explain about Chloe."

"No, you really don't have to." I ducked out of the kitchen, which was beginning to feel like one of those rooms in a haunted house where the walls close in on you. I walked toward the front door.

"I wanted to call you after that night in DC, but things are just kind of complicated."

"Honestly, it's fine," I said, trying to remove any emotion from my voice. "We broke up, you moved on. You don't owe me any explanations...or anything at all. It's fine."

"Are you sure?" I couldn't tell if I was imagining it, but there seemed to be something stacked behind his question. It could have been hope, or it could have been condescension.

"Thanks for coming by." I opened the front door, an unmistakable signal that this visit was over.

CHAPTER 19

I spent much of the first hour at work preoccupied with the fact that Jay was talking to Lindsey Davis, trying to persuade her not to make a deal with Tackett. I'd wanted to tell Holman that Jay was here just in case he decided to go over to talk to Lindsey this morning. He was probably the number-one member of the Jaidev "Jay" Burman fan club, and I wanted him to know that in this instance, Jay was working in direct opposition to us, so he could turn down the whole hero-worship thing. I called and texted but so far hadn't gotten a response. I was updating the "Inspecting the Eateries" page when I got an email from someone at the Virginia vital records department saying my request for the death certificates had been denied because I was not authorized to view those records. *Damn.* I'd expected as much, but I really needed those to find out who was listed as the Millers' next of kin—that information would go a long way in figuring out if they were subjects in *The Lonely Dead.*

I was just starting a search of how to get a copy of a death certificate of a nonfamily member when Ash texted.

lunch today?

sure

Mysa or Landrys?

mmmm meatballs.

Mysa it is. what u doin?

trying to get a death certificate of someone who died 60 years ago

journalism is fun

haha. not having any luck

just call the funeral home. we keep records forever.

OMG ASH UR A GENIUS!!!

wow if id known u were so easily impressed i would have talked funeral home director to u sooner

haha lol

glad i could help. i like to see u happy

c u at noon?

I knew that the Millers hadn't been buried or cremated in Hudson Falls, because if they'd been laid to rest in Texas, there would have been a file on record, and my old friend Elaine had already established that there wasn't. I assumed that they were buried on Chincoteague, where they died. There were three funeral homes on Chincoteague Island, but only one that had been in business in 1959. I felt like an in-person visit would increase my odds of getting them to give me a copy of the death certificates, but Chincoteague was a four-hour drive and I didn't own a car at the moment. Plus, I had missed enough work as it was and wasn't sure I could take another whole day out of the office, even if it was for the sake of a big story.

A spark of inspiration struck, and I texted Ash back and asked if I could stop by Campbell & Sons on the way to lunch. All of a sudden it seemed very advantageous to have a funeral home director interested in making me happy.

"Tell me again what you want me to say?" Ash asked.

"Just say someone has come in asking if you have the records for a family of five, the Miller family, who died in Virginia in 1959. Say something like there's been some confusion as to where the family was buried and they thought maybe it was in Tuttle County but that you think it was in Accomack County, given that's where their plane crashed..."

He looked slightly uncomfortable, so I added, "You're not lying—that's all true. Mostly."

"And you think they'll just give me that information? Without any paperwork or proof of anything?"

"Would you?"

"Probably," he said. "But only because I'm still learning the rules. In fact, until you told me five minutes ago, I didn't even know that death certificates could only be accessed by the family or legal guardian in the state of Virginia."

I sat on the edge of his desk. "I'm hoping there's a professional courtesy between you guys, one funeral home director to another? If they don't want to give you a copy of the certificate, that's fine. Just try to find out who the next of kin is. That's what I really need."

"Next of kin," Ash repeated. "Okay...I'll give it a try."

"Thank you!" I was nearly giddy with excitement.

"What'll you give me if I do this for you?" Ash said, a playful edge to his voice.

"I'll buy you lunch."

"You already owe me lunch."

"I'll buy you a drink then."

"When?"

"Whenever you want. Will you make the call already?"

"How about tonight after work? We can talk about our costumes for Toad's party over a bottle of wine?"

Ash was standing close enough to me that I could smell his cologne. Funny, I never noticed that he wore cologne before. It was a nice, clean musky scent that was light enough to be noticed only by those in close orbit. Which I guess I was.

"A bottle is more than one drink," I said, looking down.

"We have a lot to talk about."

"Just make the call."

"Do we have a deal?"

"Yes, fine. We have a deal."

"Seal it with a kiss?"

I spit on my hand and stuck it out to him instead.

Ash laughed again, then made the call.

Just as he did, my phone rang. *Holman.* I needed to talk to him, so I stepped out into the hallway to answer. "Hey. Where have you been?"

"You will never guess who I saw on the way into Lindsey's office today."

"Jay."

"Oh." Holman sounded disappointed. "I guess you did guess."

"What happened with Lindsey?" I didn't have time to explain everything to him. I wanted to get back in the office to hear Ash's conversation.

"We didn't have a chance to talk because she was meeting with Jay. Riley, I think Jay is the federal agent who's trying to block her from making a deal with Tackett."

"He is."

"How do you know this already?"

I cracked the door and could see that Ash was still on

the phone and writing something down. I lowered my voice. "I'll explain later, but he's under orders to shut it down."

"Why are you whispering?"

"Later."

"Fine. Lindsey wants to meet with both of us at one-thirty."

I could hear Ash laughing. It sounded like he was talking with an old friend. I hoped that was a good sign. "See you then."

"Technically, you will see me before then because we work in the same—"

I clicked end and walked back into Ash's office.

"Yeah, okay, okay. Thanks, Gary." He held up one finger at me. "Perfect. I'll look forward to it. And thanks again."

If he was thanking Gary, surely that meant he got it! I waited for him to end his call, and after another chorus of "You too, man" and "It's a deal," Ash finally hung up.

"So...did you get it?"

"Pffff, did I get it?" He smirked. "Not only did I get it, but I have an invitation to play golf at the Chincoteague Country Club with Gary any time I want."

"Congratulations," I said, rolling my eyes. "Where is it? Did he email you a copy or just give you the name?"

He held up a piece of paper and I snatched it out of his hand like a greedy child. I scanned the page. "Oh my God."

"Does that name mean something to you?"

"You could say that. I just met him yesterday."

CHAPTER 20

Holman had been right. Charles Miller was not from the West Coast. According to the records from the funeral home on Chincoteague, Charles Miller was from Brunswick County, Virginia, and he was the only brother of Daniel Miller and listed as his next of kin. According to the paperwork, it took nearly three weeks for Charles to be notified about the plane crash. By that time, the bodies had already been cremated in accordance with Virginia State law, but Charles Miller did sign for the remains of his brother and his family on October 18, 1959. It had to be the same man Holman and I spoke to yesterday. Why had he lied? If he hadn't been so adamant about his family being from the West Coast, I could have reasonably believed the lapse could have been the result of old age. Then again, if his memory was fading, he'd be more likely not to know where he was from as opposed to straight up lying. My gut told me he had not wanted us to make the connection between him and his brother. The big question, of course, was why.

The minute I got back to the newsroom, I called Silver Meadows and asked to speak with Charlie. Rhonda, whose voice I recognized, asked who was calling and when I said my name, her voice changed. "Charlie isn't up to talking to anyone today." I asked if he was all right and she said yes, but with a definite edge.

"What if I came back to visit him this weekend?"

"I'm sorry, honey, but that's out of the question."

"How come?" I asked, surprised.

"No visitors. Family's orders."

So, the day after Holman and I talked to Charlie Miller about his brother, his family clamped down the security? That seemed super shady. What was his family hiding? Why didn't they want to be connected to the Millers who died in that plane crash? If I couldn't get access to Charlie, I'd just have to take my questions to someone else in the Miller family. I replayed my conversation with Charlie from my voice notes to listen for any clues as to how I might get in touch with his family. He mentioned a daughter who lives in North Carolina, a granddaughter who lived in Texas, and a grandson who was a practicing CPA. I had no more information to go on than that—not even their last names, unless his daughter used her maiden name.

"Since he isn't feeling up to another interview, I wondered if I could talk to his daughter?"

My question was met with silence. No surprise there. I figured a couple of the reasons people pay the big bucks for a place like Silver Meadows is privacy and security. I followed up with, "I know you probably can't give me her name or contact information, but could you get a message to her?"

After a moment, Rhonda said, "Why not? She calls over here every morning to check on her dad. I can give her a message tomorrow morning."

"That'd be great," I said. "Just tell her Riley Ellison from the *Tuttle Times* is doing a story on her cousin, Shannon Miller."

"Shannon Miller?"

"Yes, that's right."

"Huh," Rhonda said. "Well if that ain't the darndest thing!"

"What?"

"To have the same name as your first cousin." She laughed. "I'll bet that got confusing around the family table!"

CHAPTER 21

"There are two Shannons in the Miller family?" Holman asked.

We were in the waiting room of Lindsey Davis's office. We'd arrived a little early and her assistant Anna told us she was running about ten minutes behind, so I had some time to fill Holman in on what I'd learned from Rhonda.

"Yup," I said. "Pretty strange—brothers choosing the same name for their daughters, don't you think?"

"Maybe it's a family name? Or perhaps Charlie's Shannon was born after his niece Shannon passed away...maybe the name is a tribute to her lost cousin?"

"Yeah, could be." I had my doubts, but no point in speculating. "Either way, this changes things. Flick told me to remember the name Shannon Miller. Up till now I thought she was long gone. Now it seems there's a Shannon Miller who is very much alive."

"Yes." Holman paused, then changed topics. "I take it you spoke to Jay earlier?"

"He came by this morning to tell me about Tackett offering information on Granddaddy. He didn't know I already knew," I said. "He also didn't know about Flick."

"Yes, I thought about telling him when it happened but decided against it. He wasn't close with Hal, and I figured the last thing you needed at the funeral was the extra stress that seeing Jay brings you now that you two are no longer romantically involved."

My instinct was to clap back at him, to deny that talking to Jay stressed me out, but then I remember how it felt standing in my kitchen this morning and I closed my mouth. He was right. There was a certain amount of stress that came from seeing Jay. Whether that was from unresolved feelings or the current situation, I suppose it didn't matter.

"That was thoughtful," I said. I checked my watch. It was now four minutes past our appointment time.

"Mother says hello, by the way," Holman said. "She invited me to come to a dinner party she's having this weekend, but I told her you'd already invited me to a *The Great Gatsby*–themed party."

"Was she disappointed?"

"On the contrary, she seemed pleased. In fact, she said she had the perfect costume for me to wear. She's having it couriered overnight to me."

Sometimes when I talked to Holman, it seemed like he belonged to another generation. And sometimes, admittedly, another universe.

"She's free now," Anna said. "Let me show you in."

Lindsey came out from behind her desk to shake each of our hands. She wore a slim-cut ivory pantsuit with a gorgeous champagne-colored silk blouse that perfectly complemented her dark complexion. Black patent oxfords added just the right amount of quirk and style to showcase her individuality. I took inventory of my own appearance. I had on a Forever 21 sweater that had the collar and hem of a shirt sewn in to it to make it look like I had a blouse under my sweater. *Oh God,* I thought, *I'm wearing a dickey.*

"Thanks for coming back, Will," she said. "Sorry I couldn't see you before."

"It's okay. I should have made an appointment."

"Oh, normally it's totally fine if you ever want to stop by," Lindsey said, and then it was as if she suddenly thought that might have been too forward. She added, "Not that you would want to stop by, I mean, unless we have business to talk about. But, I mean, you could, if you wanted to...but whatever."

Was Lindsey Davis, Ms. Hotshot Lawyer, getting flustered around Will Holman? This was priceless! Holman, for his part, looked like he didn't know how to react. True to form, he just blinked at her. Twice.

"I know Jaidev Burman was here to see you this morning," I jumped in, saving them from their awkward flirtation.

Lindsey motioned for us to sit down at the six-person table near the window. "Yes, Agent Burman was here. I'd spoken to him on the phone, but apparently he felt an in-person visit was necessary." There was a cool edge to her voice. *Note to self: Lindsey doesn't take kindly to people invading her turf and telling her what to do.* A woman after my own heart.

"As Tackett's arresting officer, he's been under pressure from his superiors at the DEA to get Tackett to give up sensitive information they believe he has about the Romero cartel. Is that about right?" I asked.

"Yes, and from what I could tell, the man is under a lot of pressure."

I felt a flicker of pity for Jay. I knew him well enough to know this had to be hard for him. Jay was one of the most empathetic people I'd ever met. Even though we were no longer together, it had to be hard on him to be the thing standing in the way of me finding out the truth about

Granddad. I looked down and tugged at a loose thread on my faux shirttail. "He's a good agent."

"Riley and Jay used to have a sexual relationship," Holman said loudly.

"*Holman!*"

"What?"

I felt the telltale blotchiness of humiliation creep up my neck. I could have killed him! "I'm so sorry, Lindsey. That's obviously highly inappropriate."

The corner of her lip tugged up.

Holman, as unable to read a room as ever, continued: "What? I was just providing context. After all, it's hardly fair to expect Lindsey to understand the sensitivity of the situation without knowing your history with Jay. Two people who have been intimate with each other are going to bring a certain amount of emotional baggage to the situation."

"Will," I said, through clenched teeth, "I don't think we need to tell Lindsey my entire life story..."

"I wasn't." He looked from me to Lindsey and then back again. "I only told her the one detail of your past, your sexual relationship with—"

"*Anyway,*" I said, cutting him off and turning to Lindsey. "Yes, Jay and I have a past, but that's not a factor in the situation that we wanted to talk to you about."

"Of course," she said, wiping her face of any lingering amusement.

I took a breath to reset. "We're here because we went to talk to Tackett yesterday."

"In prison," Holman added, puffing up just a bit.

"He wants us to raise public awareness by publishing a story in the *Times*, reporting that he has information about the murder of one, possibly two, community members. He thinks this will persuade you to offer him a deal," I said.

Lindsey responded with, "I see." I didn't know her well enough to know what she was thinking, but if the purse of her lips was any indication, she was thinking, *Why does everyone think they can tell me how to do my job?*

"Was he able to shed any light on what happened to Flick?" she asked.

"Not really," I confessed. "But he said he *might* know something and he *might* be willing to share that with you."

"I see," she said again. "And I *might* be willing to hear him out." It was clear she was perturbed with Tackett's arrogance, which I totally understood, but I hoped it wouldn't get in the way of her decision regarding whether or not to proceed.

"I—we—still think the two crimes are connected. Sheriff Clark said there's documentation that proves Flick was seeking a meeting with Tackett the day before he died—so it isn't just Tackett's word. Their meeting didn't happen, but it proves a connection."

"The other thing you should be aware of," Holman said, "is that Tackett says he has a recording of Albert's killer confessing to the crime."

Lindsey raised her eyebrows.

"And he says that person is a public figure," I added.

"I suppose he didn't tell you any more than that?" she asked, a slight frown forming.

"No."

"Listen, I know you're in a tough spot," I said, leaning forward. "But we really believe that Flick's and my grandfather's murders are connected, likely committed by the same person for the same reason." I then explained about Charles Miller and the record of Flick's appointment at Silver Meadows. "He was trying to track something down—probably the same something my granddad was."

Lindsey looked down at her notepad for several seconds. It was impossible to tell what she was thinking or which way she was going to come down on this. I held my breath.

"Okay," she said after a few seconds. "I think the next step is for me to talk to Sheriff Haight. If—and it's a big if—I'm going to consider offering to recommend some sort of reduced sentence to Judge Giancarlo, I will need to be certain that Tackett has credible, fruitful information."

"What about the feds?" I asked.

Something glinted in her eyes, a little twinkle of steel, perhaps. "You let me worry about them."

CHAPTER 22

I felt cautiously optimistic as Holman and I headed back to the newsroom. Lindsey seemed at least open to the idea of getting more information from Tackett about what he knew. And the fact that she was going to talk to Carl about it made me feel even better. Not only was Carl a good sheriff, he was a good sheriff in an election year. I knew he'd definitely want to be credited for apprehending an allegedly high-profile murderer who had killed one, if not two, of our own.

Ash and I had decided to cancel lunch since we were meeting after work for a drink and to talk about our costumes or whatever. I was too busy to spend much time on it, but it did strike me as odd how flirty Ash was being lately. While there'd always been an undercurrent of flirtation between us, now it seemed he was escalating things. Had he suddenly decided he was super into me? Or was he just lonely and looking for a hookup? I still wasn't sure how I felt about that. I mean, I liked Ash, of course. I liked spending time with him—he was smart and had a wickedly dry sense of humor—and there's no doubt I was attracted to him. My body practically hummed when he got close to me, but still. Something was holding me back, though I couldn't put my finger on exactly what it was. Maybe I was just afraid of getting hurt again like I had with Ryan and Jay? Maybe I was just content being alone? Maybe I was just overthinking it like Ridley had suggested? If social media had taught me anything, it was that I might be the only woman of my generation who was unable to just turn off her brain and have some fun every once in a while. And Ash would definitely be fun....

At about four-thirty, Kay asked me if I could run over to the post office and clear out the *Times* PO box. It was one of those jobs we all took turns doing and all complained about. It wasn't that the post office was far away—it was only three blocks—but its supervisor, Theresa Fielding, was what my mother would call a "chatty Cathy." When you walked in and asked Theresa how she was, she told you. In detail. Henderson once clocked her response to his polite *How's it going today?* at seventeen minutes, forty-six seconds. This is why we only cleared out the box once every couple of weeks and always waited till the end of the day. If you went in during the morning, you might not make it back to the office before dark.

It had been gray all day, and now at twilight the clouds covered the sky. It looked like it could start raining at any moment, and with the temperature dropping that could mean freezing drizzle—my least favorite kind of drizzle. Despite the weather, I decided to take the long way along the sidewalk instead of cutting through Memorial Park. Inviting Praise, Mayor Lancett's stationery shop, had a new selection of journals in the window. I had some Christmas money from my parents, and even though it should go into the new-car fund, I think we all knew it was probably going to go toward a new journal. There was just something so optimistic about all those beautiful notebooks full of blank pages. Some of mine were sentimental (they'd belonged to Granddaddy), some were made of handmade paper, some were cute and fun and said things like BE AWESOME TODAY. The one in the window I had my eye on was covered in fur and had multiple eyes and sharp teeth on it, like Harry Potter's *Monster Book of Monsters*. It was really more pet than journal, which made it that much more alluring.

I checked my phone to see if I had enough time to get in and out of the store before the post office closed and decided I didn't. I sent my monster journal a telepathic "You-will-be-mine" as I passed, and then because I wasn't looking, nearly ran right into Jay. *What the hell was he still doing here?*

"Whoa—hey there, Riley."

"Oh. Hi, Jay." After an awkward pause, I apologized for nearly knocking him over and he said it was no problem. Then there was another awkward pause. Jay and I never had trouble making conversation before, but given the circumstances I guess neither of us knew what to say.

"So, you're still here?"

"Yup," he said. "I had a couple of other meetings in the area, so..." He shoved his hands into his pockets and rocked back on his heels.

"Heading back soon?"

"Probably will wait another hour or so. If I leave now, I'll just sit on the 95. Wait," he said, suddenly animated, "did you ever get another car?"

I shook my head. "Ivan called me about a couple that he found at an auction, but it was right when everything was happening with Flick's funeral and I just didn't have the focus to make a decision."

"Ivan's the best," he said. "He'll take care of you. Until then, at least most places in Tuttle are walkable."

"True!" I looked around, unsure where to take the conversation from here.

"Listen, Riley, what I was going to say before—about Chloe—"

"Jay—I'd really rather not get into it—"

"Why not?"

It was a good question and one that I didn't exactly know the answer to. I had no idea why I was reacting so strongly to hearing about his new relationship. I just knew I didn't want to talk about it, particularly not with him. After we broke up, I put a lid on the box containing all my feelings about Jay and as long as no one opened it, I could pretend they didn't exist.

I looked down at the sidewalk. "I'm happy for you," I said, wading in slowly. "I really am, it's just...I guess it was just hard to see how quickly you were able to, you know, find someone new."

"I know," he said quietly. "But you have to know that if I'd thought there was any way that you and I could have had a chance..."

Something inside me gave way and the lid to the box popped open. "There *was* a way," I said, fixing him with a meaningful stare.

Jay's expression went from compassionate to confused in the space of a second. "What—stay here? Do you think I should have passed up the promotion? Did you expect me to give up my career for you?"

"No! Of course not," I said, more than a little defensively. "But it was like you were gone the second something came along—"

"Well, how about you?" he cut me off. "There are plenty of newspapers in DC. You could have found another job. You could have come with me."

I crossed my arms in front of my chest. "I don't recall being invited."

"Would you have come?"

I honestly didn't know the answer. We had only been together for a few months, but our relationship had felt so solid, like it was really something special. And it ending the way it did felt like someone had ripped the needle off the record mid-song. Would I have moved to DC with him? Part of me thought that I would have considered it; and part of me thought that was a ridiculous idea. But there was no way to know now. I took a deep breath and said the only thing I knew to be true, "It would have been nice to have been asked." And there it was. I hadn't realized it until the words were out of my mouth, but that was the crux of the whole thing, the reason for keeping the box locked up tight. I looked up at him, feeling courageous and vulnerable at the same time.

He looked at me for a long moment before he spoke. "I didn't think you'd even consider it." There was a sad kind of resignation in his voice. "It just didn't seem practical at the time."

"It wasn't," I said. "I guess I was hoping for something that transcended practicality."

"Riley—" he started to say, but then stopped himself. "Maybe I should have—"

"Don't...please." I wasn't angry anymore, but I couldn't listen to him explain all the reasons he hadn't fought for us. In the end, there was only one reason that mattered: He hadn't loved me enough.

He looked at the sidewalk, then turned his eyes toward the sky, anywhere but at me. It seemed like he wanted to say something, but after a few attempts, he ended up just putting his hands in his pockets and saying, "Fair enough."

"Besides," I said, "can you even imagine if we were still dating when this whole thing with Tackett came up?" I was trying to make a joke, but it fell flat. The situation with Tackett wasn't funny for either one of us.

"My hands are tied. This is my job, Riley." He was the one who sounded defensive now.

"Is that why you're still here? Why you've been here all day? Are you working another angle to block Tackett from talking to us?"

He sighed and gave me a look filled with meaning, though I had no idea what that meaning was. "Goodbye, Riley," he said and leaned down to kiss my cheek. His lips hovered there for a fraction of a second, long enough for him to whisper, "I should have asked."

Chapter 23

"See, that's the thing about black ice—it'll get you every time. This one time, my sister's boy, Roland, was driving to church on Sunday morning..." Theresa Fielding was six minutes into her response to my comment, "It's getting chilly out there."

She would talk, then make a half turn like she was going to get the stamps I needed to buy, then stop and talk some more. I'd already cleared out the *Times*'s PO box and was holding an armload of mail.

"...the pastor told the entire flock to pray for him, which was real nice 'cause everyone knew Roland wasn't exactly what you'd call a devout Christian. This one time..."

I'll admit I may have taken the opportunity during her Roland story to zone out and think about my conversation with Jay. *I should have asked*...what does that even mean? Is he trying to express regret over not asking me to move to DC with him? And if he regretted losing me so much, then what's with him moving on in record time with Chloe-the-Conceited? I mean, yes, it was true that I was starting to move on with Ash, but it had now been a respectable amount of time since our breakup. Jay started dating Chloe less than three weeks after we broke up. The more I thought about it, the more annoyed I got at that comment. It felt cowardly at best, false at worst.

"...and another time, I remember it was so icy out, we couldn't even make it to church! The pastor called everyone and told us all to stay home and watch whatshisname from TV, but I don't go in for all that TV preaching. Don't get me wrong, I love me a good sermon, but some of those preachers just seem like a bunch of snake-oil salesmen to me, 'cept for Billy Graham—God rest his soul—and Wyatt Claremore, of course." She laughed. "I remember this one time..."

Wyatt Claremore. As soon as she said the name, it hit me. I hadn't made the connection until that very moment, but once I did, it was so obvious. "Theresa," I said, my adrenaline rising. "I am so sorry, but I have to go!"

"Oh. Okay. But I was just gonna tell you real quick about this one time when Daddy went straight up to—"

"Can you save it for next time?" I said, already pushing the door open. "I really have to get back to the office!"

A cold wind rushed in.

"Oh. Sure. Okay."

"Thanks, and sorry again!"

As soon as I got back to the office, I dropped the mail on Kay's desk and rushed to my own. I opened my laptop and typed the name Wyatt Claremore into the search box. The second the screen populated, I literally blurted out, "Yesssssss!" I was looking at a spitting image of the cupped hands drawing from Flick's file. It was the logo for Claremore Ministries, a prominent megachurch out of North Carolina. I knew I'd seen it before but couldn't place it until Theresa's ramblings about TV preachers reminded me.

I had no idea what the connection between Claremore Ministries and my grandfather could have been, but this was the second religion-related clue I'd come across. First, Mom tells me that Granddad had hidden a piece of paper in his desk with a Bible verse on it, and now Flick has the logo for a megachurch in his notes. I might not have known what it meant, but I knew enough not to ignore an emerging pattern.

I picked up my laptop and went into Holman's office. "I think I may have found something."

"So, you think Flick was investigating Claremore Ministries?" Holman asked after I finished explaining what I'd found.

"Looks that way to me."

"Do you have any idea what he might have been looking for?"

"None."

He took a sip of tea, allowing himself to fully sip and swallow before speaking again. "All right. Let's start by checking if we can find a connection between Claremore and any stories Albert may have worked on. I can cross-check his obit subjects for any mention of the church, and you start looking into his background and see if you recognize any ways in which they may have personally overlapped."

I nodded and immediately typed Wyatt Claremore into my search box. Of course, Wikipedia was the first entry to pop up. Any journalist knows Wikipedia is not a valid source, but it can be useful for gathering generalized background information. When I got to the part about Personal Life, what I read stopped me cold.

"Holman?"

"Mmm?"

"I think I found something already."

He looked up from his own computer. "That was fast. What is it?"

I read from the screen: "Wyatt Claremore married Shannon J. Miller of Lawrenceville, VA, on April 5th, 1982."

Holman's response was, predictably, a slow double-blink. "That is curious. The odds of that being a coincidence are extremely low."

"I'd put them at right about zero."

Holman moved his laptop aside and took out his legal pad and began writing. "So, we know that Charlie Miller was Daniel Miller's next of kin because he signed the death certificate at the funeral home."

"Right."

"And we know that Daniel Miller had a child named Shannon Miller who died in the plane crash in 1959?"

"Right."

"And we know that Charlie Miller also has a daughter named Shannon Miller—or Shannon Claremore now, I guess."

"Exactly," I confirmed. "Add to that the fact that Flick had the Claremore Ministries logo in his notes and now we find a connection between them and the Millers...this is shaping up to be one weird story."

"All stories seem weird until you find the glue that binds the disparate facts together," Holman said. "Add the Claremore's marriage to your list of things to look into."

Holman got a call, so I took my laptop back to my desk and continued my research there. The first mention I found of the couple was their engagement announcement in the *Greenville Gazette* published in 1982:

Miller-Claremore.

Dr. Robert and Mrs. Nancy Claremore proudly announce the engagement of their son, Wyatt Clifton Claremore, to Shannon Jane Miller, daughter of Charles Miller and Rebecca Miller (deceased) of Lawrenceville, Virginia. Miss Miller is a graduate

> of East Carolina University (class of '75) where she earned her bachelor's degree in elementary education. She is currently teaching first grade to students at Harrison Elementary School in Greenville. Mr. Claremore, a graduate of Wake Forest University, is working on his doctoral degree in Theology from Duke University. The couple is planning an April wedding, after which Miss Miller will join Mr. Claremore in Raleigh-Durham.

I found it interesting that the engagement announcement came from his parents. Historically, it is the bride's parents who publish those. I did a deep dive into the archives of the *Greenville Gazette* for any more mentions of the Claremore family. Most were about events they'd attended, charities they'd supported, and causes they'd championed. Nothing appeared about Wyatt and Shannon until several years later, when they took out a home mortgage in 1990. The next mention was five years later, when Wyatt took the head pastor position at Oakwood Christian Church. I read article after article and was able to piece together a skeleton outline of his life, at least from the time he married Shannon until now.

Claremore had started at Oakwood as the youth pastor, but his charismatic preaching style quickly began attracting new parishioners from surrounding communities. When the head pastor stepped down, Wyatt was promoted in an effort to help the church grow. I found an article accompanied by a grainy picture of Wyatt, Shannon, and their two children, Ella and Nicholas. Shannon had blond hair and a wan smile, and as far as I could tell from the picture, wore little makeup and plain, modest clothing. Wyatt, by contrast, had a sturdy build with broad shoulders and perfect posture. Even with the low quality of the photo, something about Wyatt made him pop off the page. It was easy to see how he could have attracted a following—he had that indefinable allure, that X factor that made the spotlight shine directly on him. Shannon, and even the kids, seemed to fade into the background.

Once he took over as the lead at Oakwood Christian, Wyatt's name was often mentioned in the press. His pedigreed education combined with his charm made him a favorite subject of journalists, local and otherwise, on subjects ranging from religious holidays to helping the less fortunate. He published his first book a couple of years later, and from my quick search it looked like he had nearly eight books out to date, most of which had topped the charts.

His most famous book by far, though, was one he co-authored with a woman named Megan Johanning. Megan was a young parishioner at Oakwood Christian and had just been diagnosed with a form of muscular dystrophy when she and Wyatt met. She was having a hard time coming to terms with her diagnosis and what it would mean for her future, so she turned to Wyatt for counsel. Those counseling sessions led to a "complete and miraculous transformation of faith that changed the trajectory of my life," according to Johanning's quote on the back of the book.

Wyatt and Megan co-authored a book titled *Healing from Within: The Faithful's Guide to Making Peace with Illness*. It struck the market like lightning, selling hundreds of thousands of copies worldwide and becoming a beacon of hope for many people struggling with chronic illnesses. I was familiar with the title because when I worked at the Tuttle County Library, we always had trouble keeping it on the shelves. Then again, people in Tuttle Corner loved their spiritual self-help books. We had a waiting list a mile long for *The Alchemist* the entire time I worked there, despite having multiple copies and it being thirty years old.

Ash texted and offered to pick me up from the *Times* so I didn't have to walk home. I'd been so wrapped up in my research, I didn't realize the weather had deteriorated so badly. I stood up and looked out the front window. Frozen sleet was raining down in diagonal sheets, covering the already wet streets and sidewalks. With the temperature plunging, the entire town was about to turn into an ice rink. Though we did experience storms like this from time to time, Tuttle Corner was not well equipped to handle severe winter weather. The county dispatched plows with salt, but the main safety measure was to warn people to stay home and off the roads.

I gladly accepted, packed up my things, and went to say goodnight to Holman.

"You going to be okay getting home?" I asked.

"I grew up in Canada, Riley."

"Okay. Well, Ash has a giant pickup if you're worried about your Neon."

He blinked. "I'm not."

"How long are you going to stay?"

Holman looked down at the time on his computer and said, "Fourteen more minutes."

"That's oddly specific. What happens in fourteen minutes?"

"It will be six p.m. exactly."

"You're a weird one, Mr. Holman."

"I know," he said without any regret at all. "Goodnight, Riley."

"Goodnight, Will."

Just as I turned to leave, he said, "Do you realize you only call me Will when you're trying to imply emotional sincerity? Otherwise you call me Holman."

"Um...do I?"

"Yes," he said. "Why is that?"

I stopped at the threshold of his door and turned to face him. This was the last thing on my mind, but I knew these sorts of questions were important to Holman. I got the impression that trying to decode the intricacies of social interactions helped orient him in a realm where he all too often felt lost.

"I guess using your first name feels more intimate—" he opened his mouth to say something, but I cut him off, "—and before you say it, I don't mean that in a sexual way."

"Thank goodness for that," he said as the ghost of a smile crossed his face.

CHAPTER 24

I got into Ash's pickup, slightly out of breath from the cold and grateful not to have to make the ten-minute walk home. "Thanks for picking me up—it's awful out there."

"No problem," he said, pulling away from the curb. "I guess we're not going to the Shack tonight."

Tuttle's other response to a storm like this was to behave as if the apocalypse was upon us. Schools canceled classes, businesses closed early, and though I hadn't been to Landry's, I'd bet my last dollar that there'd been a run on bottled water and canned goods.

"Are they closed?"

Ash nodded. "Luckily, though, I came prepared." A wicked grin slid across his face.

"What does that mean?"

"Look in the back seat."

I looked. There was a picnic basket stuffed with goodies, including two bottles of wine, sitting on the bench in the back. My internal reaction was *How romantic,* followed up quickly by *Omg what does this mean?* "I thought I was supposed to buy you a drink tonight?"

"Next time." He smiled. "I tried to pick out your favorites. There's one of their famous charcuterie plates in there with cheese and crackers and some chocolate truffles. Oh, and a can of Pringles, of course."

I looked at the basket overflowing with all the things I love, and an emotion I couldn't readily identify swept through me. "I can't believe you did this."

"You like?"

"I like," I said, and raised my eyes to meet his. "Very much."

Ash pulled into my driveway and turned off the engine. "Listen," he said, turning toward me. "I don't want you to feel any pressure. I just wanted to do something nice for you. You may not realize this, but your friendship has been really important to me over these past couple of months. Moving here and taking over the funeral home...it was hard, and you've shown me that life in Tuttle can be...well, I don't know...good, I guess. I thought some good food and wine might make you smile, that's all."

But it wasn't just food and wine to me; it was a selfless gesture of kindness, something he did for the sole purpose of making me happy. One of my reservations with Ash was that he'd been so volatile when we'd met—up then down; hot, then cold. But I had to admit that once he'd decided he was staying in Tuttle Corner for good, he'd been more up than down. More hot than cold. Literally. I looked over at Ash with his amber eyes and sandy brown hair, and it was like some kind of switch flipped inside of me. In the space of a second, images of Jay and Chloe, Ryan and Ridley, even Tabitha and Thad flashed through my mind, and I thought, *Why not me and Ash?*

I reached over, put my hand behind his neck, and pulled him in. Our kiss was warm and sweet and full of all the things I couldn't think to say, a combination between a thank-you, an apology, and an invitation. When we finally pulled away, it was Ash who was at a loss for words. I lowered my eyes, a counterweight to our intimate moment. I wasn't exactly embarrassed, but the heat that drove me to kiss him left me feeling exposed. The silence stretched on for another few moments until I broke it. "C'mon, let's go inside. It's freezing out here."

"Not where I'm sitting it's not," he said, a distinct note of bewilderment in his voice.

Once we got inside, we ate, we drank, and we talked about what we were going to wear to the party. It was fun to focus on something superficial for a change, and by the time we'd gotten halfway through the bottle of wine, we'd gone online and ordered a cheap top hat and walking stick for him, some strands of faux pearls, a cigarette holder, and a feather headpiece for me.

"How's it going with the investigation into Flick?" he asked after we'd exhausted our party-related conversation.

I caught him up on what had happened over the past couple of days and the connection I'd just discovered between Flick's notes and the Claremore Ministries logo. "What I can't figure out is what a televangelist like Wyatt Claremore could possibly have to do with my grandfather or Flick."

"Maybe they knew each other in college or worked together somewhere?"

"I don't think so." I paused. "I just wish Flick would have talked to me about what he was working on. He was so damn stubborn about wanting to 'protect' me from whatever it was he was looking into." I braced myself against the you-should-be-careful reaction I was used to getting from people like Carl and Jay and my mom.

But Ash just shrugged. "He was old-school, that's all."

"What do you mean?"

"He was from a generation when men felt they had to

protect women and children—and to him you were both. It sounds ridiculously outdated now, but that's how they were raised. My PopPop was—is—the same way."

"How's your grandma doing?"

He held up the bottle of wine and raised his eyebrows. I did a shrug/nod combo. I probably didn't need any more, but the mild buzz I had was so pleasant, I figured what the hell.

"She's holding up okay, I guess. It's just so sad. They're each other's whole life, you know?"

"Sad," I agreed, "but kind of beautiful too. That kind of love seems pretty rare these days."

We were both sitting on the floor, leaning against my overstuffed sofa. I'd moved the coffee table and spread out a blanket so that we could have a proper picnic since he'd gone to the trouble of buying the basket and everything. (I was pretty sure he didn't just have that thing lying around his rental.) Coltrane, unmoored by this new furniture arrangement, had fled to the couch. He'd mostly been sleeping, but every now and then he'd roll his big floppy head around to keep an eye on the prosciutto. I plucked one of the remaining pieces off the board and fed it to him over my shoulder.

"That's one spoiled puppy you got there."

"Don't I know it." I gave Coltrane a kiss on his long, furry snout. "But I can't help it. Just look at that face, it's perfection."

"It sure is." From his tone it was clear Ash was not talking about the dog. I felt my cheeks begin to flush. I could feel him looking at me. "Should we talk about that kiss?" he said quietly.

"Not unless you want to." I was suddenly very interested in the hem of my shirt.

He brushed the tips of my toes with his. "I could think of a few things I'd rather do."

A current of attraction zipped through me. It wouldn't take much, a tilt of the head, a slight turn of my shoulders...I just wasn't sure. And I wasn't sure why I wasn't sure.

I took another sip of my wine. "It'd change everything, you know?"

"I know."

"Do we want to do that?"

"I think one of us does..." he said with a playful edge to his voice.

I laughed, the wine rounding the edges of our conversation.

Ash turned his shoulders so we were face-to-face, or face-to-cheek, I guess. He tucked a strand of hair behind my right ear. Then he leaned in and kissed the side of my face, leaving his lips there for one-Mississippi, two-Mississippi....

Screw it. I turned my head and let his lips find mine. The world faded out and we were lost to the energy that had been building for months. Whatever reservations I had disappeared, and it was just him and me. Everything was happening so fast—like we were racing against time, or perhaps our better judgment. He leaned me back onto the floor, his hand beneath the curve of my neck. I felt the weight of his chest against mine, his hot breath on my neck, and then suddenly he stopped.

"What's wrong?" I asked, breathless.

"Riley, are you sure about this?"

"Yes," I said without thinking, and grabbed his T-shirt and pulled him back down. I lifted his shirt over his head at the exact moment the doorbell rang. We froze in place—which for the record was me pinned underneath Ash, whose entire head was inside his T-shirt. Coltrane ran to the door and started barking.

"Who is that?" Ash whispered.

"No idea."

The knocking came again, followed by more barking. Ash reached over to get his T-shirt off the floor. He sat up and put it on; I smoothed down my hair.

"Riley?" *Knock, knock, knock.* "Are you home?" It was Holman.

Are you fricking kidding me? What the hell was Holman doing at my house at nine p.m. on a Wednesday night?

"Yeah," I called out. "Hang on."

"Who is it?"

"Holman."

As I turned to go open the door, Ash pulled me close. "Get rid of him."

My stomach fluttered in the best possible way, and I leaned in for one more kiss. Then the knocking started again. I was going to kill Holman.

"Hey," I said, opening the door just enough for him to step inside. The icy sleet was coming down sideways thanks to the brisk wind. "What's up?"

Coltrane stopped barking once he saw Holman. I'm pretty sure Holman had never once petted him, but Coltrane was nothing if not an optimist. He wagged his tail and tried to nudge Holman's hand with his nose. Holman raised his arms up by the elbows to get them out of reach. "I tried calling but didn't get an answer."

I glanced over at my phone sitting on the breakfast bar. "Sorry—we were just, um, having dinner."

Holman looked over at Ash, blinked, and then focused his attention back to me. I knew Ash wasn't Holman's favorite person in the world, but this was a cool greeting, even for him.

"My power's out," he said. "From the ice storm. My whole building is without power."

"Oh."

"And my laptop is at approximately eight percent." He paused, presumably waiting for me to react to this information. When I didn't, he said, "And I have a lot of work to do tonight."

"Oh." The good Southern girl in me knew I had to invite him in, but the girl who had been on the couch with Ash a minute ago resisted.

"And it was starting to get really cold in my apartment." Holman's voice moved one standard deviation above his usual calm tone. "And I have Raynaud's disease—it's not advisable for me to get too cold."

"What's Raynaud's disease?" Ash asked, looking somewhere between grossed out and concerned.

"It's a condition in which the blood vessels in my hands and feet narrow in response to cold or stress, causing a restricted blood flow to my appendeg—"

"—it's fine, Holman," I said, cutting him off. His medical explanation broke the lust-induced trance I'd been in. "Come on in. You can work here."

Holman, who was carrying his laptop and had a cross-body bag full of files slung across his slender frame, looked relieved. "Thank you."

Ash widened his eyes at me as I led Holman to the kitchen table. *Sorry*, I mouthed.

As Holman busied himself with setting out his files and notebooks and plugging in his laptop, Ash tried to make conversation. "I read your story on the new laws regarding medical marijuana in last week's paper."

Holman looked up but didn't offer a response. I knew him well enough to know this was because Ash's comment was merely a statement of fact—neither a compliment nor an insult—therefore Holman did not feel obligated to respond. (This wasn't the first time I'd heard someone make this sort of comment to Holman.) But Ash seemed hurt by his lack of response. He looked at me for help.

I tried to grease the wheels. "So, what'd you think?"

"It was great. Really insightful."

"Thank you, Ash." Holman seemed genuinely pleased. I hoped this was the beginning of a warmer relationship between the two of them. "Riley, do you have any green tea?"

"Sure." As I went into the kitchen to make a cup of tea, Ash threw me a look, then said in a slightly stilted voice, "Hey, do you want to watch that movie in your room, so we don't bother Holman while he works?"

Smart boy. "Um, yeah, sure," I said. "Great idea!"

"What movie are you guys going to watch?" Holman asked.

I said, *Little Women*, at the same time that Ash said, *John Wick 3*.

"I guess we'll have to negotiate!" I said, then forced a laugh. Ash faked one too.

Holman, who never faked anything, just blinked again, twice. "Good luck settling on a genre." He put in his earbuds and started typing. Ash and I hurried toward my room.

A second later, Holman's voice called out, "Hey, Riley?"

We were halfway down the hallway and out of Holman's line of sight. "Yeah?" Ash playfully pushed me up against the wall and started nibbling at my neck. I tried to bat him away. Sort of.

"I'm in communication with one of my neighbors who decided to stay at the apartment complex, Joseph in 3F—he doesn't have Raynaud's," he said. "And if the power isn't back on by eleven, would it be all right if I spent the night on your sofa? If I don't get the proper amount of sleep, my performance at work will be less than optimal."

Ash had worked his way up to my ear. "Sure. Fine. Whatever."

"Thank you."

We started toward my bedroom again.

"Riley?" Holman called again.

I hung my head. Never had this fifteen-foot hallway seemed so long in all my life. "Yes?"

"Are you going to take Coltrane with you?"

"What? Why?"

"He's doing that thing where he stares at me again. It's very unsettling."

It was true, Coltrane did like to stare at Holman. My theory is that Holman was probably the only human Coltrane had ever met who would simply not pet him, talk to him, or interact with him in any way, and he found this unacceptable. For the record, I agreed.

"Um, I'm sure he'll settle down soon and lie on the couch. Don't worry." There was a pause and I felt like maybe we were home free. For a second.

"I think he wants something from me," Holman said. "I am not sure I can work under these conditions."

I sighed. "Fine. C'mon, Coltrane!"

Coltrane trotted down the hall and the three of us went inside my bedroom. The second the door was closed Ash took a step toward me. "Are we actually alone again? Finally?"

"Oh no," I said, pushing him away. "No way."

"What?"

"Not with him here."

"He can't hear anything—he has his headphones on."

"Him." I stepped back and pointed at Coltrane, who

had jumped onto my bed and was turning around in circles, a habit he always did before he laid down.

"Are you serious?"

"Yes! I can't possibly...with my *dog* in the room. That'd just be weird."

Ash looked over at Coltrane lying comfortably among my pillows. "He looks to me like he really needs to go out."

I laughed. "You think?"

A second later, as if on cue, Coltrane let out a big exhausted sigh and rolled over onto his side. He looked as though he might never move again.

"Asshole," Ash said to him playfully.

"All right," I said, a smile on my lips. "Now for the most difficult decision of the evening: What movie should we watch?"

Daily Astrological Forecast

Scorpio

The full blood thunder moon is moving into your eighth house, creating a most unusual planetary alignment. On the one hand, this brings a new and promising social element into your life! At the same time, however, intense focus will be required at your place of business. This could be the hallmark of your short-term future, being torn in two directions, and the name of the game is balance. Strive to achieve it at all costs.

As fickle Gemini begins a three-month retrograde, you will start to see duality where before you did not. Pull back the curtain, Scorpio, as frightening as it may be. Dig deeper than you think you need to go. What you find is not likely to be what—or who—you expected. Remember: Sometimes it's the devil you know that you must fear most.

Tonight: Relax with a fun face mask or hot bubble bath!

Chapter 25

Tuttle Corner was officially in the midst of the polar vortex. The roads were covered in ice and sleet, the wind had ratcheted up to a steady twenty-five miles per hour, with gusts up to forty. Temperatures dropped to the twenties overnight, and the sleet changed over to snow. The news was warning everyone to stay home, stay inside, stay off the roads. Holman ended up spending the night on my couch, even though I offered him the second bedroom.

"But then where is Ash going to sleep?" he asked, giving me a look like I had just wandered out from under a bridge. "After all, he was here first."

So, Ash slept in the guest room, which was best considering my bed wasn't big enough for three (Coltrane fell asleep before the movie ended and basically played dead so he didn't have to move). In the morning, Holman made waffles as we watched the big, fat snowflakes pile up outside. It was kind of fun, actually, like an old-school slumber party.

Over breakfast, we chatted about the upcoming party.

"So, what did Camilla send you to wear?" I asked Holman.

"A black tuxedo. It's very elegant," he said. "It used to belong to my father."

Holman didn't talk much about his father, but I knew he hadn't seen or talked to him in years. Camilla told me that Nicholas Holman had left her and Will after it became clear to him that "Will was never going to be the son he imagined." The cruelty of that took my breath away every time I thought about it. I wondered how Holman felt about wearing his father's tux.

"I've decided to dress as a newsie instead," he said, settling the question.

Ash looked confused. "What's a newsie?"

"A newsie, you know?" Holman repeated the word, as if saying it a second time might force understanding. Ash's blank face proved that it did not. "They were young men, boys actually, around the turn of the twentieth century who used to buy up copies of the newspapers and spend all day and night trying to resell every last copy because the newspaper companies refused to buy back their unsold papers."

"Okaaaaay," Ash said.

Holman was getting agitated. "Surely you've heard of the Broadway musical *Newsies*? It tells the story, albeit the Disney version, of the famous newsboys' strike of 1899."

"Kind of, but tell me why you're going to a Gatsby party dressed like a newsie?"

Holman sighed. "Some credit that strike with the ultimate reforms of the despicable child labor practices, which by the 1920s had vastly been improved. And *The Great Gatsby* is set in the 1920s, so naturally you see the connection."

I tried to communicate to Ash with my eyes that it was best to drop it. Holman was his own man, and if he wanted to spend all night dressed as a newsboy, repeating this esoteric explanation to everyone at the party, that was his choice.

I saw Ash open his mouth, probably to say that he did not see the connection, and I decided to seize the moment to tell Holman that Lindsey was coming to the party with us. "Maybe you should see if she wants to go as a newsie with you?"

"Why?"

"Well," I started to explain, "Ash is going as Nick Carraway and I'm going as Jordan Baker—and since we're all going together, maybe you and Lindsey could coordinate too?"

Holman blinked at me. "But she's a female. Newsies are male."

"Yeah, but it's a costume."

"Yes. A costume for a male."

"I don't think gender roles really apply to costumes," Ash said.

Holman looked at me, then Ash, as if we were speaking Farsi.

"Never mind," I said. "I'm sure you'll look great."

By about nine-thirty, Ash said he was going to try to brave the roads to see if he could get home. I walked him to the door.

Holman was doing the last of the breakfast dishes and probably couldn't hear us, but Ash lowered his voice to a whisper anyway. "Thanks for letting me spend the night," he said. "I had fun."

I smiled. "Me too."

"So, I'll see you tomorrow night?"

"Uh-huh."

He leaned in to kiss me goodbye, which felt like anything but a farewell. As he pulled back, a self-conscious laugh bubbled up out of me.

"What?" he asked.

"Nothing."

"Liar."

"Nothing," I repeated, lowering my voice. "It's just thinking about last night and what almost happened...it's just kind of weird, that's all. Everything looks different in the daylight, I guess."

"You don't," he said. "You look every bit as amazing as you did last night."

My cheeks instantly flushed. I pulled the middle-school move of hitting him on the shoulder. "Stop."

"Stop. Go. Stop. Go...make up your mind, Ellison," he said, laughing. Then he gave me another kiss, this one sweeter than before.

I watched him shuffle across the icy driveway and get into his car, then I floated back to the kitchen where Holman was loading the last of the plates into the dishwasher. I knew I was probably still blushing and wondered if Holman had picked up on the change in status of me and Ash.

"Is Ash your boyfriend now?"

"No," I said quickly, then added, "I mean, I don't think so—or um, I mean, I don't know exactly what we are right now."

"You're smiling."

"I guess I am."

Holman carefully folded the tea towel and set it next to my sink. "It's nice to see you happy, Riley."

That made my smile even bigger. I refilled my coffee cup from the pot and topped off Holman's mug. "Should we call Kay and see if she wants us to try to come in today?" I asked, looking out the front window at the mounting snow.

Holman leaned against the countertop next to the sink; he was looking out the window on my back door. He didn't answer.

"Holman?"

"Is it worth it?"

"Well, if it's too icy out, we just won't go—"

"No," he said. "I mean, is getting close to someone worth the risk of getting hurt?"

There was no one who could surprise me quite the way Will Holman could. I was seized by a visceral desire to hug him, but I knew better—Holman was not a big fan of physical displays of affection. So instead I took a couple of moments to think about what to say. Holman didn't ask questions like this often, and I felt a responsibility to answer truthfully.

"Most of the time."

Holman stared at me his patented wide-eyed way and after a beat he said, "Maybe Lindsey *would* consider dressing up as a newsie?"

And that comment brought about my biggest smile of the day so far.

CHAPTER 26

The consensus of most of the *Times* employees was to stay home and work remotely. Holman and I decided that's what we'd do, and if temperatures warmed enough to start melting some of the ice, we would try to go in later that afternoon. From my makeshift workstation in the living room, I filed an update on the post office food drive and did a final edit on a piece about the effects of frost on local farmers. Once finished, I went back to my online research about Claremore Ministries. Holman, having already caught up on his work the night before, was searching the *Times* obit archives for references to Claremore and Oakwood Christian Church.

I found little information that I felt could be connected to my grandfather or Flick. Specifically, I was looking for any press mentions of the church and/or Claremore himself around the time Granddad was killed. I found nothing suspicious or even out of the ordinary. I was able to find an old edition of the Claremore Ministries newsletter from the week of Granddad's death and learned that Wyatt had gone on a mission trip to Haiti for two weeks, while Shannon stayed behind to care for Megan Johanning, who had suffered a fall. They asked for prayers for her swift and complete recovery. That was it. I didn't know what I'd expected to find, but I was disappointed all the same. I couldn't find one single thread tying Claremore Ministries to Granddad or Flick, other than the doodle in Flick's notes.

My phone started to vibrate on the couch next to me, pulling me out of my thoughts. I answered and a robovoice came through the phone, "This is a collect call from—" the line crackled and then came the signature sneering tone: "Joe Tackett."

"I'll accept." I put the phone on speaker and motioned for Holman to come listen in.

"Riley?" Tackett's voice set me on edge. I didn't like hearing him say my name.

"Yes."

"You made any progress getting me a deal yet?"

I wasn't sure how much to reveal. I didn't want him to think I was running around doing his bidding, but I didn't want him to think I was doing nothing either. I needed the information he had, and I didn't want to lose the chance to get it. "We talked to the prosecutor. She said she needs to be sure you have credible information before she can do anything."

I heard him mutter something under his breath but couldn't make it out. "Well, you better tell her to hurry her ass up. I'm getting some pressure in here." He sounded agitated, impatient.

"What kind of pressure?" Holman asked.

"Who's that?" Tackett snapped.

"It's Will Holman." He paused, then added, "Lurch."

Tackett sighed, then lowered his voice to a whisper. "When it got out that I had official-lookin' visitors a few days ago, people started talking. Damn inmates are worse than a room fulla old women. Rumors started that I'm ratting out the Romeros. If the wrong people believe that, I could be in trouble—as in the *dead* kind of trouble."

This was exactly what Jay had warned me about. I had no love for Joe Tackett, but I didn't want to see him dead—in no small part because if he died in prison, what he knew about my granddad's death would die with him.

"Aren't you kept away from the other prisoners?" I asked.

"Believe me, if they want to get to me, they'll get to me."

"Why don't you tell the prosecutor what you know now? Give them what you have, then perhaps she can arrange for your protection?" Holman suggested.

"I can't do that."

"Why not?"

"Because it's all I got. I've seen how those people operate. If I give up that recording before I have a deal on the table, I'll never get a damn thing."

Tackett had a point. Giving him a transfer or whatever it was he wanted was going to be a tough sell under the best of circumstances. I'd be willing to bet that the authorities would take any chance they could to get out of dealing with him—and I couldn't blame them for that. Tackett was a bad man, and he'd abused his power in Tuttle County for a long time.

"What can you tell us about a Shannon Miller—er, I mean Shannon Claremore?" I asked, changing the subject.

There was a taut silence on the line. "Figured out the connection, did you?"

My entire body broke out into chills. I knew we were onto something! Now, I just had to bait him a little further. "Of course we did."

"Well, good luck nailing that crackpot without proof. That's why I had to get her on tape."

Crackpot? That didn't sound like he was describing the Shannon Claremore I'd read about. My hesitation gave me away.

I could practically see Tackett's self-satisfied smile through the phone. "Ah, I see. You're on the right track, but you ain't there yet. I can fill in those blanks, but I need a deal before I say shit."

Holman and I looked at each other, both of us unsure of what to do. We had no control over what Lindsey decided to offer Tackett. It could be weeks until she spoke to him, if she decided to talk to him at all. And even if she did, what if she felt his information didn't rise to the threshold of "fruitful and credible"?

"Just give me something—anything—that I can take to Lindsey to prove that the information you say you have is relevant to the murders of my grandfather and Hal Flick. That's the only way they're going to fight the feds to help you."

For a few seconds all I heard was the sound of his breath in the receiver. "Albert found out that Shannon Claremore is not who she says she is," he said finally.

"What does that even mean?" I said. "Who is she if she isn't Shannon Claremore?"

"That's all I'm gonna say for now. Tell that lady prosecutor I'm ready to talk. But I don't know how much longer I've got."

CHAPTER 27

Holman had Lindsey on the phone less than ten seconds after I hung up with Tackett.

"He spends almost all day in a cell by himself," Lindsey assured us. "He's safe."

Holman held his phone, on speaker, in between us. I leaned forward. "He sounded scared, like he really thinks the cartel's people could come after him."

"And I'm sure that's what he wants you to think," she said. "He's trying to find a way out of there, or at least a way to reduce the amount of time he spends there, so he's busting out every trick in the book. Don't let him get in your head."

While I appreciated what she was saying, I couldn't help but feel frustrated at her lack of urgency. If something did end up happening to Tackett before she had a chance to find out what he knows about Granddaddy's death, that information could be lost forever.

"Have you decided how you plan to proceed?" Holman asked.

"The plan is to interview him at Greensville next week and have Sheriff Haight and Sheriff Clark present. Tackett is still refusing representation, which I think is a mistake, but that's his choice. If he's able to provide us with good information that the sheriffs are able to use in the Ellison and

Flick cases *and* he agrees to testify, then I would be willing to go before Judge Giancarlo and recommend a transfer or reduction in sentence, depending on what we get."

"And what about the feds?" Holman asked.

"I've all but decided that the potential of prosecuting two unsolved murders needs to take precedence over the DEA's hope that Tackett may one day spill on the Romeros."

I let out the breath I'd been holding. Tackett would be heard. I didn't feel great about helping a man like him, but I was willing to live with it. My singular purpose was to extract what he knew about my grandfather's and Flick's killer, and that came before everything else to me.

"When are you set to interview Tackett?" I asked.

"Wednesday."

"Any chance I can be there?"

Lindsey actually laughed. "Uh, no."

"Really? Even under the victim's rights statute?" I knew it was a long shot, but I had to try.

"That statute is the only reason I'm talking to you now, Riley," she said, a steely kindness in her voice. "But I can promise you that once we are able to corroborate the information Tackett gives us, I will share it with you and your family."

I scribbled on a scrap of paper, *Do we tell her what T said about Shannon Claremore?* and held it up to Holman, who shook his head.

He then took the phone off speaker. "Lindsey, there is one other nonlegal matter that I was hoping to discuss with you..." he said as he walked down the hallway for some privacy. I assumed he was going to pitch her the idea of them going to the party as newsies. I sent a silent prayer out into the ether for him.

I spent the next several minutes looking over the notes

I'd taken during my conversations with both Tackett and Lindsey. *Okay,* I told myself, *This is good. Things are happening.* Tackett is going to have his chance to tell the authorities what he knows, and then Lindsey says she will tell me. I still had an inkling of doubt that Tackett could deliver what he says he could, but there was no way to know if he was lying yet. He also confirmed that there is something shady going on with Shannon Miller Claremore, which lined up with Flick's research as well. *This is progress,* I reassured myself again.

I wondered about the audio recording that Tackett claimed to have. Where was it? Obviously, he didn't have it with him in prison. He probably stashed it somewhere like a safe deposit box or with a relative perhaps. God, if I could just get my hands on that tape, I wouldn't need to deal with Tackett at all.

"She's in," Holman announced, looking triumphantly dazed as he walked back into my living room. "She was quite familiar with the newsies and loved the idea."

"That's great!"

"Mm-hm."

"Why don't you look happy?"

He walked over to the kitchen table. "I am happy," he said. "I'm just not sure what is expected of me."

"What do you mean 'expected of' you?"

"I did not technically ask her out as my date for the evening—as a point of fact, I am actually your invited guest. I don't even know the host. However, since we are going as part of a foursome, in which two of you are a quasi-couple, we, as the remaining two, are necessarily paired. But it's a forced pairing, not one of intention or choice, so that begs the question, is this a date or not?"

I stared at him, my mouth slightly agape. As an

overthinker myself, I was familiar with the twists and turns of an analytical mind, but this was over the top even for me. The best thing I could do for him was to provide some certainty. "Yes," I said. "It's a date."

Holman swallowed. "Okay then." He started to gather up his files and laptop. "I have to go."

"Go where? What about the ice?"

"I am perfectly capable of driving in snow and ice." He put on his puffer jacket and began winding a dark blue scarf around his neck. "If I am going to be a proper escort for Lindsey tomorrow evening, I'd really better get going on some preparations."

"Preparations?" I followed him to the door. "What does that even mean? I thought we were going to do more research for the story?"

"The fact is that until we know more about what Tackett is alleging, it's like looking for a polar bear in a snowstorm, to use a timely metaphor."

"Huh?"

"You know, like trying to find a black cat in a coal mine."

"What?"

He blinked. "A needle in a haystack, if you prefer."

"I don't prefer!" I said. "How is researching information about Shannon Claremore like any of those things?" I let my shoulders sag. "I'm confused, Holman."

"My point exactly," he said and tapped the side of his nose twice just before slipping out through my front door.

CHAPTER 28

Holman may have been too keyed up about his impending date to focus on work, but I was not. As soon as he left, I went back to my notes on Granddad's case and picked up where I'd left off when Tackett called. I once again read over the paperwork that Elaine at the Hudson Falls record office had sent me; I saw my notes about Jane Smith. I had almost forgotten that someone else had been sniffing around for information on the Millers the same day I had. I'd gotten her phone number (thanks to Elaine and my imaginary cat Nibbles) and had meant to look up whom it belonged to days ago, but I'd gotten distracted by Tackett's letter. I knew now that the 252 area code was from Greenville, North Carolina. I also knew now that that was where Shannon and Wyatt Claremore lived. Google didn't produce anything useful on the number, so I decided to check it out the old-fashioned way. I took a deep breath and dialed the number. It rang once, twice, three times. After the fifth ring or so, the voicemail clicked on: "Hello, you've reached Shannon. Please leave me a message and I'll get back to you as soon as possible. Thank you and have a blessed day."

The voicemail beeped and I had to make a split-second decision. Do I hang up or leave a message? The phone would have a record of my number and I wasn't unlisted, so she could easily find out it was me calling. Besides, I'd left this number with Rhonda at Silver Meadows. I'd come this far; there was no point in hanging up now.

"Hi, Shannon. This is Riley Ellison, I'm a reporter from the *Tuttle Times*. I'm doing a story on a plane crash in 1959 in which several of your family members perished and I was hoping to get a quote from you. I've spoken to your father, Charlie, already but would like to interview you as well. Please give me a call back when you have time. Thanks." I pressed end, my heart hammering in my chest.

So, Shannon Claremore was Jane Smith. Why on earth would she be trying to access her own family's records from Hudson Falls using a fake name? As family, she had a right to those records. All she'd have to do is show proof of who she is, and they'd give her everything. Tackett's words reverberated through my mind. *Albert found out Shannon Claremore is not who she says she is.* Who the hell was she then?

It was like the universe heard my question and provided an answer in the form of a ringing phone. Shannon's number flashed on my screen. She was calling me back already. My heartbeat ticked back up. "This is Riley."

"Hi, Riley, Shannon Claremore returning your call."

I thanked her and recapped my reason for the call—at least my fake reason. When I finished, she said, "Yes, I understand you and an associate visited my father at Silver Meadows. I believe he told you we aren't related to any of those poor folks who died in that plane crash."

Apparently, she was going to stick with the party line. I would have to get more aggressive. "Actually, I have information that indicates you are."

"What information would that be?"

"I've come across some records that show a signature from Charles Miller as the next of kin."

"Death certificates are private."

"I didn't say it was a death certificate."

She said nothing for several seconds. I waited, frozen with anticipation. "It must be a different Charles Miller. It's a pretty common name, you know."

"Could I ask him about it?" I said. I wanted her to know I knew she had blocked me from being able to interview her father again.

"I'm sorry. That's not possible. My father is old and unwell. His memory isn't what it used to be."

"All right," I said, trying to keep my tone as cool and even as possible. "It'd be easy enough for me to cross-check the signature on the form with one from your father—the DMV keeps records on these sorts of things, you know." This was not true. For starters, I didn't even have a copy of the form from the funeral home on Chincoteague—the funeral director had just read off that information to Ash over the phone. And even if I could get a copy, I doubted the DMV would give me, a lowly reporter, a copy of Charlie Miller's signature. I ignored the ever-more familiar feeling of ethical dissention from my brain. *I needed this information,* I thought. If I had to tell a few lies to get it, then so be it.

"I don't understand why you're arguing with me about this," she said, sounding irritated. "I'm telling you that we are not related to that Miller family. Period. End of story."

"Do you know a man named Hal Flick?"

"No."

"Are you sure?"

"I meet a lot of people, so I can't say for certain that I've never met anyone by that name, but I don't recall if I have. Why—who is he?"

"*Was*—who was he," I corrected her, barely controlling my anger as I said the words. "He was a journalist who was killed in a car wreck a month ago."

She was quiet for a moment, then said, "No, doesn't ring a bell."

"How about Albert Ellison?"

"Isn't that your last name?"

"Albert Ellison was my grandfather. He's dead now."

"I'm sorry." Perhaps for the first time in the conversation, she sounded sincere.

"The thing is," I said, wandering into unchartered territory, "he was working on a book about the Miller family who died in that plane crash, but he was murdered before he could finish it."

"Oh dear." She had the decency to sound shocked at the word *murder*—but not to ask how or why. "And now you're finishing it for him?"

"Something like that," I said.

She was quiet for a long moment and then said, "Well, I'm sorry I can't be of more help. If you need anything else from me, I'll ask you to please go through my personal assistant, Megan Johanning. You can reach her through the Claremore Ministries switchboard. And I'd appreciate it if you didn't try to contact my father again. He's very frail and any upset to his routine is hard on him." She was clearly giving me the brush-off.

"I'm not going to drop this, Shannon. I'm going to continue looking into your family's connection to this story."

I thought I heard a note of desperation in her voice when she said, "I really wouldn't do that if I were you."

"Why—what do you mea—" I said, but she had already hung up.

CHAPTER 29

Had Shannon Claremore just threatened me? I replayed the sentence in my mind—dissected her tone of voice, cadence, the places in which she paused. *I really wouldn't if I were you.* It wasn't an explicit threat like, "Drop it or else," but it felt like she was almost begging me to let it go. What I didn't know was if that was for my benefit or hers.

Given that the last two people who had looked into the Claremore/Miller connection were dead, I decided it was a good idea to let a member of law enforcement know about this, even if I didn't really have anything concrete to tell them. I called Sheriff Clark and gave him a rundown on my odd conversation with Shannon.

"And you felt she was threatening you?"

I bristled at his tone, which was somewhere between amused and skeptical. "I don't know if she was or not, but it felt like it."

"All right." He cleared his throat. "I'll make a note, but there's not a lot I can do about a veiled threat by one person against another person—neither of whom live in my county."

"I just thought..." I said, suddenly feeling very foolish. "It's just that Joe Tackett called me this morning and said he's worried that he might get killed by the cartel's spies, and so he gave me this weird clue about Shannon Claremore not being who she says she is—"

"Wait—*what?*" He interrupted me. "Back up."

I filled him in about Tackett's phone call earlier and his accusation that Shannon Claremore is hiding something and how he was worried about his safety in prison and was looking to tell his story as soon as possible. That seemed to get the sheriff's attention.

"I think I ought to call Lindsey Davis," he said. "Maybe I should go over to Greensville and talk to Tackett sooner than later."

"Yeah, great." I was surprised by his sudden enthusiasm. "I think the sooner we can find out what he knows, the better. But if he's worried about the appearance of talking to the authorities, wouldn't that just exacerbate the situation?"

"I can arrange it with the warden so no one would know he was being pulled out to talk to me."

"Wow," I said, surprised and happy at the same time. "Do you think you could get in to see him today?"

"It's possible."

If Sheriff Clark was able to talk to Tackett today, I could be hours away from finding out the truth. It was almost too much to hope for. "Will you let me know what he says?"

"I can't make any promises." His tone was clipped, but after a beat he added, more softly, "But if I can, yes."

We hung up with promises to talk again soon. I couldn't believe that this might work—emphasis on *might*. With the roads being what they were, Lindsey would not be able to get to Brunswick County today even if she wanted to, so if she insisted on being present for the interview, it would be a no-go. But since Sheriff Clark would be the one who would need to follow up on any information Tackett gave regarding Flick's death, she might allow him to get first crack, especially given his fear that he was in imminent danger. Of course, I also knew it was possible Tackett made up that whole "danger" thing to speed up the process. And while I hated to think it might have worked, I hated the idea of his secrets dying with him even more.

Energized by the sudden turn of events, I suddenly felt restless. I had been stuck in my house for less than twenty-four hours because of the weather and I was already getting cabin fever. This is why I could never live in upstate New York. Well, that and the fact that I doubted you could get a decent sweet tea anywhere north of DC. I stared out my bedroom window searching for signs of life. None of the three driveways I could see had any tire tracks on them, and it looked like the only cars that had been down my street were Holman's and Ash's.

There were two sets of footprints leading away from Oliver Pruitt's front door, one human and one canine. From the looks of it, Pruitt had braved the weather for his beloved dog, Chortle. Chortle, in all her ginger-furred glory, was the Juliette to Coltrane's Romeo. They absolutely adored each other. Oliver and I...not so much. He'd lived in this neighborhood for eons and used to complain that Granddad didn't cut his grass short/often/well enough back when Granddad was alive. I'll never forget when he came to my door on the day I moved in. I assumed he was there to welcome me to the neighborhood or possibly to say he was sorry to hear about Albert's death, but instead, when I opened the door, he simply handed me a wooden ruler and said, "Two and a half inches is the optimal height for Kentucky bluegrass." Ever since then, our relationship had been chilly. But our dogs loved each other and, on the not-so-rare occasions when Coltrane would get out without his leash, he would run straight over to Mr. Pruitt's front door and start barking. It was sweet—the lovesick-canine version of throwing pebbles. Mr. Pruitt did not find it nearly as cute as I did. The last time it happened, his exact words were, "Keep your mongrel away from my little princess." I wanted to snap back something about who names their "little princess" Chortle, but I kept my mouth shut. Silence is the better part of valor, after all, and it wasn't the dog's fault she'd been given a name that sounded like someone choking on a chicken bone.

Desperate for some fresh air, I geared up with two coats, a hat, mittens, and my warmest boots to take Coltrane for a walk. I knew my look was slightly more insane bag lady than I was used to, but I was prioritizing warmth over fashion. Once I was sufficiently outfitted, instead of our usual route around the neighborhood, I took us toward town to see what was going on around the square. I figured the paths in Memorial Park had the best chance of being shoveled or salted, since it was the heart of Tuttle Corner.

I was wrong; they hadn't been touched. I guess the town had used most of its resources in other areas. Since there was no one around to mind, I let Coltrane off his leash so he could run through the park. The exercise would do him good. Most of the shops and businesses looked closed, except for Mysa. I was too far away to see much, but I could tell their lights were on and it looked like there were some people sitting at the tables by the windows. I should have known that Ridley wouldn't let a little thing like Mother Nature turning into Queen Elsa come between her and her customers.

Coltrane and I made our way in that direction, partially because I wasn't quite ready to go home yet and partially because a cup of Swedish hot cocoa sounded like heaven.

As we got closer, I could see that although it wasn't as busy as it would normally be on a Friday during the breakfast shift, there were several people inside. Mayor Lancett and her weaselly nephew/personal assistant Toby sat at one of the tables by the window—she was reading the *Times* and he was looking down at his phone. I couldn't see his shirt, but he was wearing a black beanie that read "Gym Beast." At the table next to them, Jonathan Gradin and Mel Druing were deep into a game of Scrabble, and Skipper Hazelrigg sat at a corner table by himself with a yellow notepad and his laptop, probably working on his campaign.

Ryan was chatting with a man at the counter, and Ridley stood beside him laughing at something the man must have said. I knew I couldn't bring Coltrane through the front entrance without Mayor Lancett having a complete breakdown (her stance on no animals inside businesses was well known: *"Are we in Paris, France? I don't think so!"*), so I knocked on the front window hoping to get Ryan's or Ridley's attention and they could let us in the back, or maybe even just bring me a hot cocoa to go. As soon as I knocked, every head in the place turned, including the man Ryan had been talking to at the counter. I was surprised to see it was Jay. *Jay again.* Jay still here in Tuttle. He said he was leaving. Curiosity got the better of me, and I opened the door and marched inside.

Mayor Lancett jumped up out of her seat. "Oh no, Riley Ellison, you cannot bring that anim—"

"Just a minute, Shaylene," I said as I walked past her and right up to Jay. "Hey."

"Hi, Riley," he said with a warm smile, as if his hanging around Tuttle Corner every day was a normal occurrence.

Coltrane whined with excitement, and Ryan rushed out from behind the counter. He shot me a look and murmured,

"Geez, Riley. Right in front of the mayor? I'll take him to the back."

I started to apologize, but Ridley cut me off. "It's fine," she said. "I'll send over a banana Nutella crepe and she will forget all about it." She winked at me as she, Ryan, and Coltrane went through the swinging door to the back.

"I'm surprised you're still here." I crossed my arms in front of my chest, suddenly remembering I had sixty-four layers on. I must have looked deranged.

"The roads were too slick to drive home last night, so I got a room at the Ottoman Inn. Heather and Mike were thrilled to see me. I think I'm the only guest there right now."

"Are you sure that's the reason?" The snow had stopped at least an hour earlier, and while I'm sure road conditions weren't ideal, there had been plenty of time for the main highways to be cleared and treated. He wasn't stuck here. There had to be another reason Jay hadn't left Tuttle Corner.

He let out a little laugh and swiveled his eyes to the side. "Um, yeah. What do you mean?"

"I just get the feeling there's something else going on. You're working on something to do with Tackett."

Jay put his hands into his pockets and shrugged. The very picture of innocence.

"Okay," I said. "If you don't want to tell me, that's fine."

Ridley came out from the back holding a plate filled with the most delicious-looking crepes topped with powdered sugar and thinly sliced bananas. "I call this the 'All Is Forgiven,' " she said as she floated past us to deliver the plate to Mayor Lancett.

"Well, hope you make it home before spring," I said with more than a little sarcasm and started to walk into the back to retrieve my dog.

Jay grabbed my arm as I passed. "What's the matter?

Why're you so mad at me?"

I looked down at his hand on my arm. He released it immediately.

"You are actively standing between me and the thing I want most in the world."

"This isn't personal, Riley."

"It is to me," I said, then spun on my heels without so much as a backward glance, momentarily reveling in my own self-righteousness.

Coltrane was happily chomping on a large bone in a small room right off the back door of the restaurant. Ryan sat in a nearby chair watching him.

"Sorry I brought him in here," I said. "I didn't mean to cause trouble."

Ryan looked up. "You okay?"

I lifted a shoulder and let it drop. "There's just a lot going on right now with...stuff."

"Yeah, I figured." He paused. "Are you and Jay getting back together or something?"

I hadn't thought about it before, but Ryan and Ridley probably thought the issue Jay and I were fighting about was a personal one. "No—he's here for work."

"And you're upset about that because..."

I shrugged again. "It's complicated."

"Does this have to do with Sheriff Tackett?"

That got my attention. "Why do you ask?"

"No reason, I just overheard Jay on the phone, and I swear I heard him say the name Joe Tackett."

"Do you remember what he said about him?"

"Not really. I wasn't trying to listen in. I just heard him on the phone when I was refilling the pastry case."

"*Think.*" I took a step closer. "It could be really important."

Ryan was quiet as he tried to remember the details of what he'd heard. "I think he said something about going to see Tackett in prison before..."

"Before what?"

He ran a hand through his hair and rested it on top of his head. "God, I just can't remember...I think he said, 'Thanks for letting me know,' and then—" Ryan broke off for a minute as he thought—"he said something like, 'We should get in there before he talks to her.' Does that mean anything to you?"

Before he talks to her. That had to be Lindsey Davis. "Yes, it actually does." I grabbed the bone out of Coltrane's mouth and picked up his leash. "Thank you so much, Ryan. You have no idea how helpful you've been."

"Are you the 'her' he was referring to?" Ryan asked as he followed me to the back door.

"I don't think so. Why?"

"Good. The whole thing sounded kinda ominous."

"What do you mean?"

"I don't know. It was like the way he said it or something. 'We need to get the information before he talks to her.' " He sounded like he was doing an impression from *Goodfellas*.

"Wait." I stopped. "He said, 'We need to get the information'?"

Ryan nodded. "I'm almost positive."

"Any clue who he was talking to? Did he say any names at all other than Tackett's?"

Ryan looked like he was concentrating so hard, I thought he might sprain something. After a few seconds, he said, "I think he said, 'Thanks, Mike' before hanging up. I'm not a hundred percent, because like I said I wasn't paying a ton of attention, but we just hired Mike Skelton as a busboy, so the name must have caught my ear."

I didn't want to jump to conclusions, because Mike was about as common a name as you could get, but I did anyway. I wasn't three steps out the back door of Mysa before I had my phone in hand dialing the number of Sheriff Michael Clark.

CHAPTER 30

The person who answered the phone at the Brunswick County Sheriff's office refused to share Sheriff Clark's whereabouts with me, even after I told her I had already spoken to him and that he told me he was going to try to go to Greensville Correctional to see Joe Tackett. She said she could neither confirm nor deny. So, after I got Coltrane home, I quickly changed clothes and texted Holman to meet me at the *Times* office ASAP. When I got in, Kay Jackson was there and I told them both about the morning's developments.

"And you think Jay was talking to Sheriff Clark?" Kay asked.

"That's my guess, but obviously I can't be sure. It's just strange. There's a reason Jay is still hanging out around here."

"It could be the road conditions," Holman said, a note of hope in his voice. I knew how much Holman idolized Jay. It was going to be hard to get him to realize that on this issue, Jay was our adversary.

"I checked with VDOT and 1-95 is showing pretty clear. Fifty-eight, on the other hand, is a mess—not to mention the other small roads that lead in and out of Brunswick County. Greensville would be hard to get to from here, given the weather, so maybe he's waiting for those roads to be cleared?"

Kay took a sip from her ever-present mug of coffee. "So, let's assume for a minute that it *was* Sheriff Clark that Jay was talking to on the phone. What would that mean?"

I bit the corner of my lip.

"What?" Holman said.

"Nothing. It's just—"

"This is not the time to hold back, Ellison." Kay crossed her arms.

I was hesitant to voice my theory, in part because it was based on a lot of speculation, and in part because it did not reflect well on Jay. I guess Holman wasn't the only one having a hard time thinking of Jay as a rival.

"Well," I started slowly, "I told Sheriff Clark this morning that Tackett said he felt threatened because there was a rumor going around the prison that he was cooperating with the feds, right?"

Kay nodded.

"Tackett's afraid he could get hurt—or worse—if the cartel thinks he's informing on them. But from Jay's perspective, that would almost be a good thing, you know?"

Holman furrowed his brow. "How so?"

"Jay told me yesterday that he thinks if they can put enough pressure on Tackett—make him 'uncomfortable' enough—he will make a deal. How much more uncomfortable can you be than to think you could be attacked at any given moment?" I paused, hesitant to make the connection out loud. "A visit from the sheriff would certainly bolster the perception that Tackett is cooperating with the authorities...what if Jay and Sheriff Clark are working together to create that perception?"

"That's what he could have meant by 'We need to get the information before he talks to her,' " Kay said, leaning forward. "*Her* could be Lindsey Davis. They need to get the information on the Romeros before Tackett talks to Lindsey and she offers him a deal for his information about Albert..."

I nodded. "The DEA is prepared to offer him some sort of protection, but Tackett said that the cartel could get to him no matter what. That's why he's so anxious to make the deal with Lindsey—giving up *that* information won't get him killed."

Holman blinked. "I guess he believes that whoever killed Albert and Flick is less of a threat to his personal safety than the Romeros."

"Or he's making it all up," Kay said grimly. I opened my mouth to protest, but she held up a hand to stop me. "It's a possibility, is all I'm saying. We have to stay open to the idea that this all might be an elaborate trick. You know I'm right, Riley."

I did. But I wasn't happy about it. "So what's the plan?" I said.

"We should tell Lindsey about these new developments," Holman said. "If Tackett is working with the feds in direct opposition to her case, she deserves to know. It might change her timeline on interviewing Tackett."

"I'll keep trying to reach Sheriff Clark," I said. I hadn't told Kay much about the other direction Holman and I were pursuing with the Shannon Claremore/Miller plane crash theory, mostly because I wasn't sure what it all meant. But I hadn't forgotten about my strange phone conversation with Shannon and definitely planned to look more closely into her family's connection to what my granddad was writing about.

Holman and I went back to his office and decided we would divide and conquer. He would call Lindsey and fill her in; I would go talk to Carl Haight. He may not have had jurisdiction over Flick's murder, but Granddad had been killed in Tuttle Corner, which made that crime definitely his to investigate.

Gail was on the phone when I got to the sheriff's office, but she gestured toward the break room, which I took as an invitation to walk in.

"Are you suggesting Sheriff Clark is up to something?" Carl asked, doubt dripping off every syllable. "I don't know..."

"I'm not saying that," I said as I followed him from the break room back to his office. "He probably believes he's acting in the interest of the greater good by helping the DEA get something on the cartel."

We walked into his office and I closed the door. "You said yourself that it was a little weird that he hadn't looked into certain things about Flick's death. What if he's slow-playing that investigation in order to give Jay more time to persuade Tackett to flip?"

Carl sighed. "There is something to be said for getting information on the Romero family..."

"That's not his job!" I didn't quite yell, but I came close. "I'm sorry," I said, lowering my voice. "But the job of the county sheriff is to enforce the laws of the county, to investigate crimes that happen within the county limits. His job is to figure out what happened to Flick, not worry about the Romeros."

Carl tilted his head toward me. "I'm not arguing with you. I'm just sayin' it could be that Sheriff Clark figures better to get the information we know Tackett has—the dirt on the cartel—than the stuff he *says* he has but has offered no proof of."

"Yeah, I get it. I'm not even saying I completely disagree.

But the fact is that two good men have been murdered and it seems like no one cares." I sighed and leaned back in my chair. "I know that whoever did it might not be as bad as the Romero family, but shouldn't they be held accountable for their actions? Are we all supposed to just forget about finding out who killed Flick and Albert because the one person who knows who's responsible might also know some other stuff? Where is the justice in that?"

Carl's face grew serious. If there was one thing I could count on, it was Carl Haight's commitment to seeing justice served. He'd been that way since he was line leader of Mrs. Emerson's fifth-grade class. No one got away with butting in line when Carl was on duty. "Okay," he finally said.

"Okay what?"

"I'll reach out to Tackett."

"Will you go see him?"

"Weather's iffy. I'll see if I can't get him on the phone first."

"Thank you, Carl." I wanted to jump up and down, but I restrained myself.

"If I can persuade him to give me something concrete, something to prove he knows what he says he does, then I can take that to Lindsey and see about getting him moved to a safer location or increase his security. Not sure he'll cooperate, but if he's truly scared for his life, he might just be willing to let a little more of his leverage go."

I stood, anxious to let him get to work. "Let me know what you find out?"

"You know I used to work for the man, Riley," he said, his voice taking on a dark edge. "Tackett is one of the most gifted liars I've ever met—and that's saying something. He's not to be trifled with and not to be trusted."

"I know."

"Do you?" He arched one eyebrow. "Because it seems to me that you're putting an awful lot of faith in Tackett. I know you're desperate to find out what happened to Albert and Flick—"

"I'm not *desperate*," I shot back, but even as I said the words, I knew how false they sounded. I was desperate, and anyone could see it.

"Tackett is out for one person and one person only: himself. He will lie, cheat, steal, and worse to get what he wants. Do not put too much stock in what he's telling you."

CHAPTER 31

It was still cold out, and gray clouds filled the sky, clumping on top of one another like balls of dirty socks, making it seem much later in the day than it was. Cars had begun to populate the streets again, but there was definitely less activity than there would be on a normal weekday in downtown Tuttle. I had just started walking back to the *Times* office when Ash texted.

Something weird just came up. Can you come over?

The funeral home was only a couple of blocks out of my way, so I decided to detour and head over there before going back to the newsroom. I turned the corner onto Broad and saw Ash standing outside the funeral home as I walked up, wearing his usual rumpled jeans and plaid shirt. He was waiting for me. My belly swooshed as I got closer and his eyes locked onto mine.

"Hey."

"Hey," I responded, an involuntary smile edging across my face. "What's up?"

He held the door open for me and I stepped inside. "I wish I could say this was all just an elaborate ruse to get you to come see me."

"It's not?"

He laughed but shook his head. "I just got a call from Gary, from the Chincoteague funeral home."

"Okay."

"He said he was telling his wife about talking to me the other day and she got a funny look on her face, and when he asked her what was the matter, she said someone had come by the funeral home about a month ago asking about the same family—the Miller family who died in a plane crash."

A tingle started to creep up the back of my neck. I had a feeling about what he was going to say next.

"It was Flick."

I knew it. I wasn't surprised, but that didn't stop the pounding feeling building inside my chest. Flick had been onto something big. He'd tracked down where the Millers died, had a meeting with someone, and then headed over to Brunswick County—either to see Charlie Miller or Joe Tackett in prison.

"There's more."

"Okay..."

"Gary's wife gave Flick a copy of the death certificate, the one with Charlie Miller's name listed as next of kin on it. He told her he had a meeting with some very powerful people who were trying to cover up 'a lifetime of lies' and needed it as proof."

"A lifetime of lies?"

Ash nodded. "That's what Gary's wife said."

"The powerful people he was talking about must be the ones he referred to as the 'pack of professional liars.' "

"I thought you'd want to know," Ash said. "And I didn't want to put this all down in a text, just in case. All of this stuff is starting to feel really cloak-and-dagger."

I agreed. "Good thinking."

"You okay?"

"I will be."

Ash took my hand and squeezed. "I know you will."

For a split second the feeling of his skin on mine took me back to last night, and all I wanted to do was lose myself in the moment, to block out all the confounding puzzles I was trying to unravel, the crushing weight of trying to chase down the truth. But when Ash let go, the feeling faded. This was no time for passion; it was time to get back to work.

He offered to drive me back to the office, but I told him I'd rather walk. Fresh air always helps me think, and I certainly had a lot to think about after hearing that bit of news. I wondered who Flick had shown the copy of Daniel Miller's death certificate to. And where was it now? It certainly wasn't in the file, and it hadn't been found in his car after the crash. If Flick had figured out, as we did, that Shannon Claremore was really Charlie's daughter, he could have reached out to her. Was that who he had been meeting with on Chincoteague? Shannon denied that she knew Flick when I asked her on the phone, but it wouldn't have been the first time someone lied to me. Or maybe Flick used a different name. If he was afraid he was getting close to the people who killed Albert, maybe he was trying to be extra careful? The thought caused a squeezing sensation deep inside my chest.

I felt with almost one hundred percent certainty that Shannon Miller Claremore and her father were lying about being related to the Miller family from the crash. The question, of course, was why. Shannon Claremore was married to one of the most high-profile and influential Christian leaders of our time. It seemed a little far-fetched to think that she could somehow be involved in not one, but two murders. However, there was definitely something weird going on with her. Tackett said Albert found out Shannon wasn't who she said she was...what did that mean? If she wasn't Shannon Claremore, who was she? It felt like I was trying to put together a jigsaw puzzle without using the picture on the box.

I didn't care about Shannon's warning—I needed to talk to Charlie Miller again. If I could tell him I knew he was Daniel Miller's brother and that his daughter was hiding something, he'd have to provide some explanation. The problem was that Rhonda would never allow me back in. And she'd already seen Holman too, so he wouldn't be able to get in either. I was thinking about the possibility of asking Kay to do it, when I looked up to see Ridley walking along the sidewalk toward me.

"You left before I had a chance to say goodbye," she said, looking resplendent in her long ivory wool coat (what new mother wears ivory?). She leaned in for her traditional greeting of the double-sided cheeks kiss and handed me a white cardboard box. "You looked like you could use one of these."

It was one of Mysa's giant iced cinnamon rolls. A swell of gratitude rose inside my chest. Or possibly my stomach. "Thanks, that was really sweet of you."

She fell into step with me as I headed for the *Times* office. "Is everything okay? Ryan said you were upset about something to do with Jay?"

"Oh, it's not that," I said. "I'm frustrated because I need to interview someone and can't get access." As we walked the remaining couple of hundred feet to the door, I explained the broad brushstrokes of the situation with Charlie Miller and Shannon Claremore. I left out the details about Tackett because it seemed like whenever I said his name, people started warning me to be careful.

I pulled open the office door and held it for Ridley.

Holman and Kay must have been in their respective offices because the newsroom was empty. We took off our coats and sat down in my cubicle—well, I sat and Ridley leaned against the partition.

"Let me do it," she said.

"Let you do what?"

"Go interview this Charlie Miller. I can do that. I'm not banned from seeing him."

"No way."

"Why not? You can tell me the questions you need answered and I will ask them," she said with a shrug, as if it was the simplest thing in the world. "You know I am very good at getting men to talk to me."

Ridley had helped me out a few months ago on a story in which I needed to elicit information from a pervy pharmaceutical executive. He'd been all too happy to talk to me with Ridley by my side.

"Uh, he's old—like in his nineties."

"Even better." She smiled. "Old men love me."

I was fascinated with how Ridley unapologetically owned and acknowledged her near-universal appeal but never came off as arrogant or full of herself. "I don't know..." I said.

"What? It solves your problem, right?"

"I guess, but—"

"And I love to help with your investigations—you know that!"

I thought about what Kay would say (No) and what Holman would say (also No) and what Ryan would say (Hell no). I bit the corner of my lip.

She raised one eyebrow in challenge. "You know how you hate it when the people around you tell you to be careful all the time and try to protect you even though you're perfectly capable of making your own decisions?"

She had me there. Ridley was a grown woman who had proved herself more formidable than most. Who was I to protect her from herself? I pointed a finger directly at her chest. "Okay, but you will do exactly as I say and will not give anyone your real name and you will quit the minute I say quit." I glared at her, trying to convey the seriousness of the situation.

"Of course," Ridley said, flashing a triumphant smile tinged with a smidge of irony. "You're the boss!"

Chapter 32

We made a quick stop at Mysa to check in with Ryan, during which Ridley gave him a vague explanation of where we were going. Then Ridley and I set off in her car for Silver Meadows. I convinced myself that this kind of subterfuge was justified, even if it veered just a teensy bit outside the ethical lines. Shannon Claremore had tied my hands by refusing to talk to me and refusing to let me talk to her father. The information he had could be the key to finding out who killed my grandfather and Flick. If I had to extend my toe across the line to get it, I could live with that.

As I watched Ridley walk into the lobby of Silver Meadows, I gripped the steering wheel of her Yukon so tight, my knuckles were literally white. I closed my eyes and exhaled as I loosened the death grip on the wheel. I needed to relax. We'd been over the plan several times on the drive down here. Ridley knew what she was supposed to do.

The plan was for her to pose as a member of the Greenville, North Carolina, Town Council, there to speak with Charlie regarding his daughter Shannon's nomination for Citizen of the Year. It seemed like a plausible enough story—after all, the Claremores were prominent members of the community, active in several local charities in addition to their own ministries. It was late December, when all of the year-end lists were coming out, so it felt like the idea worked. Hopefully, it was at least strong enough to get past Rhonda. If she gave Ridley any trouble or asked to call Shannon to approve the visit, Ridley was going to tell her that the award must be kept secret from the nominees or they'd be disqualified.

Once Ridley got in front of Charlie, she was supposed to ask some softball questions about Shannon—What she was like as a young girl? How she did in school? Stuff like that—and then ask if there are any other family members she could talk to aspart of the process. If he said yes, then we would walk away with more potential sources about the Miller family. And if he said no, well, that would provide the perfect opening to bring up the plane crash. I told Ridley to tread lightly but mention that she'd read somewhere that Shannon was related to the family who died on Chincoteague in the fifties. If he denied it, she should say she'd seen his signature on the release forms from the Chincoteague funeral home. Surely once he realized he'd been found out, he would come clean. Or at least slip up and say something that would help us figure out what this man and his daughter were hiding.

I sat in the parking lot facing the large green lawn. There were a few other cars in the lot, but I was the only person out there as far as I could tell. It was still light out but wouldn't be for much longer. The days were short this time of year in eastern Virginia. I tapped my fingers on the wheel. I was not good at waiting or at trusting someone else to do the interviews that I wanted to do, but in this case, I had no choice. The minutes ticked by. In need of something to do to busy my mind, I opened Words with Friends.

I don't even know how much time had passed, but I'd just scored sixty-two points for the two-letter word *za* (accepted slang for pizza) when Ridley's knock on the window nearly sent me flying into the roof of the car. I fumbled for the door-unlock button, my heart racing.

"Well, that was interesting," she said, a crease appearing above her nose.

"Did they buy it? I mean, did they believe you were from the town council?"

"Of course." Her tone was breezy, but there was a look of concern on her face.

"What did he say? Did you confront him about the form at the funeral home?"

"We never got that far."

After all of this effort, Ridley never even asked Charlie Miller about signing the release form? Never confronted him about why he was lying to us? I didn't want to come down too hard on her, but I was disappointed. "What happened?"

"Charlie told me—insisted, actually—that he doesn't have a daughter named Shannon."

Of all the things I expected her to say, that was not one of them. "*What?*"

"Yeah, he kept referring to his daughter as Bethany. Each time, I corrected him by saying, 'You mean Shannon?' and he'd shake his head and say, 'My daughter is Bethany.' He started to become agitated, so after a bit I went and got Rhonda. I told her what was happening, and she said he must be having one of his 'off days.'"

"Off days? Like memory-wise?"

"That's what she seemed to indicate."

Shannon had told me on the phone that her father was not well, but I had no idea that's what she meant. I'd talked to him just a few days before and he seemed completely lucid. I didn't know a whole lot about how memory loss in the elderly...was it possible that one day he could know his daughter's and grandkids' names and a couple of days later not know them?

My frustration was mounting. "Well, I guess that was a giant bust."

"There was one other thing." She took out the small notebook I'd given her and read from one of the pages. "He said Bethany was a good girl and that he was so proud of how far she'd come since the night of the accident."

The night of the accident? What the hell did that mean—if it meant anything at all? Given the fact that Charlie couldn't even remember his own daughter's name, the reference could have been just a random artifact of a diseased mind.

"Any idea what accident he's talking about?" I asked, more out of frustration than any expectation that Ridley might actually know what the old man was referring to.

"Well," she said, giving me a look that was one part warning and one part pride. "I did a quick Google news search of the name Bethany Miller, Charles Miller, and the word *accident*. Here's what came up." She handed me her phone.

It was an article from the *Hudson Falls Chronicle* from November 1969. I read the story. Then I read it again. Then I read it yet again. This must have been what my grandfather and Flick had discovered, what Tackett meant when he said Shannon Claremore isn't who she says she is. If I was jumping to the right conclusion, Charlie Miller was not losing his memory. He knew exactly who his daughter was.

Chapter 33

In November 1969, fifteen-year-old Bethany Miller, daughter of Charles and Rebecca Miller of Hudson Falls, Texas, was driving her father's pickup truck downtown just before midnight. She had only a learner's permit, no driver's license. Bethany's mother had recently died, and both Bethany and Charlie had sort of "fallen apart" after Rebecca's death, according to neighbors interviewed for the article. The police report said that Bethany ran a red light in downtown Hudson Falls and hit a Ford Mustang that was making a left turn across the intersection. The driver of the Mustang was killed instantly. He was seventeen-year-old Jason Wells, the son of Judge Garrison Wells, a municipal court judge in Hudson Falls. Bethany pleaded guilty to vehicular homicide and was sentenced to twenty-seven months in a juvenile detention facility.

As I read the story and began reconciling it with what we already knew, a picture began coming into focus. After weeks of stumbling around in the dark, it suddenly felt like someone had switched the lights on. Shannon Miller and Bethany Miller were cousins who were born in the same year, 1954. Shannon died in a plane crash along with her entire family at the age of four. Bethany Miller got into serious trouble as a minor, went to prison, and was released at the age of seventeen. There were no searchable mentions of

Bethany Miller from Hudson Falls after 1971, which was the year that Shannon Miller, now Shannon Claremore, would have enrolled in college—the wedding announcement said she graduated from East Carolina University in the class of 1975. I knew I had a long way to go before I could bring any of my theories to the authorities, but for now I just needed to say it out loud. I turned to Ridley. "I think Bethany Miller stole her cousin's identity and started a new life for herself after she got out of prison."

Ridley looked at me, eyes wide, and for one awful moment I thought she was going to start laughing or tell me I was crazy, but instead she said, "How does a person even do something like that?"

I let out the breath I'd been holding. She didn't think it was crazy...or at least she didn't think I was. "Identity theft in 2020 looks very different than it would have back then, but it definitely happened," I said. "I took a class in college on the counterculture literature of the 1970s..."

Ridley shot me a sideways look.

"It's relevant, I promise," I said. "As a part of the class, we read this book—more of a glorified pamphlet, actually—called *The Paper Trip*. It was all about how to steal the identity of someone who died. It gave detailed instructions."

"Really? Is that even legal?"

"Identity theft, no, but the book was protected under free speech. Anyway, the point is that it used to be way easier to become someone else back before the internet and before everything was digitized."

"And you think Bethany Miller started living as Shannon Miller after she got out of prison?"

"Obviously this is all just guesswork right now, but think about it: Bethany would have been released from detention when she was about seventeen. What if she wanted to go to college or get a job? She'd have a hard time doing that with a felony conviction on her record. Juvenile records aren't sealed or expunged until five years after a crime is committed in most states. And," I said, my excitement mounting as I made more connections, "as next of kin, she would have had access to all of her cousin's information, like her social security number, date of birth, etc. Or at least her dad would have."

"You think that's what she and Charlie are trying to hide?" Ridley sounded excited now too.

"Let's say Bethany got out of prison and wanted a fresh start. And here she had this first cousin who died way too young, same age, same everything—it's like a premade blank slate! I could see someone in that position thinking, 'What's the harm in using her name and social?' Bethany 'becomes' Shannon Miller, she and Charlie move to North Carolina, and she enrolls in East Carolina University. All is well. It's practically a victimless crime."

Ridley's eyes were glued to mine. She was utterly absorbed in the tale I was spinning, however speculative it might be.

"Then, a few years later she meets and marries Wyatt Claremore," I continued. "She becomes Shannon Claremore and thinks the whole mess is behind her. The only one who knows about her old life is her father, and he's not telling. She's succeeded in completely transforming her life." My wheels started turning faster and faster. "Years go by and then one day Albert Ellison comes along asking questions about the Miller family who died in the plane crash on Chincoteague. He wants to know why they were laid to rest without a funeral, why no one mourned them or wrote an obituary for them. He gets in touch with Shannon Claremore and maybe Charlie as well. Maybe he figures out the connection between Shannon and Bethany."

"Do you think that's what got him killed? Uncovering an identity theft?"

"I don't know," I said. Hearing it out loud made it sound even more outlandish than thinking it. But there was something there, something about it that hit a note of truth for me. "The wife of one of the wealthiest and most recognizable moral authorities out there would certainly have a lot to lose if her secrets were revealed."

"Yeah, but..." Ridley crossed her arms in front of her chest and leaned back against the chair.

"I know...it's pretty out there."

"So," she said. "What are you going to do now?"

I looked out the window at the rural Virginia landscape as we rolled down the highway toward Tuttle Corner. It wasn't lost on me that this was the same road Flick had traveled in his search for the truth. I thought about where this had led him and my grandfather. "It's time for this to end," I said. "So that's what I'm going to do. End it—one way or another."

CHAPTER 34

Ridley dropped me off at the *Times* office even though it was after business hours. I had texted Holman and told him to stay there until I got back. When I walked into the office, Kay Jackson was waiting too.

"What did you learn?" Holman asked before I even had a chance to take off my coat. "And why wouldn't you tell me over the phone?"

Call me paranoid, but after realizing how vulnerable we all are due to the technology we rely on, I was hesitant to talk about any of this stuff over the phone—and I certainly didn't want to put any of my suspicions in writing over text. For all I knew, Shaquille O'Neal could somehow be listening to every word I say. Granted, that was a crazy thought, but this was nothing if not a time of crazy thoughts. Ash had put it perfectly: All of this felt very cloak-and-dagger. Nothing seemed out of bounds.

As soon as I started to explain what I'd learned, a crease appeared between Kay's eyes and stayed there throughout the telling of my entire story. The more I talked, the more nervous I became. I knew it sounded bizarre—a half-century-old identity theft and two murders to cover it up were just way too far-fetched. Kay and Holman were journalists, first and foremost; they weren't exactly big supporters of wild conspiracy theories. When I finished talking, they both gaped at me.

"Well?" I said. "Say something. Do you think I'm crazy?"

"You're definitely crazy," Kay said, and my heart sank. "But it fits."

I looked up at her, then at Holman.

He blinked at me, twice. "The problem is going to be how to prove it."

Thank the Lord, they believed me. Or at least were willing to follow the theory to see where it led. I was so happy, I felt like I might float up to the ceiling. I opened my notebook to check the list I'd made during the car ride home from Silver Meadows. "I'm going to contact Greensville Correctional to make another appointment with Tackett. We definitely need to see him again. I want to tell him I know about Bethany Miller and lay out my identity-theft scenario for him."

"And you think he'll tell you if you're right?" Kay looked skeptical.

"If we're on the right track about Bethany, he may get scared that we're going to discover who killed Albert and Flick without him. The more we know without him, the less useful he becomes—and the less likely it becomes that he'll get a sweeter deal out of Lindsey."

"What about the recording that supposedly proves who the killer is?" Holman asked.

"Yeah," Kay said. "We need that tape."

I tapped my pen against my lip as I thought that through. Kay was right. We needed that tape, but Tackett wasn't going to give it up easily. "I wonder if we could come at this from the other direction, by putting pressure on Shannon. I have half a mind to call her and just tell her I know about her secret," I said. "That would at least force her to do or say *something.*"

Holman, ever the rational one, said, "I think we should

be cautious about whom we share this information with."

Kay, equally as rational but more economical with words, simply said, "That is a dangerous idea."

"Fine, then we're going to need to get documents," I said. "Everything we can find relating to Bethany and Shannon Miller—a picture of Bethany Miller before she went to juvie would be ideal, but something tells me we won't be able to find that. I also want to see if we can access any newspaper stories mentioning a Charlie or Rebecca Miller back in Hudson Falls. Small town, maybe they had their photo in the paper at some point?"

Kay and Holman took notes as I spoke, and it occurred to me (in a very meta-moment) that it was like I was the assigning editor in this case. I was telling them what information was needed, what leads to track down, what sources to hit up. And they were listening. The me of one year ago would never have believed it. A warm glow flared deep inside me and I had to fight to keep the happiness from showing up on my face.

"Should I ask Lindsey to come by?" Holman asked.

"The DA could be a big help in getting some of those arrest records you're talking about," Kay added.

"Good idea." I got out my cell. "I'll call Carl too. No point in explaining this thing a thousand times."

Pizza never tasted so good. Lindsey ordered in from West Bay Pie, and the five of us sat in the conference room figuring out what our next steps were going to be. To my surprise, no one rejected the premise that Shannon Claremore had stolen her cousin's identity and was really Bethany Miller. Where we diverged, however, was on how that figured into Granddaddy's and Flick's murders.

"I just don't see a woman like Shannon Claremore being a cold-blooded killer, Riley," Carl said. "She doesn't fit the profile."

"Even if her secret coming out would mean she could lose everything—her husband, her children, the life they'd built together? She's broken like a million laws, right?"

Lindsey was sitting next to Holman at the far end of the table and they were deep in private conversation. "Right, Lindsey?" I said, slightly louder.

She looked up when she heard her name, a blush spreading across her cheeks. "What? Oh, right. Well, I don't know about a million laws, but yes. She would definitely be looking at fraud charges, and possibly more depending on whether or not she had any financial motivation in the crime. But it's important to note that identity theft didn't become a federal crime until the Identity Theft and Assumption Deterrence Act of 1998. It carries a maximum prison term of fifteen years and 250,000 dollars."

I looked at Holman, whose eyeballs practically turned into little red hearts as he listened to Lindsey reciting statistics.

"The legal ramifications aren't even her biggest problem," I said, ignoring Holman's lovesick gaze. "Can you imagine what it would do to her husband's reputation if it came out that he married a felon who had spent years lying to him and everyone else? It would be a scandal for sure."

"I wonder how much Wyatt Claremore knows about her past," Kay said.

"I wondered that too," I said. "But there's really no way to know."

"There's one way," Holman said. All eyes turned to him. "We could ask him."

"Oh no." Kay was shaking her head from side to side.

"Way too early for that. We are not about to start making wild accusations about a very powerful religious leader's wife without proof."

"Kay's right," Lindsey said. "We have to get Tackett to tell us what he knows—and better yet, give up that recording he has. If it's Shannon Claremore admitting to a role in Albert's death, then there would certainly be cause to move forward. We need something concrete—either proof of her identity theft or proof of crimes committed to conceal that—before we can take any sort of prosecutorial steps forward."

"But *we're* not prosecutors," I said, gesturing to the side of the table that Kay, Holman, and I were sitting on. "What if we told Tackett that we found his tape—even if it's not true—maybe that'd get him to slip up and say something about where it is or what's on it?"

"We are journalists, Riley, not the gang from *Scooby-Doo*," Kay said with more than a little judgment in her tone. "Our job is to report the facts of a story, not get involved in altering them."

My cheeks stung like I'd been slapped. She was right, but still. I got up from the conference table to fill up my water bottle (and hide my humiliation), and a few seconds later Holman joined me at the sink. Our backs were to the others, who carried on with their conversation.

He lowered his voice. "We will figure this out, Riley. We have the resources of law enforcement behind us. Going off and doing something impetuous would only harm our chances of bringing those responsible to justice."

I titled my head to look at him. "But we're so close... don't I owe it to Granddaddy and Flick to do whatever I can to find their killer?"

Holman's eyes were magnified by his thick glasses, and at this close proximity they looked about three times bigger than they actually were. "They were both scrupulous journalists; you owe it to them to be one too."

Damn, I hated it when he was right. We rejoined the others and spent another hour or so talking through what we knew, what we suspected, and what each of us was going to do in service of finding the truth. Carl and Lindsey were going to Greensville first thing in the morning to interview Tackett. They debated whether or not to include Sheriff Clark in the interview and ultimately decided not to.

"I'd like to ask Tackett what he and Clark talked about today, if they did indeed talk," Lindsey said. "If Clark is working on behalf of the DEA to try to persuade him to flip on the Romeros, we need to know that."

Kay told Holman to try to schedule an in-person interview with Shannon Claremore. I tried not to be offended when she gave him that task instead of me. I knew it was because she didn't trust me to stay within the lines on this case, which I guess was fair, but it still hurt. This whole investigation had been my baby so far. We were working off leads *I'd* chased down, theories *I'd* pieced together. My earlier sense of pride and accomplishment evaporated, leaving a dull resentment in its place.

Kay assigned me the job of digging into Charlie and Bethany Miller's past to see what information could be found on that branch of the Miller family in Hudson Falls in the late 1960s. I was to try to determine what became of Bethany Miller after she was released from the juvenile detention facility. I would do my best to find any old friends from high school and see if they knew what became of her, but I had a feeling this would yield nothing. If Bethany Miller had gone to all the trouble to steal a new life—and had killed twice to protect it—I imagine she cleaned up her trail of breadcrumbs long ago.

Weekly Tarot Card Forecast

Card of the Week: The Wheel of Fortune

Thank you for purchasing the optional Weekly Tarot Card Forecast for an additional $4.99.* You clicked on the Wheel of Fortune card, also known as the Wheel of Karma. It is chosen to remind us that what goes around, comes around. It can also signal a major shift in perspective in the coming week. Alternately, it could mean that some sort of sacrifice may soon be needed. Only time will tell. Drawing the Wheel of Fortune often means you will experience some uncomfortable shifts in the days ahead, but it can lead you to a much-needed release of negative past patterns that are no longer serving you. Ask yourself what have you been holding onto? How have these beliefs held you back? Would you be better off if you were able to just let it all go?

Note: Your Wheel of Fortune card was reversed, which means your luck and fortune may take a turn for the worse. You may experience unexpected change, or negative forces could be at play, leaving you feeling powerless and vulnerable. This tarot card signals that factors outside your control are at play, as though the universe is toying with you. This is one of the challenging aspects of the Wheel of Fortune, since no matter which way the wheel turns, it is impossible to try to change it. It's critical to remember that you always have choices in life. Some choices will lead you to better days, some will not. The more you trust your intuition and allow the Universe to guide you, the better the outcomes will be.

*Weekly Tarot Card Forecast requires four-week commitment at a rate of $4.99 per forecast, billable to the credit card on file.

CHAPTER 35

I woke up, still in my clothes, with light streaming through my bedroom window and a cold, wet snout in my face. I must have passed out at some point while I was doing research, which meant I hadn't let Coltrane out before bed like usual. Poor guy was probably dying.

"C'mon, baby," I said to Coltrane, hoisting myself off the bed. "Sorry I forgot about you." He forgave me in the form of a wagging tail and followed me into the kitchen. I opened the back door to let him out into the fenced yard. The cold morning air flooded into the kitchen, and the second he was out the door, I closed it. I knew from experience that Coltrane would be a while and there was no point in bringing down the inside temperature to freezing while waiting for him to do his business.

I made a pot of coffee and was just about to pour myself a large cup of it when my cell phone vibrated. It was a text from Jay.

I know it's early but can u talk

Another early morning powwow? This could not be good.

Sure

I'm outside. Can I come in?

This *really* could not be good. Once again, wrapped in my puffy peach robe, I trundled to open the door for my ex-boyfriend.

"Tackett's been attacked," he said, before he even stepped inside.

I felt a rush of blood to my head and had to grip the edge of the door to steady myself. "When? What happened?"

"Early this morning. The warden has no idea how anyone got to him, maybe someone paid off the guards, who knows. They're looking into it." Jay stepped inside, and I closed the door behind him.

"Is he...?"

"Not yet." His face darkened. "He was severely beaten with a metal pipe, lost a ton of blood, but by sheer luck one of the CUs arrived for his shift early and heard Tackett's moaning. He found him lying on the floor in a pool of blood and called for help. He's in the ICU at Southern Virginia Regional right now."

I performed a quick survey of my emotions. I was a little surprised at my own callousness, but my only concern was for what Tackett knew. His life meant nothing to me beyond what he could tell me. "Will he make it?"

"Don't know. All I've heard is that he's in critical condition."

We migrated from the entry into the living room. I sat on the couch, while Jay took the chair, both of us silent as we thought through what this meant to our respective objectives. Jay broke the silence by saying, "There's a good chance this was done on orders from the cartel."

"Oh, you think?" The words fired out of my mouth like machine gun bullets. I was angry. Jay was the reason

Tackett hadn't given up his information yet. Jay was the reason his secrets might die with him.

"Listen—" he started to say, but I cut him off.

"No. *You* listen. You knew this was a possibility and you let him stay in prison, like a sitting duck. You wanted him to feel that pressure, to be scared, so that you could get your precious information out of him. That's all you care about!"

"Don't sound so righteous," Jay said, color starting to spread upward from his collar. "You don't care what happens to Tackett either. You're hoping to use him every bit as much as I am."

He was right, of course, but I was too busy being sanctimonious to give in to him at that moment. I opted instead for the always mature, "Whatever."

Jay leaned forward, his elbows on his knees. He took a deep breath before speaking again. "Listen, there's a lot you don't know, Riley."

"Oh, like how you've been working with Sheriff Clark behind the scenes to make sure Tackett doesn't cooperate with Lindsey Davis?"

"What are you talking about?"

"Yeah, I overheard you talking to 'Mike' on the phone at the diner the other day. You were talking about visiting Tackett in prison and said you needed to get that information 'before he talks to her.' One question, Jay," I said, cocking my head to the side. "By 'her' did you mean Lindsey Davis or me?"

Jay stared at me silently for a moment, probably thinking back on the conversation in Mysa. "You weren't there when I was on the phone. You walked in after."

Damn his excellent memory. I said nothing.

He thought for a moment, then rolled his eyes. "Ryan."

"It doesn't matter." I lifted my chin. "I know that you tried to interfere in Lindsey Davis's attempts to make a deal with Tackett. That's playing dirty, Jay."

"You have no idea—"

"I heard you!"

"First of all, *you* didn't hear anything," he said, his voice dipping low into that serious tone he reserved for when he was really frustrated. "Second of all, you're dead wrong." He stood up, putting one hand on the back of his neck. "You do this all the time, Riley. You jump to a conclusion and then you just go off chasing leads down pathways you know nothing about without concern for your safety or—"

Not to be outdone in the moral outrage department, I rocketed to my feet. "So now you're going to lecture me on how I do my job? You don't get to do that, Jay. You're not my boyfriend anymore!"

"I never said I was—"

"I don't even know why you came here. You should probably just go."

We were both seriously pissed off now. This was getting out of hand. We weren't dating anymore—hell, we were barely friends. There was no reason for this kind of knockdown-drag-out.

"I came here to tell you something," Jay said, his voice a touch softer than before. "If you'll just listen to me for a second, there's something you need to know. After that, I'll go. I promise."

"All right. Talk." I folded my arms in front of me.

Jay sat back down on the armchair and sighed. When he spoke, it was in a calm, clear voice—the voice of a professional, not an ex-lover. "The 'her' that Ryan heard me refer to on the phone was not you and it was not Lindsey Davis either. It was Gina, my boss."

"Gina?" I asked, surprised.

"She's hell-bent on getting Tackett to talk. He's in a unique position to share some very detailed information about the Romero organization—their supply chains, distribution network, etcetera. She knows if she could flip him, it would be a huge win for the department."

"And her personally," I said, reading between the lines.

"She's an ambitious woman," he said without judgment. "And she knows busting up the Romero cartel would do big things for her career, not to mention get a lot of drugs off the street."

I waited for him to explain why he felt so strongly that I needed to know this.

"You should also know that the 'Mike' that Ryan heard me on the phone with was not Sheriff Clark," he said, letting that sink in.

My cheeks began to burn. "Jay, I—"

He shook his head, as if to save me the humiliation of having to apologize for my conclusion-jumping. "He's a confidential informant I work with who's housed in Greensville. Sometimes prisoners hear things from other prisoners...it's a controversial methodology but one we've had some luck with nonetheless." He cleared his throat. "Anyway, he's helped me out in the past, and I reached out to him the other day unofficially to see if he could get anything out of Tackett."

"Why unofficially?" I asked, confused. "I'd think if Gina was so hot to flip Tackett, she'd authorize you to use whatever resources you needed."

A look passed over Jay's face that I couldn't name. "This wasn't for Gina, Riley. It was for you."

"Me?" Even as I asked the question, understanding was beginning to scratch its way through my thick skull.

"I asked him to see if he could get Tackett to say anything about Flick or your grandfather."

So this whole time that I'd been convinced Jay was working against me to cut my chances of finding out what Tackett knew, he'd really been doing the complete opposite. And not only that, he was risking his job in order to help me. To say I felt like a self-centered fool would have been an understatement. "I don't know what to say." My throat felt dry. "I'm—"

"Gina has been frustrated with my inability to flip Tackett and was planning to come down here to speak with him herself. She mentioned pushing for Tackett to be moved to solitary until he talks, or requesting he be transferred to a facility in upstate New York where he'd most certainly face even *more* pressure from Romero's people. I hung around here so I could go see Mike yesterday and ask him to accelerate his investigation before Gina swoops in and takes over."

"I—I..." I stammered around and after a few false starts I managed to say, "but you could have gotten fired..."

He looked down at his shoes. "Flick was a good man. And I know how important finding out what happened to him and your granddad is to you."

Tears pricked the backs of my eyes as a current of shame and gratitude washed over me like a tidal wave. Jay had risked so much to help me, and in return I'd been cold and childish. I'd shouted at him and refused to let him explain time and again. "I don't know what to say...Jay, I'm so sorry, I—"

He shook off my apology. "I don't need you to apologize. I understand. It was just important to me that you know I'm always on your side."

I was literally speechless. I knew Jay was a good man

when we'd dated, and I even knew it when we broke up, but being confronted by his "goodness" like this was almost too overwhelming to process. He risked his job to help me and didn't want anything in return. Holman had been right to think of Jay as a hero; he truly was one. *When people show you who they are, believe them....*

"Thank you," I said quietly. "I know you don't want an apology, but I'm giving you one anyway. I acted like a spoiled brat and the whole time you were—" I broke off. I took a breath and then continued, "Needless to say, I acted badly, and I'm sorry."

He swiveled his eyes to the floor. I was embarrassing him, I could tell. "I didn't tell you this to make you feel bad."

"I know."

"There's actually more," Jay said, shooting me a warning glance. "Mike *was* able to talk to Tackett before he was attacked. He got something."

It was like all the air went out of the room, and I felt my pulse begin to pound. I managed to eek out only one word. "What?"

"I think I might know where Tackett hid the recording."

Chapter 36

"My office?" Carl Haight stared at us like we were half a bubble off plumb.

Jay and I had raced straight over to the sheriff's department and basically insisted that Carl talk to us even though it was barely eight a.m.

"Tackett told an inmate at Greensville that he had a trump card that he could play at any time to get a better deal," Jay said.

"The tape?" Carl asked.

"He didn't say what it was, just that it was being protected by none other than the sheriff of Tuttle County himself."

Carl frowned. "What the hell? I am not—"

"No one is suggesting that you're somehow in cahoots with Tackett on this," I said quickly. "But remember, this used to be Tackett's office."

"That's why we think he must have hidden it somewhere in here before he was sent to prison."

"Does anyone else know about this?" Carl asked. I knew he was thinking about what Skipper Hazelrigg would do with this information during the campaign. I could practically see the headlines myself: *Sheriff sits on evidence of local murder for years without knowing it.*

"No," Jay said, "not at this point. But I can't promise it'll stay under wraps. The sooner we find whatever he's hidden, the better."

Carl sighed. "All right, let's get to it then."

The three of us each started in different corners of the room, feeling along walls and baseboards for anything that seemed out of place. We looked under shelves and behind light switches, and double-checked every creaky floorboard.

"If the attack was the work of the cartel," I said as I checked under a chair in the corner of the room, "they won't be happy to hear the job's not done. Tackett could still be in danger."

"I talked to Sheriff Clark this morning," Carl said. "They've got security outside his room."

"DEA has issued an order for all agents who have informants working with the Romero cartel to keep an ear out for any plans they hear about concerning Tackett," Jay added, as he felt along the top of the shelving unit on the back wall of Carl's office. "We think Tackett must be in a position to deliver some very valuable intel if the cartel attempted to take him out so brazenly."

That couldn't be good. The Romero cartel was known for being extremely well organized, thorough, and ruthless. "What if they just wanted to scare him?" I asked, trying to find some glimmer of hope. "Maybe they don't care if he's dead as long as he doesn't talk?"

Jay made a doubtful sound. "He's a loose end—and the Romeros don't like loose ends."

Carl unscrewed a vent cover on the wall to check behind it. He paused and turned to Jay, "Do you people have a plan if he recovers?"

I couldn't help but notice the slightly adversarial tone in Carl's voice with the use of the words "you people." I understood where he was coming from—I mean, my tone had been way worse not even an hour earlier—but now that I knew Jay had been on our side all along, I felt defensive, and maybe even a little protective of him. "Jay wants to find out who killed Albert and Flick as much as we do, Carl," I said.

It felt like my words had landed on the floor with a dull thud. No one said anything in response. I looked up from the book I'd been thumbing through. Carl and Jay had stopped what they were doing too—Carl's mouth formed a thin line, and Jay looked down at the ground.

"What?" I said, looking from one to the other.

An excruciating few seconds of silence ticked by. Finally, Jay said, "Given what happened, if he survives, Tackett's likely going to be transferred to another facility."

It took a couple of seconds for me to realize the implications of this. I slowly, carefully set the book I'd been holding back on the shelf. "But—but that's what he wanted all along," I said. "Now he'll have no incentive to tell us anything. The only reason he was even willing to talk in the first place was to get out of Greensville. Now, if he recovers, he'll never talk." I felt defeated, like everything I'd been hoping for had just burst into flames.

"That's why it's so important that we find the recording," Jay said, trying to refocus me. "If we find it, we don't need Tackett."

Carl looked at me and nodded. "C'mon. Let's keep looking."

We spent the next hour going over every square inch of Carl's office. We found nothing. By the time we replaced the last knickknack back on the last shelf, we were all thoroughly demoralized. Our optimism had been replaced by a growing sense of doubt regarding the likelihood of finding Tackett's recording.

"I'm gonna call Sheriff Clark and check on Tackett," Carl said as he walked me and Jay out to the reception area. "I'll be in touch if I hear anything."

Jay excused himself and went back to the Ottoman Inn, saying he had phone calls to make, and I decided to head over to the *Times* office. There were a few things I needed to do as well, having spent more time than I should have on this over the past couple of days. Besides, I was ready for a break from thinking about how all my hopes and dreams of finding out what happened to Granddaddy and Flick were about to die with Joe Tackett.

Chapter 37

Memorial Park was practically empty, which was not surprising, given the weather. It was still unseasonably cold for Virginia, but at least the sun was shining. It bounced off the white snow, giving it an almost iridescent, multicolored quality. Icicles hung from tree branches and melted slowly, the droplets of water making tiny plunking noises on the ground below. I was no fan of winter, but I had to admit there was a kind of peace to it. I actually closed my eyes and took a deep breath, allowing the chilly air to fill my lungs while the sun warmed my face.

The past few days were like being on an emotional rope swing. I'd been flying between anger, hope, fear, and frustration, all while clinging on for dear life to avoid falling into the abyss. For seven years, I'd been desperate to know what had really happened to my granddad, and then the one person who was helping me had been murdered himself. It seemed impossible that this should go unpunished, yet that was beginning to look increasingly likely. The only evidence we'd been able to dig up connecting Flick's and Albert's deaths wasn't even really evidence of anything, except possible identity theft. And the one person who could give us all the answers we needed was a lying psychopath who was inches from death, and oh, by the way, even if he did manage to claw his way back to life, no longer had any reason to cooperate with us.

I stood under the sun, letting the brisk air renew and reset me for a long time. Eventually, my phone vibrated in my pocket, pulling me out of my reverie. Blocked Caller.

No good has ever come from a blocked caller. "This is Riley," I answered. There was a weariness to my voice that even I could hear.

"Hi, Riley. This is Megan Johanning, Shannon Claremore's personal assistant."

"Hi," I said, suddenly more alert.

"I understand you've been in touch with Pastor Claremore's wife with some questions about her family."

"Yes, that's right."

"Well, Shannon has so much on her plate right now, what with her ailing father and all, so she's asked me to take up as point person for the rest of your questions." The subtext was crystal clear: Leave Shannon alone.

I debated how to play this. If I challenged her, I risked cutting off the stream of communication with Shannon. But I also didn't want her to think I was a pushover. My issue was with Shannon Claremore, not her assistant.

"And how is it that you would be able to help answer questions about Shannon's family?" I asked, careful to keep my voice light.

"Oh, I've known the Claremores for years," she said. "Wyatt and Shannon helped me through one of the most difficult seasons of my life. You see, I was diagnosed with facioscapulohumeral muscular dystrophy at the age of nineteen."

I knew her story from her book. "Yes, I'm so sorry."

"Oh, don't be!" Her voice was bursting with cheery optimism. "I may have my challenges, but through the grace of Jesus Christ I am living my life's purpose more fully than I ever would have had it not been for my disability. I consider it one of my greatest blessings."

I didn't know what to say. Megan Johanning was clearly a brave and faithful fighter. I could see why she'd been an inspiration to so many. What I couldn't see was the reason for her phone call. "Ms. Johanning," I said carefully. "I'm sorry, but I'm just having a little trouble understanding why you're calling me."

She continued as if I hadn't asked the question, as if I hadn't spoken at all. "I was ready to give up on everything—my family, my God, myself—and Wyatt healed me. He helped me to see that God had a bigger plan for my life."

"That's great, but—"

"And where Wyatt brought me back to life, Shannon made it worth living. She's positively been my angel through the years. When I fell on a patch of rough sidewalk, Shannon nursed me back to health. When I lost the ability to raise my arms over my head, it was Shannon who helped rearrange my entire house so I could reach everything I needed. When my ankle muscles deteriorated to the point that I could no longer drive, Shannon had my car outfitted with all the necessary adaptations."

"That's amazing," I said, not sure where she was leading with all this.

Then Megan's voice lost its trademark pep. "One thing she hasn't been able to help me with, though, is smiling. My facial muscles have weakened, and I can't smile anymore." She paused. "Do you have any idea what it's like to go through life without being able to smile?"

"I can't even imagine. I'm so sorr—"

"Oh no no no, remember: Don't be sorry!" Her chipper voice came back and cut me off like a guillotine. "What I lack in physical strength, I more than make up for in mental fortitude."

I was starting to feel unsettled by this conversation, though I couldn't have told you why at the time. I only knew I wanted it to end. "I appreciate the call, Ms. Johanning, really, but the questions I have for Shannon are probably best kept between her and me for now."

"She's really just too busy at the moment. I'm sure I can help you with whatever you need. As I've said, I know just about everything there is to know about the Claremores!"

I hesitated for a fraction of a second, calculating whether or not I wanted to test the waters. "Um, well, my questions are from a time *before* she was Shannon Claremore."

There was the briefest of pauses. Had she gotten my meaning? Did she know what I was trying to so cleverly say-without-saying?

"Riley," she said, her voice taking on a knife-like edge. "Anything that happened before Shannon married Pastor Wyatt is ancient history. Much like he did for me, Wyatt transformed her through prayer and grace. Their marriage was like a baptism, a rebirth, if you will, and whomever she was before that is dead and gone."

I felt a whooshing sensation in my gut. What were we talking about here? Did Megan know Shannon was really Bethany? Or was she just one of those people who spoke in religious riddles to try to sound profound.

"Still," I said, slightly more forcefully, "I really need to talk to Shannon directly."

"I just had a thought, Riley." The tone of spontaneity in her voice was so false, it was almost like she was being sarcastic. "Would you like to meet in person to talk more about this? Perhaps at your little house? On Salem Street..."

The blood running through my veins turned to ice. I was aware of a fuzzing pulse pounding behind my ears, and the hand holding my phone began to shake. My body was responding on a primal level, but my brain thought there might still be a chance I was somehow misinterpreting what she said. "What?" My voice came out in a cracked whisper.

"The house that used to belong to your grandfather, right?"

Chapter 38

"In through the nose, out through the mouth," Holman said as he watched me melt into a panic. "Then count backward from five."

"What? No—"

He ignored me, taking a deep breath of his own. "Five... four...three..."

"Two, one!" I sucked in a quick breath and blew it out at him. "There. Are you happy?"

"No, not particularly—"

"*Holman!*" I shouted. "We have to do something! I think this Megan person could be the person behind everything." My mind flew back to the night Coltrane had gotten spooked on our walk. I remember there'd been a car at the top of the street...could it have been her?

"Tell me again what she said to you?"

"I think she was threatening me," I said, my heartbeat still several clicks above normal. "Why else would she mention where I live? Or that it was my grandfather's house? How did she know that? Oh God..." I was starting to spin out. I told him exactly what she had said to me again, recounting every detail I could. What I didn't tell him was how my hand started to shake so much, I could barely press the end button. Or how I could hear her saying, "Riley? Riley? What's the matter?" through the speaker as I ended the call.

"She could have found your address online," Holman suggested.

"How did she know it used to belong to Granddaddy then, huh?"

"Well," he said. "I'm sure you're on the record somewhere talking about that..."

"On the record? What are you even talking about? I'm not a public figure. I'm a nobody reporter."

"She could have—"

"Why are you fighting me on this?" I slammed my palm on his desk. "I'm telling you the woman was threatening me. Why don't you believe me?"

Holman folded his hands together neatly, the gesture giving him time to formulate a precise response. "Megan Johanning wrote an entire book about how God's grace healed her. And she's disabled."

"So?"

"So that isn't exactly the profile of a killer," his voice was maddeningly calm. "Besides, what would her motivation be?"

"To protect the Claremores!" I shouted. "You didn't hear her—she was creepily into them. I'm telling you, Holman, there is something off about her."

He drummed his long fingers on his desk. "What is it that you think we should do then?" There was a patronizing tinge to his voice that really chapped my hide.

I crossed my arms in front of my chest. "I think we should go see Carl."

"And say what?"

"Tell him what happened...what I think she was implying..." Even as I was saying the words, I remembered Sheriff Clark's dismissal when I told him I thought Shannon Claremore had threatened me.

He sighed. "All right. Fine. If you want me to go with you, I will."

It wasn't exactly a brick wall of support, but it would have to do. For now.

"He's out, honey," Gail said as soon as we walked in.

"Do you know where he went?"

"Official business is all I can tell you." She winked. Gail was Ryan's cousin and I'd known her practically all my life. "Hey, can you hang on a quick sec? I wanna show you something." She was already up and out of her chair before I could answer.

Holman looked at me and raised his eyebrows. I shrugged. No telling what Gail wanted to show me—it could be a new jacket or something weird that just came in as evidence on a case. With Gail, there was no telling. She was full of surprises.

The walk over to the sheriff's office had given me some time to calm down, and I was feeling a little less freaked out than I'd been right after the call. I took the opportunity while Gail scuttled off toward the break room to take a couple of deep breaths. I let my eyes wander over the familiar room. I was struck again by how similar it was to the Brunswick County Sheriff's office, and I wondered if they all looked this way. American flag/American flag. Sheriff star logo on the wall/sheriff star logo on the wall. Framed pics of the governor and president/framed pics of the governor and president.

"All these small-town sheriff offices look the same. Have you noticed that?" I said to Holman.

"Of course."

"Why is that?"

"There are a host of reasons. First, there is a uniformity of function. Second—"

I wasn't in the mood for a lecture or for the real answer, for that matter. "No, I mean, like why can't each sheriff's office have its own personality? Seems to me it'd be nice if every office was allowed to make their own choices about color and décor...maybe it'd improve morale? My mom told me about an article she read in *Better Homes & Gardens* about how the color blue has been shown in studies to slow down heart rates and reduce stress."

"That's entirely impractical, Riley," Holman said. "This is a place of business, not a place to showcase one's individual personality."

"I just think they could jazz it up some, that's all," I said, annoyed at Holman's bah-humbug response.

Gail came back from the break room holding an index card in one hand and a white paper bag in the other. Sounding slightly robotic, she said, "How would you like to reduce mood swings, improve mental clarity, and generally support your ultimate health and wellness goals?"

"Riley might be interested in reducing mood swings," Holman said, deadpan.

I shot him a look.

Gail looked down at her card and read, "We all want to feel our best, but it's easy to get bogged down in the stress of daily life. Work, kids, volunteering at school..."

Kids? Volunteering at school? What the hell was she talking about? "Gail, are you feeling all right?" I said, confused.

"Oh, forget it!" She dropped the card onto her desk. "I can't do this. I'm sorry."

"Can't do what?"

"I got roped into selling these essential oils as part of

one of those multilevel-marketing deals, but I can't even make it through the sales pitch without wanting to shoot myself." She let out a self-conscious laugh. "I've never heard such a load of horsepuckey in my life. That's the last time I let Darla Jensen ply me with 'free' margaritas."

Holman raised a long skinny finger. "Point of fact, essential oils have been used since ancient times in religious observances, food preparation, preservation, and for medicinal purposes."

"Maybe you should sell 'em then," Gail joked.

"I already have a job, but thank you."

"Well, I guess I do too," she said, laughing. "And I'd better get back to it."

"When the sheriff comes back, will you let him know we came by?" I asked.

"Sure thing, hon. And happy new year, by the way!"

The day had been such a long, weird one that I'd almost forgotten it was New Year's Eve—and that I had a party to go to. I checked my phone. Ash would be picking me up in just a few hours. Holman was itching to get home, so I told him to go ahead. There was nothing I could do about Megan Johanning right now anyway. Besides, maybe there was an innocent explanation for her knowing where I live? I doubted it, but the slight room for doubt helped me move on. At least for the time being.

I swung back by the *Times* office and gave the Christmas Lady obit feature a quick once-over before uploading it to the shared server. I sent Kay a message apologizing for it being a few hours late. I texted Jay to thank him again for what he did to help and wished him a happy new year. I figured he was probably already halfway back to DC to celebrate with Chloe. After that, I made my last phone call of the afternoon, to Sheriff Clark.

"No change," he said. "Doctor says Tackett sustained some pretty serious injuries. He isn't out of the woods yet."

"I heard a rumor that he'll be transferred if he survives," I said, purposefully vague about the source of my information. "Is that true?"

"That's above my pay grade, Riley. But between you and me, survival ain't looking super likely."

"All right," I said with a sigh. "Hey, before I let you go, did you ever have a chance to look into Flick's cell records on the day he died? As the executor, I have a request in, but my lawyer tells me it'll take a month minimum to get them."

"I have them here, actually. Phone company responds a little faster to law enforcement, I guess."

"Any chance I can get a copy?"

"Why not? You're gonna get 'em eventually, I suppose. I'll scan and email it over to you when we hang up."

I felt badly for suspecting Sheriff Clark of obstructing earlier. He was a good man, like Carl said, probably just overworked and underpaid, like most small-county sheriffs. "Thanks. You have a happy new year."

Sheriff Clark let out a wry laugh. "New Year's Eve takes on a whole new perspective as sheriff," he said. "Last year, we had seventeen DUIs, five illegal possession of firearms, and nine drunk and disorderly arrests. Not exactly my favorite night of the year."

"Wow," I said. "Well, hope you have a boring New Year's...is that better?"

"Much," he said. "I'll send that stuff over just as soon as I can."

Coltrane and I took an abbreviated version of our usual walk, mostly because it was cold, but also because I'd gotten some fake lashes to wear as part of my costume and

I knew I would need extra time to get those suckers on. We walked down Salem Street and had just turned onto Beach when I noticed there was a car behind me driving very slowly. A Prius. My mind flashed back to the night that Coltrane growled a warning. *Wasn't it a Prius that had been out that night too?* I looked over my shoulder, hoping it was someone slowing down to look for an address or turning into a driveway, but it just kept inching along the road. No turn signal, no signs of stopping. *Could someone be following me?* Then I thought of Megan's eerie warning about knowing where I lived. I quickened my pace.

The car crept along, hanging back just far enough away that I couldn't get a good look at the driver, despite my frequent glances. Sweat started to form at my temples and I realized I was practically racewalking. Thoughts—crazy thoughts—of the car jumping up onto the sidewalk to mow me down started to flood into my mind. Is this what happened to Flick...did he notice someone following him right before they forced him off the road? If he did, I'd bet my last penny that he thought he could outrun them. Flick was nothing if not brave and stupid; there was no way he'd have done something sensible like call for help or drive to the sheriff's station.

But I was not brave—or stupid—and I was not going to fall victim to the same heroics that got him killed. I took a deep breath and with one last backward glance at the car, I yanked on Coltrane's leash and took off running through the Wilson's yard, into the trees behind their house. I knew that it let out on Bishop Street just down from Ryan and Ridley's house. It wasn't much, but it'd buy me about a minute until the car could catch up. I got to their house and banged on the door, my heart thundering. "Ryan! Ridley! It's me—open up!" I yelled. My desperate voice echoed out into the quiet afternoon.

"Riley?" I heard Ridley say as the deadbolt clicked open. As soon as Ridley opened the door, Coltrane and I bounded inside, nearly knocking her over. "Is everything okay—"

"Close the door!" I said, panting.

"What's the matter? Are you okay?"

I peeked out of the sidelight next to her door. The street was completely empty. My fear started to give way to confusion...*the car had been following me, right?*

"I'm fine," I said, stepping into their dining room to look out the large front window. There was nothing there. No cars at all. "I'm sorry...I just thought someone was..." I let my words trail off. I was starting to feel embarrassed at how scared I'd been over a threat that now seemed unlikely, if not completely invisible. "I thought someone might be following me, but maybe my imagination got the best of me."

Ridley, eyeing me cautiously, took Coltrane's leash from my hand. "Lizzie's napping. Why don't you come into the kitchen and I'll get you some water?"

I pulled off my gloves and hat and followed her down the short hallway and into the kitchen. It occurred to me that this was my first time inside Ryan and Ridley's house. Given how sleek and modern Mysa was, I guess I expected their home to have a similar aesthetic. It did not. The aesthetic here was less Swedish minimalism and more American disaster zone. And not a *we-just-moved-in* sort of disaster—the kitchen looked like a carload of drunk monkeys had ransacked it looking for bananas. Every square inch of counter space was filled with some sort of pot or pan or kitchen utensil, cabinets hung open, boxes of cereal, bags of pretzels, and other kitchen flotsam littered the countertops.

Ridley didn't seem the least bit troubled by the mess

as she got down a glass and filled it with water. Coltrane started to lick up some sort of oatmeal-colored glob from the floor.

"Did I catch you at a bad time?" I said, stepping over what looked like a bubble wand on the floor near the fridge.

"No. Why?"

Because it looks like you were just robbed. "Um. No reason."

"So," she said, handing me the glass. "Tell me what happened."

I leaned against the edge of the island. "I was walking Coltrane and there was this car. I thought it might be following me...I don't know. Saying it out loud makes me realize how stupid it sounds."

Ridley didn't look like she thought I sounded stupid. She looked concerned. "Do you think this is connected to what we discovered yesterday?"

I told her about my unsettling conversation with Megan.

"And this woman knows where you live?"

"Apparently," I said. "But that's crazy, right? I mean, she's like a religious icon or something. Surely she isn't some sort of psychopath..."

"Those two things are not mutually exclusive," Ridley said, bless her loyal heart. "What kind of car?"

"A Prius. Silver."

Ridley frowned.

"What?"

"Nothing," she said, not meeting my eye. "It's just that the Matthews' daughter just got a Prius."

"Oh." Edward and Helen Matthews lived about four houses down Bishop. Their daughter, Stella, was a senior at Tuttle High School.

"I think I have their number," Ridley said. "Do you want me to call and check if it was her?"

"No!" Gossip traveled around Tuttle Corner like a high-speed train. The last thing I needed was for word to get out that I thought someone was following me. I was embarrassed enough already. "Thank you, but no. I'm sure that's who it was. That makes a lot more sense than..."

Ridley gave me what could only be described as a pity smile. "If you're sure?"

I brought my glass over to the sink. "I'm sorry for barging in and ringing the alarm bells," I said. "It's been a stressful couple of days, and I think I just got paranoid for a second."

Ridley handed me Coltrane's leash and gave him one last scratch behind the ears. "No worries. I'm glad I was here." We said our goodbyes and I headed out for the short walk home.

On the way, I passed by the Matthews house and sure enough, there was a silver Prius sitting in the driveway. *What an idiot,* I thought. I can't believe I actually believed that Megan Johanning had come all the way to Tuttle to run me over in her environmentally responsible car. There was something seriously wrong with my brain these days. My fear had been real, though, and I took it as a sign that now more than ever I probably needed to take a break from thinking about brutal attacks, identity thieves, and murderers for a while. And yes, even the beloved men I'd lost. I'd been in a near-constant state of anxiety for a month now, and it was obviously beginning to take its toll.

Holman, Kay, and I had some good solid leads on what Flick and Granddaddy were looking into when they were killed, and we had the support of law enforcement to follow those leads. True, I would have felt a lot better if we could find Tackett's recording, but there was little I could do about that. We would keep looking, and if we weren't able to find it, there was a still a chance, however small it might be, that Tackett would recover and be motivated to exchange the tape for something he wanted. In any case, I felt confident that there wasn't anything else I could be doing to track down the truth. Especially at six p.m. on New Year's Eve. I made a mental decision that I was done thinking about the story for the night. Tonight, I decided, was going to be about having fun.

CHAPTER 39

Ash stepped into my entryway wearing a black tux, white waistcoat, white shirt, and white bow tie. His tawny eyes sparkled, and his brown hair, which was normally messy, tonight had been gelled, parted, and slicked back into the perfect twenties style.

"Wow," I said.

"You look pretty wow yourself." Ash's eyes wandered up and down the length of me. "That dress..."

I had on my mother's ivory beaded dress and had layered on strands of pearls and draped a feather boa around my neck. I'd tied my hair back into a lose bun, letting strands of hair fall out from under the headband. It was a look I'd tried to copy off Pinterest, with some success if Ash's wide-eyed stare was any indication. I'd put on way more makeup than my usual mascara-and-lip gloss combo and had—after considerable effort—affixed the faux lashes to my own. It was definitely more of a va-va-voom look than my usual attire. "You like?" I posed, jutting my hip out.

"Uh...*yeah*."

"Good." I turned toward the kitchen, my beaded dress making a deliciously sophisticated swishing sound as I walked. "Drink?"

Before Ash got there, I'd dimmed the lights, put on a Spotify playlist called "Jazzy Nights," and lit several candles around the room. My parents had given me a bottle of champagne when I'd gotten my first front-page story at the *Times*, and I'd stuck it in a salad bowl full of ice (I didn't own an ice bucket) and set out some wine glasses (I didn't own any champagne flutes) along with a small bowl of strawberries. It was not exactly Instagram-worthy, but I thought it had a certain charm.

Ash let out a low whistle. "Champagne? Strawberries? Candlelight? You better be careful, Miss Ellison, or we might not make it to the party..."

"Calm down, Romeo." I laughed. "Holman and Lindsey are meeting us here. I thought it'd be fun to have a drink together before we go."

That was partially true. The other part was that it had been a long time since I'd been to a party, let alone a costume party, and I was a little nervous. I wasn't the most socially gifted person who ever walked the Earth, so I thought a pre-event drink would help me feel more comfortable in a room full of costumed strangers. I nodded to the bottle in the bowl. "Do you mind opening? I'm not sure I know how."

Ash twisted the bottle until it made the obligatory pop and poured us each a glass. "To a year full of new experiences, new friendships, and new possibilities."

"Cheers!"

We took a sip and then set our glasses down. The moment was artificial but sweet, and I had to fight the impulse to say something sarcastic to counterbalance it. One of my flaws had always been that I had trouble being serious in a serious moment. It was a product of immaturity, no doubt, and something I was determined to change. So as the silence between us stretched on, I took another sip of my champagne to swallow my urge to say something stupid.

Finally, Ash broke the tension. "Look at us in our fancy

clothes drinking champagne by candlelight. Who *are* we?"

I almost spit out my drink with relief. "I know, right? I feel like a total imposter."

"Imposter? Nah, I feel like I should be on a red carpet somewhere. I look *good* in this tux."

"My, but someone has a high opinion of oneself," I teased.

"What? You don't think I could give Tobey Maguire a run for his money in this?" He spun around to give me the full view.

"You watched the movie!" I said, clapping my hands together. "What'd you think?"

"It was kinda sad," he said. "But it looked like they had one hell of a party before things all went to shit."

"Maybe we should drink to that: one hell of a party before everything goes to shit." I raised my glass into the air.

"I'd rather drink to having a date with the prettiest girl in town."

I rolled my eyes. "That tux is turning you into a cheese ball."

"I'm dead serious." Ash was looking at me the way a lion might look at a gazelle. Or Holman might look at a doughnut. He said, "I can't remember the last time I was as proud to go anywhere with anyone as I am to go to this party with you tonight."

"Ash—" That was maybe the nicest thing anyone had ever said to me, and I didn't know how to respond. Luckily, the doorbell rang and I didn't have to finish my sentence. And, double-luckily, there could not have been a more effective antidote to the intimate moment than what I saw when I opened my front door.

Holman and Lindsey stood before me, both wearing pants that I think were called knickers, drab-colored button-down shirts under even drabber vests, and flat newsboy caps. Holman had a parchment bag slung across his chest filled with newspapers. Lindsey's accessory appeared to be dirt she'd that smudged onto her cheeks to perfect the "street urchin" look. I was both horrified and impressed.

"Whadaya know, Riley!" Holman said in that nasal tone familiar to old movies.

"Jeepers! You look swell!" Lindsey chimed in.

"Wow," was all I could say.

Ash walked over to the entry. "Man, you guys look... wow...you really went all out, didn't you?" he said.

Holman beamed at what he perceived as a compliment, and Lindsey patted at the base of her hat where she'd tucked up her beautiful hair. "Thanks, daddy-o," they said in unison, and then looked at each other and laughed.

I led them in and offered them champagne. Lindsey accepted and Holman declined, as he was our driver for the evening. Earlier in the day I told him we'd be happy to take Uber to and from the party so he could have a drink, but he'd insisted on taking his car. "What kind of gentleman takes a woman out and does not see to her safe return home?"

"Uber is 'seeing to her safe return home,' " I'd told him.

"It's outsourcing the job," he'd said with more than a hint of judgment in his voice. "Besides, wouldn't it likely be your mother driving the Uber?"

"Good point," I said. I mean, I love my mom and everything, but having her drive me and my friends to a party was way too high school flashback for me.

We spent the next thirty minutes or so making excited chitchat, all of us careful not to bring up anything having to do with work. This was a night for celebration, and we were all determined not to let the weightier issues of the day spoil it. When it was time to leave for Toad's party, we piled into Holman's Dodge Neon. After a lengthy process of him putting the party address into his navigation system while Ash kept repeating, "Dude, I can just tell you where to go," we were off.

Toad lived in a subdivision about two miles outside of Tuttle Corner. The narrow road was still snow covered from yesterday's storm, but it was a well-traveled route, so the snow was packed down, making for an easy drive. The night was cold and clear, and the bright moon reflected off the snow, bathing everything around us in dark periwinkle. As Ash and I sat in the cramped back seat, our knees touching, he reached over and threaded his fingers through mine. An old song from Holman's weird but oddly perfect "Roaring 20s" playlist drifted through the small car, and for a brief moment I actually felt transported to another time, or at the very least to another age.

People had often told me I was an old soul—Granddaddy, when I'd devour his old Agatha Christie novels, and Ryan, when I'd suggest we blow off a party in college to stay home and watch a movie. Granddad had meant it as a compliment, and I'm pretty sure Ryan did not—but either way the epithet had been okay with me. There's a certain peace that comes with knowing who you are, and while I was far from Miss Confidence, USA, I'd always been comfortable with that part of myself. I dipped my head onto Ash's shoulder as we rode in silence, enjoying the closeness as he gave my hand a meaningful squeeze.

"I think this is it," Lindsey said as we pulled onto a street lined with cars.

"I'll drop you ladies at the driveway," Holman said, "so you won't have to walk in the snow."

For a guy who didn't date much and didn't often dwell

on the subtleties of human interaction, Holman was being quite the gentleman tonight. I knew that must have been a testament to how much he wanted to impress Lindsey. I hoped it was working.

We pulled up to the house, and I couldn't help but smile. White twinkle lights filled multiple trees out front, the path to the front door was lined with white-paper-bag luminaries, and music spilled out onto the street. You could also hear a roar of lively conversation all the way from the driveway, and I'll admit I felt a flutter of nervous excitement ripple through my belly.

"You know anyone who's coming?" Lindsey said to me as we stood on the driveway waiting for our dates.

"Ryan and Ridley," I said, my breath visible. "And I'll probably recognize some people from high school—but other than that, no." I noticed she looked a little nervous. I wanted to ask how it was going with Holman, but I knew he'd be along at any moment. "Your costume looks great, by the way."

"Thanks," she said. "Truthfully, I'd probably rather have worn a cute dress like yours, but Will was so excited about the newsies idea, I just had to go along with it."

"That was really sweet of you."

She smiled, an unspoken answer to my unspoken question of how things were going between them. Just then Ash and Holman walked up, their cheeks red from the cold. Ash leaned over and whispered in my ear, "Um, he keeps calling me 'old sport.' "

I stifled a laugh.

"You gals ready to bust into this gin joint and sip on some giggle water?" Holman said, reviving his old-timey voice from before.

I was about to tell Holman that he didn't have to talk

like that all night, but then Lindsey said, "That'd be the bee's knees!" and I felt like I'd be a total wench to try to tame their enthusiasm. Lindsey was clearly trying to get into the spirit and so should I.

"Sure thing, daddy-o," I said.

Holman's face lit up with excitement. "Nice use of Prohibition-era slang, Riley!"

Ash, on the other hand, looked at me like I was speaking Russian.

"When in West Egg..." I trilled as I took his arm to walk inside.

CHAPTER 40

We stepped inside the house, and it didn't even feel like we were in Tuttle Corner anymore. The entire first floor had been transformed. Toad must have moved out all his furniture, because huge centerpieces with giant white feather plumes and pearls sat on bar top tables that were scattered about the room. Muted gold and clear teardrop balloons hung from the ceiling on fishing wire, giving the effect that we were standing inside a bottle of champagne. Everyone was dressed to the nines, wearing their best twenties costumes. I'd never seen so many flappers and gangsters and top hats in one room in all my life. Everything looked so festive, it was impossible not to feel so yourself. Even Holman was scanning the room with a look of wonder on his face.

We hadn't been in the house for three seconds before a tall, thin man in a black tux came walking toward us with his arms spread wide. "Glad you could make it, cuz!"

This must be Toad. Ridley was right—he looked nothing like a warty, swamp-dwelling creature. He was about as tall as Holman but looked like he spent much more time in the gym. He had the same coloring as Ash, but his face was longer, and he wore wire-framed glasses. He wasn't what I'd describe as traditionally handsome, but he oozed the sort of charm that would have made good looks almost too over-the-top. As it was, he was the kind of guy you liked immediately.

He and Ash embraced and clapped each other on the back in the traditional bro greeting. "This is Riley Ellison, my date," Ash said, "and our friends Will Holman and Lindsey Davis."

Toad took my hand and kissed the back of it, a gesture that were he to have done it in any other setting would have been kinda creepy, but in this one was sort of fun. "Lovely to meet you. I can already tell you are far too good for my degenerate second cousin."

I smiled and might have even blushed.

Then he turned to Holman and Lindsey, his hand on his chin as he looked them up and down. Just before the moment turned awkward, he snapped his fingers. "Newspaper boys...am I right?"

"Well done, Mr. Toad," Holman said, shooting Ash an I-told-you-so glance. "Thank you for allowing us to come to your party."

"The more the merrier," Toad said as he threw his arms up in the air. He proceeded to give us the lay of the land: beer and wine were in the living room, hard liquor in the kitchen, food in the dining room. "At midnight, we're gonna have a toast and do the traditional banging of pots and pans, so be sure to grab one off the pile by the patio door before then."

"It wards away the evil spirits," Holman said with a discreet nod of the head.

Toad looked slightly unsure whether or not he was joking, but raised his glass and said, "To banishing evil spirits! And annoying the crap out of your neighbors!" We all laughed, and with that, Toad was off to greet other guests.

Ash and I made our way through the crowd toward the

wine and beer station. Lindsey said she wanted to try Mr. Toad's Wild Ride, the signature cocktail of the evening, so she and Holman went in search of the kitchen. The music was loud, and I could barely hear Ash ask me what I wanted to drink. "Whatever you're having!" I shouted. A few minutes later he was back with two bottles of beer.

The next couple of hours were a blur of drinking, laughter, and conversations starting with, "Tell me again what your friends are dressed up as?" Ryan and Ridley showed up at some point—she looking ridiculously stunning in a gold-fringe flapper dress, and he dressed like Al Capone, complete with a toy machine gun and stick-on black mustache. Eventually, the 1920s music was replaced with more current selections, and the large living room turned into one giant dance floor. Ash, as it turned out, could really *dance*. I probably should have been embarrassed at my lack of coordination, but I'd had just enough beer not to care. Holman and Lindsey mostly stood off to the side, talking and watching the dancers, but they looked like they were having fun in their own way.

It was about eleven when I excused myself to go to the bathroom. There was a long line at the closest one to the living room, but I remembered Toad saying there was a powder room off the kitchen. I made my way over there and was glad to see there was only one person ahead of me in line. As I waited, I checked my phone and saw I had gotten an email from Sheriff Clark. It was probably the copy of Flick's phone records. There was a little voice inside my head telling me not to open it, that whatever was in there could wait. I was supposed to be taking the night off from thinking about this stuff. But then my little voice started fighting with another little voice that pointed out that Sheriff Clark had gone to all the trouble of sending it and it wouldn't take but two seconds to open it. Maybe I should just peek real quick and see if anything jumped out at me. I looked around (as if anyone knew or cared what I was doing) and clicked on the attachment.

I scanned the document, which listed the date, phone number, and duration of each call. There were no names associated with the numbers, so until I could cross-check the phone numbers on the internet, this list offered little information. I saw my own phone number on there a couple of times; the last entry was from the day before Flick was killed. My heart ached at the memory, but I pushed past it.

There were several calls in between the one to me and the end of the log to what looked like two numbers, both with a 252 area code. I recognized that as Greenville, North Carolina, which was, not incidentally, where both the Claremores and Megan Johanning lived. Megan's call had come to my phone as Blocked Caller, so I had no way of knowing if one of these numbers was hers, but I did have Shannon's number from the records I'd received from Hudson Falls. A quick toggle over to my outgoing calls confirmed that one of the 252 numbers was indeed Shannon Claremore's. I started to get that excited-slash-nervous feeling I got when I was onto something. Flick had called Shannon Claremore, which means she lied to me when she said she didn't know him.

The woman in line behind me tapped my shoulder, prodding me to look up. The bathroom was free, and now there were at least four people in line behind me. I stepped inside the small powder room with only one thing on my mind: Who did the other number belong to? I knew I shouldn't be doing this now, that I should wait until tomorrow when I could attack this with a clear head and a plan, but patience had never been my strong suit. Leaning against the sink, I keyed in the other 252 number, the last phone number Flick ever called. I held my breath as the phone rang. After three or four rings, I heard the distinct click of someone on the other end of the phone, though no one spoke.

"Hello?" When I got no response, I covered my ear with my free hand and tried again. "Hello? Who is this?"

"Happy New Year, Riley." The voice was unmistakably Megan Johanning's.

"Megan?"

"That's a real pretty white dress you're wearing."

Darkness edged in on my field of vision, and for one brief moment, I thought I might black out. "Where are you?" I asked, my voice a hoarse, urgent rasp.

"Let's just say I'm nearby."

"What—why—" My mind was frantically trying to make sense of this and having a hard time with it. "It *was* you..." I thought of the car that had been following me earlier. "You won't—"

"YOU," she said, her voice slicing through me, "would do well to be quiet and listen to me. I'm giving you a chance to avoid any future *unpleasantness*. Drop this whole thing, Riley. Stop looking into Shannon Claremore's past. Stop the investigation into Mr. Flick's accident. Honor Albert's memory by letting this go."

"Don't you dare say his name!"

"Why not?" Megan said calmly. "Albert and I made a deal. Your safety was his main concern, his last request, if you will."

I was vaguely aware of someone knocking on the door and voices. *Hurry up! C'mon!* But it felt like I was rushing through time at warp speed—everything around me faded into the background as I struggled to hold onto what she was saying. *Granddad's last request.*

"I gave him my word that you'd be safe," Megan continued. "I'd hate to have to go back on it."

Someone outside the door started to knock loudly. "Hey, are you almost done? C'mon!"

"Is that a threat?" I asked, the fear in my voice obvious even though I was trying to sound tough.

"I don't make threats," she said. "You know that by now. You've already lost two people over this situation. It would be such a shame to lose anyone else—that handsome boyfriend of yours? Or your partner from the newspaper? He drove you all there tonight, didn't he? It's a dangerous business driving on New Year's Eve. So many accidents..."

My knees literally buckled, and I had to grab the sink for balance. The pounding on the door was getting louder.

"But how?"

She made a tsk-tsk sound. "People always underestimate the physically disabled, don't they? When they look at us, they only think of the things we can't do, not what we can. For instance, some of us can drive far better than we can walk. And the hand controls on cars these days result in amazing precision."

She was talking about Flick. She'd been driving the car that had forced him to crash. My mind was racing to catch up. "But...but...I have—"

"What you have is fair warning. You're the only person—well, the only person currently alive and conscious—who has made the connection between Shannon and who she used to be. This can all end with you, Riley. Tell your friends you were wrong. Throw them off the trail."

The only person currently alive and conscious. My brain made the connection in an instant. "You arranged the hit on Tackett..."

"Alas, no," she said, sounding truly disappointed. "Let's call that a happy coincidence."

It sounded like more than one person outside the door now. Somewhere in the back of my brain I thought I recognized Lindsey's voice, then Ash's. *What's going on? Who's in there? Is she okay?* The door handle rattled again.

"You can't—you're not going to—"

"Yes, I am." She cut me off. "Because if you even so much as *think* about telling anyone about this or asking your friend the sheriff for help, I will know." Her voice turned into a low growl. "The second I find out anyone is asking around about Shannon's identity or my involvement in any of this, I will consider my arrangement with Albert null and void."

She sounded like she was describing a real estate contract. "You're truly insane..."

I don't know if she didn't hear me or didn't care. Either way, her response was, "I know you're going to need some time to think about this, so I'll let you go."

My shock was morphing into numbness. All my fight, my bravado from before—my I'm-going-to-find-out-who-did-this-and-make-them-pay attitude disappeared like smoke in the wind. I was as scared as I'd ever been in my life.

"I'll be in touch soon," she said. "Till then, you be a good girl, okay? None of this trying to be a hero. We all know how that worked out."

I don't know how long it was between when the line went dead and when the door burst open, but suddenly Ash was there, Lindsey and Holman behind him, along with a sea of onlookers. Their eyes swept over me for some sign of injury or trouble.

"What is it?" Holman pushed past Ash. "What happened?"

I looked up at him through blurry, tear-rimmed eyes but couldn't make myself speak.

"Let's get her out of there," Lindsey said. She and Ash got on either side of me and led me out of the bathroom toward the front door. I could feel people staring, but I was too numb with confusion and fear to care. Ryan and Ridley must have seen what was going on because the next thing I knew, they were there too. As we stepped outside onto the concrete patch in front of the door, the cold night air hit me like a slap to the face. My breath felt ragged, sharp, and shallow and my shoulders shook, more from fright than cold. Ash took off his jacket and placed it around me.

"What happened?" he asked softly.

I looked to the left and then to the right. The street was filled with cars, but I didn't see any people. Megan knew where we were. She knew Holman drove us here. She could still be here, watching us, waiting. She'd know if I said anything. She could be close enough to hear me. "N-n-nothing," I said.

"That's crazy—look at you—you're terrified," Ryan said.

My eyes searched the dark street and saw nothing, but that only meant that I couldn't see her coming. She was out there. How else could she have known what I was wearing?

"I'm s-s-sorry," I said, silently willing myself to calm down. "I just had too much. I'm fine. Really. I'm fine."

"The hell you are," Ash said.

"Give her some space." Ridley gestured for everyone to take a step back. There was a small iron bench on the porch, and she took my elbow and led me to it. I sat, still trembling, the icy bench doing nothing to help the situation.

Holman bent down, his big buggy eyes stared directly into mine. "Riley, does this have to do with the story? With what happened today?"

I wanted desperately to tell him everything—to scream that it was Megan, that it had been her all along—but I didn't say a word. I believed that she was nearby, and I was terrified that anyone who knew the truth about her would be in danger. After all, hadn't she just basically threatened Ash and Holman on the phone? *None of this trying to be a hero. We all know how that worked out.* Flashes of past conversations came to mind—all the times Flick refused to answer my questions, refused to even acknowledge that there was anything to look into. *I was trying to keep you safe. Albert made me promise to keep you safe.* I started to shake again.

It was Lindsey this time who spoke up. "She's had some sort of a shock. Let's get her home and we can figure out what happened later. Will, can you pull the car up?"

"No!" I screamed, wild with panic, and all eyes turned to me. "Ryan, can we take your car? *Please?*"

"That's silly. Holman's car is right there," Ash said, sounding like he was explaining something complicated to a small child. "He hasn't had anything to drink."

"No, please." Tears filled my eyes as I pleaded with him, with all of them. "You have to trust me. Not that car. *Please.*" I looked at each of them, trying to convince them that though I couldn't explain it, they needed to listen to me.

"Sure, we'll take our car," Ridley said, her voice soft and comforting, like a hug. She nodded toward Ryan.

"Yeah, right. I'll go get it."

Ash put a hand on my shoulder. "I'm just going to go tell Toad that we're leaving so he doesn't worry, okay?"

I nodded. He was in and out in under a minute, and by the time he came back, Ryan had pulled up to the base of the driveway. Ridley helped me up from the bench, and she, Lindsey, Holman, and Ash all huddled around me protectively. Ridley held one of my elbows and Ash had the other. Holman held my purse. We walked slowly toward the truck. My eyes swept from left to right for any signs of Megan's silver Prius. All I saw was darkness in both directions. When we got to the truck, Ash helped me step onto the running board and hoisted me up into the back seat of the cab. My friends made a semicircle around me, waiting until I got safely in the truck before moving an inch. If someone had been looking at us from a distance, it would have looked like they were the Secret Service and it was their job to protect me. The irony, of course, that no one could know but me, was that it was actually quite the opposite: It was now my job to keep each of them safe.

Voicemail transcript: Jeannie Ellison to Riley Ellison.
Thursday, January 6, 3:21pm

Hi honey, it's mom. Um, I haven't heard from you in a few days and I'm starting to get a little worried...it's not like you not to call me back. I know it's a busy time with work and all, but I want to hear all about the New Year's party! Was your dress a hit? Did Ash just die when he saw you all dressed up? I'll bet he did!

Anyway, I ran into Dr. H yesterday at the library—I was picking up the latest Louise Penny—[lowers voice] you know how I just love that Inspector Gamache. By the way, did I tell you that the girls from book club and I are thinking of making a pilgrimage to Three Pines? Anyway, like I was saying, I ran into Dr. H who said he saw you rushing through Memorial Park the other day and he tried to wave to you, but you just walked right on past like you didn't even see him. He said it looked like you were carrying the weight of the world on your shoulders. [Sigh.] So, like I said, I'm just a little worried. Could you call me when you have a chance? Or come by the house? Just give your old Mom a little sign that you're doing okay...

Oh, and speaking of signs, how are you liking the daily horoscopes? Aren't they just the most fun! Confession: I got myself a subscription too [laughs]. I've been having the best time with them. The other day, my horoscope said that soon I would meet a stranger who would rock my—[Click]

Voicemail transcript: Jeannie Ellison to Riley Ellison.
Thursday, January 6, 3:23pm

Hi honey, it's mom again. Well, never mind about the horoscopes, just call me when you have a minute and let me know you're okay. I know you're a grown woman, but I still worry. [Laughs] All right! That's it for now. Love you, racoon. [Mumbled: What? wait—okay, okay.]

[Full voice] Dad says hi, honey...and he says he loves you too...and he says if you stop by he'll give you some black-eyed peas for good luck in the new year. Skip, she doesn't like black-eyed peas, you know that! [Pause] Well, she has the right to like any kind of food she wants to and you just can't force these things on—[Click]

CHAPTER 41

It's amazing how quickly—and slowly—time goes by when you've been blindsided by a homicidal lunatic. It had been just over two weeks since Megan Johanning threatened to hurt the people closest to me if I didn't thwart the investigation into Shannon Claremore, and I'd spent every moment since then trying to do just that. It hadn't been easy.

I managed to convince everyone that while in line for the bathroom at Toad's party, I'd found an old voicemail from Flick that I hadn't previously known about. I told them hearing his voice, combined with the alcohol, had upset and confused me, and that was the reason for my odd behavior. Eventually, they all accepted the explanation; I had been so emotional right after his death that it wasn't a far leap to think I might have had a grief-induced setback. Explaining why I wouldn't let us ride home in Holman's car had been more difficult, but I'd just kept repeating that I'd had a lot to drink and who knows exactly what was going on in my mind at the time. This had prompted frequent lectures about the perils of binge-drinking and several emails with the times and dates of AA meetings from Holman. *Fine*, I told myself. *It was worth it if my plan worked.*

Joe Tackett succumbed to his injuries and died on January 2nd. The secret of where he'd hidden the recording—which I knew now was almost certainly that of Megan Johanning—died with him. And so ended any hope of prosecuting her for her crimes. She was going to get away with it all. After all, as she pointed out, I was the only one left alive who knew, and I wasn't going to tell. As much as it sickened me, I would not put anyone else in the path of this madwoman. I'd seen what she was capable of, what she was willing to do to protect this secret. I simply would not put the people I loved at risk. I'd already lost too much.

Over the course of the past couple of weeks, Megan was like an evil puppet master, feeding me the lies I was to use to persuade Holman, Kay, and Lindsey that I'd been wrong about Shannon Claremore's involvement in Flick's and Granddaddy's deaths. It required me to push the limits of both my theatrical and ethical boundaries. In short, I had to do a lot of lying and faking of evidence.

My first task was to dispel our assumption that Bethany Miller had stolen her cousin's identity after getting out of the juvenile detention center. Since I'd been the one who'd done most of the legwork thus far, no one questioned it when I managed to unearth a paper trail that showed Bethany Miller was very much alive and well, though estranged from her family and living under a different name. It was all fake, with evidence supplied to me by Megan or simply made up out of thin air. But I was careful to make it look like this information came out in drips and drops, planting the slightest seed of doubt about our identity-theft theory and slowly building the case against it. I was also careful to appear crushed when it became clear we were wrong. Whenever it seemed like the lies were too much, just when I'd think maybe I could take all of this to Carl or Sheriff Clark, Megan would call and remind me why I was doing it. *It'd be a shame if anything were to happen to your parents,*

Riley. She haunted me like a ghost.

"Twins?" Holman asked, when I walked into his office holding the fake documents Megan had given me. "Charlie Miller didn't say anything about having twin daughters?"

"I was shocked too," I said. "But here, look." I showed him the two birth certificates she'd sent me. One was for Shannon Miller and one for Bethany Miller, both with the same parents, same hospital, same 1954 birth date. I didn't know how she did it—but they looked legitimate enough to convince Holman that it was true. The story was that Bethany and Shannon were Charlie's girls, twins. Daniel Miller also had a baby girl named Shannon (named after the matriarch of the Miller family), but she died in the plane crash.

I told Holman that I'd tracked down an old friend of the Miller family who'd given me the whole painful history. Charlie Miller fell to pieces after his wife died (which was true) and Bethany had started to get into trouble (also true). Megan told me to say that Bethany's twin, Shannon, was a good girl and tried to help her sister. But Bethany blamed her father for her problems, and after she was released from juvenile detention, she changed her name and moved out to California. I recounted the fake details Megan fed me and told Holman they were from an interview I did with Shannon Claremore in which she admitted the existence of Bethany, her twin. She explained that the reason she hadn't mentioned it before was that it was particularly upsetting to her father, and that his memory of Bethany was starting to fade, which was a blessing.

It had been disturbingly simple to craft a believable story and falsify documents to support that story. After all, my co-workers trusted me. They never suspected for one minute that I was lying the whole damn time—and that kept me awake, wracked with guilt, nearly every night since

New Year's Eve.

Without any evidence of identity theft, Shannon Claremore was no longer a suspect, which meant that Megan Johanning wasn't either. After building the case brick-by-brick over the course of three weeks, Holman and Kay were on board—and just as disappointed as I was in our failed conclusions.

Of course, there'd been some collateral damage to my personal life. I'd necessarily pulled away from Ash. I could not in good conscience start out a relationship among all these lies. And I knew the only way I could keep my distance from him was to literally keep my distance from him. It had been so hard to suddenly start treating him with indifference, refusing to explain why I didn't want to hang out anymore. *I'm too tired. I can't tonight. I don't think so.* He stopped by my house one night, mid-January, and demanded to know what was going on with me.

"Just tell me what I did wrong?" When I refused to invite him in, he'd stood outside my front door.

"Nothing. I just need some time to myself."

"But I don't understand. Everything seemed to be going so well with us." To his immense credit, he seemed more confused than angry.

"Don't make this a bigger deal than it has to be, Ash," I'd said, coldly.

I fought back tears after he left but reminded myself that the shame and regret I felt was a small price to pay for his safety. After weeks of unreturned calls and texts, he'd sent me a message that he was going back to Texas to get his stuff, and when he came back, he'd leave it up to me whether or not to get in touch.

It's for the best, I told myself. That had been my constant mantra over the past couple of weeks—every time I thought I'd break, that I couldn't tell Holman one more lie, or shut Ash out one more time. I knew that at least for right now, the fewer people I was close to, the better. I'd chosen to make a deal with the devil in order to protect the people I loved, and I would accept the consequences of that deal.

But on all those nights that I laid awake unable to sleep lest the nightmares set in, I began to look at things another way. Megan had robbed me of my sense of safety, control, honesty, and optimism. Because of her, I'd not only lost two of the most important men in my life, I'd lost so much of my sense of self. Night after night in the still of the early morning hours, I perseverated over everything that woman had taken from me. And I decided I wasn't about to walk away from her empty-handed.

CHAPTER 42

It was ten minutes past the meeting time we'd set; Megan was late. I sat on a bench facing the small man-made lake and braced myself against the icy air. I pulled my coat tighter around me as a gust of wind whipped up, sending the detritus of a long, cold winter swirling around my feet. Dead leaves, sticks, and rocks scattered on top of the muddy ground. Redemption Lake, the newest addition to the Claremore Ministries campus, was not yet officially open. The man-made lake was filled, but the surrounding area was still under construction. A concrete path stretched from the main cathedral all the way down to the lake, where it gently sloped into the water. It would be the ultimate zero-entry baptism experience. Just behind the benches, there was a framed outbuilding that wasn't quite finished. I guessed that would be where families could gather before the ceremonies, a place to celebrate the renewal of baptism, the beginning of a blessed life.

Everything looked gray and dirty under the winter clouds, and I closed my eyes and imagined what this place would look like with the inevitable rebirth of spring. It would be lovely, no doubt. The finished park would be perfect and beautiful, and no one would remember how ugly it had been before.

I patted Coltrane's big, furry head as he watched a

couple of birds flying high over the lake. I'd brought him with me mostly for moral support, but it didn't hurt that he was a skilled attack dog. I knew the code word that would turn him from fuzzy companion to trained killer but didn't expect to have to use it. Today's meeting was to be a simple business transaction. An eye for an eye, so to speak.

Another seven minutes passed before I saw Megan coming down on the path from the main church. Her power wheelchair was almost completely silent and seemed to be traveling at high speed. Within seconds, she came into focus. Though I'd seen pictures of her online and we'd spoken on the phone more times than I cared to think about, I was startled by her appearance. She had thinning brown hair and large gray eyes the color of wet concrete. She was thinner and younger than I expected, with papery skin that clung to the bones in her face. Her left shoulder caved inward back toward her body, while her right shoulder protruded. Her legs were thin and bowed in at the knees. Despite her physical fragility, she radiated a sense of strength and intimidation. And it wasn't just that I knew what she was capable of—there was something in her aura, for lack of a better term, that emanated a kind of fortitude that must come from singularity of purpose. Or, perhaps, criminal insanity.

She rolled up to the bench and put her chair in park using the hand controls. As she turned her hand over, I saw a small tattoo on the inside of her wrist: "26:7." The bible verse Granddad had written on a scrap of paper. It had been a clue. Tears stung the back of my eyes. *If I had only figured it out sooner.*

Her eyes came to rest on Coltrane, who stood up immediately and assumed a protective stance. It was obvious he did not like her.

"He remembers me," she said.

It had been Megan following me the night I saw Ryan taking out his trash. She'd admitted to me later that had Ryan not been outside, she was planning to "have a little chat" with me right there in the street.

"This is Coltrane. If you're nice to me, he'll be nice to you," I said, tightening my grip on his leash.

She laughed, but because she was unable to smile—and because she was a complete psychopath—it sounded all wrong. "You have something for me?"

I nodded. "But first, I want to know why. You owe me that much."

She rolled her eyes. "You wouldn't be trying to record me, now would you, Riley? Get me to confess to all my sins on tape and then take that to your friends in law enforcement?"

"I already have a tape of you confessing to murdering my grandfather," I said, the words coming out sharp and bitter. "If I wanted to turn that in to the police, I would have already done it."

In the end, it had been Jay who figured it out. After Tackett died, he'd gone back to his source inside Greensville to try to squeeze out more details about what Tackett had told him. "He just kept calling it his trump card," Mike the informant told Jay. "Tackett kept saying, 'The sheriff was guarding his trump card,' and then he'd get this weird, smug smile on his face, like he was laughing at some private joke."

"So what does that mean?" I'd asked Jay over coffee one morning at Mysa about a week ago.

"I've spent time in a lot of sheriff's offices, Riley, and there are two things that are a constant in each and every one of them. One is an American flag, and one is—"

"A picture of the President of the United States," I'd

finished his sentence, almost in disbelief. "His Trump card...capital 'T.' " That sneaky sonofabitch.

I arranged a meeting with Carl offsite under the guise of wanting to talk to him about his upcoming debate with Skipper Hazelrigg, and Jay walked into the office about ten minutes later. He'd done some consulting work for the Tuttle County Sheriff's Department a while ago, so everyone knew him and knew he worked for the federal government. When he said he'd been tasked with checking the government-issued photographs as a part of the Presidential Image Task Force, Gail didn't bat an eye. "Have at it," she'd said. "Just don't cite us for excessive dust buildup!"

Jay said it had taken him less than two minutes to find the spot on the back of the frame where the paper had been peeled back, locate the jump drive, and put it all back together. The recording was short, but listening to it had been painful. It was a phone conversation between Megan and Tackett on the night Granddad died. Megan called Tackett, told him she'd witnessed Albert Ellison commit suicide, and offered him 10,000 dollars to get over to the house and close the case as quickly as possible.

"What do you care how I handle the case?" Tackett said without reacting at all to the news that a man was dead.

"Albert had something that belonged to me, some unauthorized research. I've taken what's mine from the scene and don't want anyone to read anything more into that than what it is, so I think an expedited investigation would be best for all parties concerned," she'd answered.

"You were there when he offed himself?" Tackett asked, a clear challenge in his voice.

"Let's just say I bore witness."

"Mmm," Tackett had said. "Albert Ellison's a pretty

happy guy as far as I've ever known. Seems awful out of character for a guy like that to shoot himself. Oh, and he doesn't own a gun. See, as the Sheriff I remember that sort of thing about my constituents." He was threatening her, ever so subtly letting her know he knew she was lying.

"Would 15,000 help you forget, Sheriff?" Megan hadn't exactly confessed to the murder, but there was enough there to open an investigation.

Megan's voice brought me back to the moment. She nodded at Coltrane and said, "Just like you have your guard dog here, I have mine. And if you were to somehow get me arrested or have Cujo here eat me alive, he has been instructed to carry out my very specific, well-thought-out, and unpleasant plans for your friends and family."

"Yeah, you've been clear about that," I said through gritted teeth. I knew Megan had to have had help with some of the things she'd done, but I had no idea who it was. I supposed it didn't much matter at this point. "I'm here for the money and an explanation. After that, this all goes away."

Once I had the jump drive in hand, I'd called Megan and offered to sell it to her for 25,000 dollars. At first, she'd responded by making more wild threats against my parents, Holman, Ash, Ridley—basically everyone I knew. But I assured her I didn't plan to turn it over to law enforcement. "I'll put it somewhere you'll never find it, and you'll have to live with the knowledge that it's out there—or," I'd said, "you can pay me a finder's fee and it becomes yours to do with what you want."

"And how do I know you haven't made copies or saved it onto your hard drive?"

"Because I know what will happen if I do," I'd said, honestly. "I told you, Megan. I won't lose anyone else to this insanity."

She'd eventually agreed, and I said I'd come to Greenville

and meet her in a public space. I didn't trust her to not just kill me and make it look like an accident (her specialty, apparently). So here we were, and as much as I wanted my pound of flesh, I was willing to settle for a pile of cash and an explanation.

"I just need to understand why protecting Shannon—or Bethany—Miller's secret was worth killing for," I said, reiterating my demand.

Megan looked over toward the main church building. "We are all called to do certain things in this life, Riley, and my calling is to faithfully protect those who are here on Earth doing God's work, like Pastor Wyatt. He's a true prophet of the Lord, and he's saved thousands upon thousands of people, including me. Do you have any idea how broken I was when he found me?"

I said nothing.

"The course of my life had just been changed forever when I was diagnosed with this cruel disease. There is no cure, no treatment, no advice other than to live while you can until your body fails and decomposes around you. I was nineteen years old, completely alone, and facing a bleak future. I came very, very close to ending my life," she said. "And then Pastor Wyatt found me and healed me, spiritually. He helped me realize that I was given this particular set of challenges because of my inner strength, *because I had what it took to handle it*. He told me I was special, sanctified."

I was beginning to lose my patience with this psycho. Most of what she was telling me had been in her book, minus the creepy, reverent tone she used when she talked about Wyatt Claremore. "Yeah, that's all very interesting," I said. "But let's get to the part where you killed my grandfather to protect Wyatt. Did he ask you to do it? Did he tell you that God wanted you to commit murder to protect the image of his 'perfect wife,' his 'perfect family'?"

"Wyatt doesn't know about any of this," she said calmly. "He is pure of heart and mind. This is Shannon's burden. She only confessed it to me because I overheard her talking to her father about it one day back when I was living with them. Albert had started asking questions, and she was distraught at the thought of her secret coming out and destroying the life they'd built. She was going to tell Wyatt everything, but I stopped her. I told her I would take care of it." Her eyes sharpened. "And I did."

She held out her wrist for me to see the tattoo: " 'You shall chase your enemies and they will fall by the sword before you. Leviticus 26:7.' Wyatt needs a clear path and a clean heart in order to do his good work. Shannon's revelation would have destroyed him, possibly even destroyed his ministry. The way I see it, the lives lost were a small price to pay."

I felt sick hearing what she'd done and her twisted rationale, but there was a tiny part of me that felt some peace at finally knowing what happened. "So, you killed him...you killed my grandfather." Hot, angry tears pricked the back of my eyes, but I held her gaze, forcing her to look at the pain she'd caused. Not that she had the capacity to care.

"He was going to expose Shannon and Wyatt," she said as if that was supposed to justify her actions. "I gave him chance after chance to drop it, but he wouldn't. So, one night I showed up at his house—your house now—with some photos I'd taken of you at college. I knew where your dorm room was, your class schedule, the restaurants you went to. I told him I was done playing games and this had to end. I could not allow him to destroy the Claremores. The time had come to make a choice: his life or yours. He chose you."

A sob escaped from somewhere deep inside my chest,

and I fought it back. "You're a monster," I whispered.

"Do you know how many lives I saved through that one act of violence? Thousands probably!"

"And what about Flick? That was a *second* act of violence."

"That was a snap decision." A crease formed between her eyes. "Shannon and I met with him on Chincoteague and explained to him that he was mistaken. We brought the fake documents and everything—used the same 'twin' story that I fed you—but Flick didn't buy it. Said he was going to talk to Shannon's father in the morning. I had to do something. Shannon and Wyatt have touched people all over the globe, they—"

"Megan?" A man's voice curled out from inside the half-built structure behind us.

Megan had to turn her chair to see who it was, and when she did, her face drained of what color it had.

"Tell me this isn't true..." Wyatt Claremore stepped out of the building. Jay was behind him.

"Wyatt," Megan said, her voice a shocked whisper.

Jay walked over to stand beside me and Coltrane. He wore street clothes, not his usual suit. He was here today as a concerned citizen, not a government employee.

Wyatt's face was contorted with pain and shock, and he looked like he might become physically ill. "Just tell me this isn't true. Tell me you didn't hurt those people."

Megan's eyes went wild. "I did it for you, for Shannon, for the kids," she said, her voice rising with panic. "They would have exposed what she did—" she broke off. It was clear by the horrified expression on his face that Wyatt would never understand, never absolve her.

He stared at her for another long moment, before turning to me. He spoke in a low voice, laden with sorrow. "I don't know what to say, except I am so deeply, profoundly sorry, Miss Ellison. I had no idea...about any of this."

I nodded. What was there to say? I believed that he hadn't known anything about Shannon or the horrific things Megan had done in his name. But should he have? Had he been willfully ignorant of what was going on around him? That was a question for another day.

"Would you like me to call the authorities?" Jay said to Wyatt.

He turned to Megan, ignoring Jay's question. "Does Shannon know what you've done?"

She simply stared back at him, refusing to answer.

After a moment, he turned away, dropping his head into his hands. I heard the sound of muffled weeping as his shoulders shook with anguish. Jay took a few steps away to make a call, presumably to the local authorities. I dabbed my eyes with a tissue, and when I looked up I saw Megan's near-silent chair hurtling full speed down the concrete path toward the lake.

It happened in a matter of seconds. She plunged into the water, the chair tipping forward as it became submerged. As soon as I realized what was happening, I started screaming, which started Coltrane barking. Jay reacted immediately. He dove into the lake, grasping and clawing at the chair, trying to grab hold of it as its weight pulled it down into the murky water.

"She's strapped in," he yelled.

I turned to Wyatt, who seemed paralyzed, and yelled at him to call 911. Then I dropped Coltrane's leash and ran into the water to try to help Jay. In the few seconds that it took to get there, the chair had sunk deeper beneath the surface. It was barely visible under the opaque mask of slate blue. Jay dove underwater again and again, as he desperately tried to free Megan, taking great gulps of air in between efforts. When it became clear he was not going to be able to loosen the safety belt, Jay told me to grab hold of the chair. The lake wasn't deep, but I couldn't stand and therefore couldn't get the leverage to pull the chair up.

"Help us!" I called to Wyatt, who stood frozen on the concrete. He didn't move. Coltrane was barking and pacing frantically along the water's edge.

"I'm gonna try to pry the harness off," Jay said as he sucked in another big breath and dove under the water. He was under for longer this time. After what seemed like an eternity, he crashed through the surface, Megan's limp form slumped over his left shoulder. Jay swam toward the edge of the lake, crawled onto the bank and gently laid Megan out on her back.

Jay was hovering over her performing CPR, but I had no idea if she was alive or dead. I pulled myself out of the lake and went to her side. "Is she...?" I said, panting.

I saw Jay make the barest shake of his head as he continued to compress her disease-ravaged chest. I took her wrist to feel for a pulse, my fingers resting directly on the inked "26:7." I left them there for several seconds but felt nothing.

"She's gone," Wyatt said, his voice suddenly full of authority. He put a hand on Jay's shoulder, but Jay wouldn't stop. His training had taken over, and there was no way he was going to give up until he was certain that there was no hope of resuscitation. I rocked back on my heels and sank down in the mud, feeling numb as much from the freezing water as what had just happened. Coltrane orbited around me like a nervous mother, and Wyatt started to recite the Lord's Prayer.

CHAPTER 43

The story made front-page news, not only in Tuttle but in newspapers across the country. Holman and I shared the byline. It had taken some time to sort everything out, but once Megan had been declared dead at the scene, Shannon Claremore—the woman born as Bethany Miller—started talking. And once she did, she didn't stop.

As we'd suspected, she had started living under her dead cousin's name after she'd gotten out of juvenile detention. "By the time I met Wyatt, I'd almost forgotten that I'd ever been anyone else. I didn't tell him because I didn't think it would hurt anyone...I had no idea..." she said in the police interview, just before breaking down into tears.

She explained that when Albert first reached out years ago to ask her about the plane crash, he just wanted to know why it had taken so long for the bodies of the Miller family to be claimed. Shannon told him the truth, which was that Charlie *had* technically claimed the bodies of his family over the phone, but at that time he was an alcoholic who had a hard time holding down a job. They didn't have the money to pay for the cost of a funeral and burial for six people, so Charlie simply let the three-month time limit run out, and when the state cremated the bodies, he went to pick up their things. Daniel Miller's small estate was left to Charlie, as his closest living relative, and Shannon said the money helped pull her family up out of hardship—at least until Rebecca died.

It wasn't until Granddad discovered the unusual coincidence of there being two Shannon Millers the same age in the same family that he came back with more questions. He called back several times asking more and more questions, and Shannon Claremore became convinced that Albert was going to discover the truth. She said she was sick with nerves over the situation and had decided to come clean to Wyatt. That's when Megan intervened and offered to take care of things.

"I had no idea what she was planning," Shannon said, her red-rimmed eyes raw with guilt and shame. "She just said she'd deal with it, and I never heard another word about it. I didn't even know that man had died until a few months ago. By that time, it was too late."

She went on to say that she thought the whole thing had just gone away until Flick reached out to her last fall asking the same questions. He was the one who told her Albert had died under suspicious circumstances. She admitted to having a fleeting thought that perhaps Megan had "done something bad" but had never asked her directly.

"After Mr. Flick called and started asking questions, Megan came up with the idea to say that I had a twin sister. She took care of getting all the documentation we needed to make it look convincing, and then we arranged to meet Flick on Chincoteague Island. I thought if we could just explain it all away, then everything would be fine..."

When pressed by the detective, Shannon admitted that she had a feeling Megan was capable of violence. "Looking back, I remember that she got that tattoo on her wrist the same year Albert called with questions," Shannon said. "I remember asking her about it at the time. She said it was a signal to everyone that she was a soldier for the ministry. I swear I never made the connection until it was too late."

I wasn't sure, legally speaking, what Shannon Claremore would be charged with, but I hoped that whatever it was, it carried a significant punishment. She'd willfully ignored the warning signs of a homicidal zealot because it served her interests. I'll admit that the thought of her sitting in a cell, thinking about how her cowardice caused two good men to die, gave me a small measure of comfort.

While it could never be officially confirmed, police suspected that Megan had an accomplice in the actual killings, a guy named Tay Drogden. He was a recovering addict and longtime Oakwood Christian Church parishioner who credited Wyatt Claremore with saving his life. The day after the news of Megan's death came out, he was found dead in his home of a heroin overdose. Wyatt told police that Megan and Tay had been extraordinarily close, and he suspected that Tay would have done anything Megan asked him to. When the police found him, they said he had a fresh tattoo on his wrist of the same bible verse that Megan had: "26:7."

Wyatt Claremore stepped down as the head of Claremore Ministries on the day the story broke. He made a public statement expressing his shock and grief about what had happened. He said he planned to stand by his wife as she atoned for her sins, both spiritually and according to the letter of the law. He said they would seek God's grace to help them move forward after this terrible tragedy. The cynic in me would bet good money that he signed a tell-all book contract within minutes of the press conference.

The past few weeks had been some of the most difficult of my life, but I was getting through it, determined to put my life back together in the aftermath of Megan's reign of terror. I'd practically thrown myself at Kay's feet and apologized for lying to her about the Claremore/Miller story. I spent nearly an hour crafting an entire speech about how and why I'd done what I'd done, promising to start from scratch to build back her trust, swearing to stay well within all ethical boundaries on all stories from this day forward, etcetera, etcetera. I'd gotten eight words into my speech when Kay said, "Totally get it, Ellison. We're all good." Classic Kay.

My conversation with Holman had required slightly more explanation. He was hurt that I hadn't come to him with what I knew. "You could have trusted me, Riley," he'd said. "Don't you know by now that I will always be on your side?"

I tried to explain to him how powerless and frightened I felt after New Year's Eve, how Megan seemed to know everything I said and did, how I was terrified that confiding in him would lead him to the same fate as Flick and Granddad. He listened to me and was quiet for a long time after I'd finished my explanation. Finally, he'd said, "You think of me in the same category as Flick and Albert?"

"I do."

"Okay then," he'd said. "I forgive you."

I can't say for sure, but I had a feeling that Lindsey helped Holman work through some of his conflicted feelings about it all. They'd been spending a lot of time together lately and I'd never seen Holman happier. In fact, their relationship was the one thing that had made lying to him easier. I knew that even if he hated me and never wanted to speak to me again once the truth came out, at least he'd have Lindsey. Holman deserved at least one person in the world who adored him. Now he had two.

After having explained things to Kay and Holman, it

was time to sort things out with Ash. I knew he must have seen the headlines about what happened, but he hadn't reached out. About three days after the story ran in the paper, I'd stopped into Campbell & Sons to see him. He'd listened to my emotional explanation of everything that happened and why I'd made the choices I did. I told him how I truly believed it was the only way to keep everyone, him included, safe. He responded by saying he was glad I was okay and that'd I'd finally gotten answers. That was it. I didn't know what I'd wanted or expected him to say, but I'd been a little surprised at his cold response. I tried to crack through his tough shell.

"I just wanted to tell you in person how sorry I am for—"

"It's fine." He cut me off.

My cheeks burned, but I persisted. "I never wanted to hurt you," I said. "It felt so horrible to push you away like that."

"Tell me about it," he said with a biting sarcasm.

The conversation felt all wrong. Everyone else in my life understood—or at least tried to understand—what a horrible position I'd been in and why I felt like I had to do what I did. But Ash was acting like this was personal. He was so wrapped up in his own hurt feelings that he didn't care what I'd been through. *When someone shows you who they are, believe them.*

I swallowed the lump in my throat. "For what it's worth, I am really sorry. I'll see you around," I said and walked out the door.

I was halfway down the front steps of the building when I heard the door open behind me. "I would have understood, you know," Ash called after me. "If you would have just told me what was going on, I would have helped you figure out what to do."

I stopped and turned around slowly, taking a few extra seconds to formulate my response. I fought the urge to apologize again and the stronger, angrier urge to point out that I'd made a decision about what the best course of action was and I didn't need him second-guessing my choices. Or implying that his help would have somehow changed things. Yes, I'd hurt him, but I did it because I was trying to do the right thing. Plus, I'd apologized sincerely, and if that wasn't enough for him, then he wasn't enough for me. I wouldn't beg for his forgiveness. "This was something I needed to deal with on my own," I said simply.

He just looked at me, his face a mixture of anger, pain, and pride. He didn't say anything else, so I walked away. And he let me go.

Daily Astrological Forecast

Scorpio

You are in store for some much-needed calm after the intensity of the past few weeks. This has been a time of much tumult and regeneration, but thankfully the worst is over. Jupiter sparkles in your self-esteem sector, giving you just the confidence you need to take things to the next level, both personally and professionally. You have a lot to offer, Scorpio darling. By taking big risks that position you outside of your comfort zone, you'll continue to recognize and trust your own power.

A new astrological season begins today when the Sun cruises into Libra's domain, putting you in the perfect position to touch the sky. Go and get it, girl.

Tonight: Reach out to an old friend. You just might find they've been waiting for you to make the first move to reconnect.

CHAPTER 44

I met Jay for coffee at Mysa on a Friday afternoon. He was involved in some loose ends that needed tying up at Greensville Correctional, and he stopped through Tuttle on his way back home.

"The investigators think Tackett engineered the attack on himself," he said, after Ridley brought us each a cup of black coffee. And me a cinnamon roll.

I shouldn't have been surprised. I knew Tackett was a lying dirt bag—the fact that he'd go to those lengths to get what he wanted was perfectly in character for him.

"DNA evidence pegged an inmate named Sammy Parish as having been the one who beat Tackett to death. When they questioned him, Parish swore that Tackett paid him in cigarettes and ramen noodles to do it. He said Tackett told him he needed to make it look like the Romeros were after him," Jay said. "Could be that Parish didn't mean to kill him. The coroner said what killed him was one blow that severed an artery in his brain. Could have been an accident of bad luck or bad aim."

"Do you think?" I asked, skeptical. If Tackett had arranged the attack himself, he was certainly playing at a risky game. Then again, Joe Tackett had never shied away from risky behavior before.

"Parish doesn't have ties to the cartel that we know of,

but we're still investigating. I also think he could be saying that to reduce his charges from murder to manslaughter, but they did find a big stash of ramen in his cell." Jay shook his head. "Prison currency is a strange thing."

"If it is true, it's almost too ironic," I said, still stuck on Tackett having arranged the attack himself.

"How do you mean?"

"Tackett always was his own worst enemy."

He smirked. "Ain't that the truth?"

"Keep me posted, will you?"

He nodded. "You doing okay?" He gave me a meaningful look. He was obviously referencing my emotional state.

I smiled and said, "Pretty good." Which was the honest truth. I didn't mention the nightmares, which were becoming less frequent but always the same. We were back at the edge of Redemption Lake, and Megan stared at me from under the surface of the water, begging me through some silent form of communication to help her. I'd reach into the water and she'd instantly disintegrate into a million tiny grains of sand. The trauma of what happened to Megan—of all of it, really—would be with me for a while.

I offered Jay a bite of my cinnamon roll, which he politely declined. "I'm trying to cut back," he said with a self-conscious laugh.

"Getting ready for Belize?" Jay and Chloe had planned a weeklong trip to an inclusive resort in the Caribbean. I'd be lying if I said there wasn't still a part of me that had a hard time hearing about their relationship. Old jealousies die hard, I guess. But Jay was about as good a man as there was in this world, and he had shown me the sort of devotion and loyalty that earned him a forever-place in my heart. Because of that I truly wanted him to be happy—even if that meant being happy with Chloe.

"Actually," he said, tracing the handle of his coffee cup with his finger, "the trip is off."

"Off? Why?"

Jay's cheeks started to color. "Well, she didn't really want to go to Belize with me after I broke up with her."

I didn't know what to say. I was surprised and, without examining it too closely, pleased. But lest I reveal myself as a horrible person, I said the obligatory, "I'm sorry."

"Thanks." Jay shrugged. "But it's better to be alone than with the wrong person."

We shared a look. A second before it went on too long, he changed the subject. "How about you?" he asked. "Are you going to take any time off after all of this?"

"Nah," I said, looking down. "I think the best thing for me right now is to get back to work."

"You really love your job, don't you?"

I smiled. "I can't imagine working anywhere else."

"You headed back there now? I can drop you off on my way out of town?"

I shook my head. "I've got a stop to make first, but thanks," I said. "For everything."

CHAPTER 45

It was early March and the air was cool, but not cold, which was a welcome change after the brutal winter we'd had. I took my time on the five-minute walk, enjoying the feel of sunshine on my face and the crisp breeze blowing past but not through me. It was the cusp of spring, and the cold and ice felt like friends made at summer camp, distant memories as soon as the season changed. The sky was the color of my favorite crayon when I was growing up, Cornflower Blue, and I paused at the entrance to Stern's Cemetery to reflect on how beautiful the grounds looked bathed in sunlight, almost as if the heavens had opened up directly overhead.

I made my way over to Flick's grave, following the winding path by memory. Not enough time had passed to set a gravestone, but we'd placed a temporary marker after his burial. It was a simple black metal sign on a straight stake. The inscription card read simply: "Hal Flick. A man of honor and loyalty, who left this world too damn soon." I liked to think he would have appreciated the slight saltiness of the epithet.

I'd never really felt the presence of the dead after they passed, as much as I wish I could sometimes, but it had been important for me to come here all the same. There was something I wanted him to know, and this seemed like the best place to tell him. I knelt down and placed my hand on the earth below. "We got 'em, Flick. Thanks to you, we got 'em." Emotion crept up on me, and I sniffed it away as I stood up and whispered, "You can rest in peace now, my sweet friend."

Granddaddy's grave was marked by a tall, thick rectangular headstone with rough-hewn edges. The inscription was a quote by Ralph Waldo Emerson that my father had chosen. It had been one of Granddad's favorites. *Do not go where the path may lead, go instead where there is no path and leave a trail.* I had visited this spot many times in the years since his death, but today felt different. I felt a sense of peace that I hadn't before. It was as if finding out the truth of what happened had helped me let him go. I would always miss my grandfather, but the jagged edges of my grief felt smoother now.

Granddad used to say that the best obituaries answer the question, "What can we learn from this person's life?" And while I could never quantify all that I'd learned from Albert Ellison, it wasn't until I discovered the truth about how he died that I could fully understand the man he'd been. His death, ironically, told me all I needed to know about his life—which had been a living, breathing testament to unconditional love and sacrifice. He'd made a heartbreaking choice to allow my story to go on knowing that it meant his would end. The weight of that would never leave me. He gave up his life for mine, and that was a gift I would not waste. I kissed my fingertips and placed them on the top of his headstone. "Thank you, Granddaddy," I said. "I love you."

As I walked out along the path, the hum of new life buzzed all around me. The early spring sunlight glinted off the stone monuments, setting off bits of sparkle where the light caught them just right. There was so much beauty here, so much love. There was sadness too—the undeniable sorrow that comes with death—but mostly this was a place where memories burned bright. It struck me that a graveyard was in many ways like a well-written obit: filled with beginnings and endings, mourning and celebration, reflection and renewal. I'd come here today to pay tribute to two men I'd lost, and for the first time in a long time, instead of feeling the injustice of the way they left this world, I was inspired by the spirit of how they lived. It filled me with a kind of optimism that I hadn't had for a long time.

As I approached the gate, an impatient sort of anticipation started brewing inside me. I looked back over my shoulder one last time. I wanted to remember this place in this moment. I knew I'd be back, but I had a feeling that it would never look quite the same to me again. My eyes found the top of Granddad's stone, and I could just make out the first line of the engraving. *Do not go where the path may lead...* A soft, smiling gust blew through the cemetery and landed gently on my back as if to say, *It's time to go.* Who was I to argue with the wind? So, I turned and walked out, excited by the certainty that although I would always be guided by those who had come before me, the time had come for me to set off on a trail of my very own.

ACKNOWLEDGMENTS

The biggest thank you of all goes to you, dear reader. In a world where there is so much competition for everyone's time and attention, I so appreciate your giving me yours. It is an honor, and I am truly grateful.

My sincere thanks to Emma Sweeney and Margaret Sutherland Brown at the Emma Sweeney Agency, who work so expertly and thoughtfully on my behalf. Your sound counsel and staunch support is a guiding light. Plus, you are a pleasure to work with, plain and simple.

A huge thank you to the entire team at Prospect Park Books. I know that not every author gets to work with a team that is as hardworking, supportive, talented, and fun as you are. I feel incredibly lucky to get to create books with you. Caitlin Ek, Julianne Johnson, Katelyn Keating, Dorie Bailey (who has moved on from PPB, but not before making this book better), and of course the amazing Colleen Dunn Bates. I want to add an extra layer of thanks to Colleen, whom I consider a friend, mentor, and general role model for how to be a super-smart-and-nice-yet-still-totally-badass-boss-lady.

A great big shout-out to the incredibly talented cover design team of Nancy Nimoy and Susan Olinsky for creating what might be my favorite cover yet. And, as always, a million thanks to Amy Inouye, Margery Schwartz, and Leilah Bernstein for their detailed work in polishing this book to its best advantage.

Sincere gratitude to my friend and legal expert Dan Knight, who patiently answered all my questions and talked me through the prosecutorial process on more than one occasion. All inaccuracies are mine. And speaking of inaccuracies, please know that I am in no way a trained astrologist. The horoscopes in this book are a combination of language I learned from legitimate astrology websites like Refinery29, Allure, and Astrotwins—and a heaping helping of BS.

To Melinda Jenne, my "how long can a voicemail be" consultant, thank you for sharing your expertise on this issue. Please continue to test the limits of voicemail capacity, preferably by calling me. A message from you always makes my day better.

A special thank you to the real Megan Johanning, who is nothing like the character who shares her name. The real Megan is charitable, strong, hardworking, funny, and brave. Thank you for sharing your story with me and being up for the adventure of being fictionalized.

To Laura McHugh, Jennifer Gravley, Ann Breidenbach, and Nina Mukerjee-Furstenau, my beloved "writing beasties." I can't imagine writing without having you all in my corner.

Thank you to my many girlfriends for every moment you've shared with me along this journey. I say it often because it's true: I have the best friends. And while I'm bragging, I might as well just say: I have the best family, too. Much gratitude to my mom and Jack, my dad, Scott and Cheryl, Eddie and Dawn, and Allison and Pete. Thanks for the many ways in which you support me.

Thank you to my son Fletcher and my daughter Ellie for your unwavering support. You guys are the best thing I will ever create. You make me proud every single day.

And last, but never least, thank you to Jimmy. You are the yin to my yang, the hot to my cold, the macaroni to my cheese. There is nothing in my life that isn't improved by having you by my side. Thank you for encouraging me to follow my dreams.

ABOUT THE AUTHOR

Jill Orr is the award-nominated author of the Riley Ellison mystery series, which has been called "delightfully comic" and "highly amusing" by *Publishers Weekly*. In a starred review, *Booklist* said the series is perfect for fans of Janet Evanovich's Stephanie Plum and Kyra Davis's Sophie Katz books.

Before writing novels, Jill wrote a parenting column in *COMO* magazine for more than ten years. Her work has also appeared in *Waterways, National Horseman,* and the *Columbia Business Times*. She was a speaker at the inaugural *Listen to Your Mother* show in St. Louis, and she posts humor essays on her blog, *An Exercise in Narcissism*. Jill is a proud member of Sisters in Crime, Mystery Writers of America, and International Thriller Writers.

Originally from Chicago, Jill moved to Columbia, Missouri, to attend the University of Missouri, where she received her bachelor's degree in Journalism and her master's degree in Social Work. These days, the only social work she does is at cocktail parties, and she sometimes wishes her degrees were in What's for Dinner and Decoding the Teenage Eye Roll. Jill lives in Missouri with her husband and two (usually delightful) teenage children.